ENFLAMED

KNIGHTS OF 5 BRETHREN

Books by Jody Hedlund

Knights of Brethren Series
Enamored
Entwined
Ensnared
Enriched
Enflamed
Entrusted

The Fairest Maidens Series
Beholden
Beguiled
Besotted

The Lost Princesses Series
Always: Prequel Novella
Evermore
Foremost
Hereafter

Noble Knights Series
The Vow: Prequel Novella
An Uncertain Choice
A Daring Sacrifice
For Love & Honor
A Loyal Heart
A Worthy Rebel

Waters of Time Series
Come Back to Me
Never Leave Me
Stay With Me

The Colorado Cowboys
A Cowboy for Keeps
The Heart of a Cowboy

To Tame a Cowboy
Falling for the Cowgirl
The Last Chance Cowboy

The Bride Ships Series
A Reluctant Bride
The Runaway Bride
A Bride of Convenience
Almost a Bride

The Orphan Train Series
An Awakened Heart: A Novella
With You Always
Together Forever
Searching for You

The Beacons of Hope Series
Out of the Storm: A Novella
Love Unexpected
Hearts Made Whole
Undaunted Hope
Forever Safe
Never Forget

The Hearts of Faith Collection
The Preacher's Bride
The Doctor's Lady
Rebellious Heart

The Michigan Brides Collection
Unending Devotion
A Noble Groom
Captured by Love

Historical
Luther and Katharina
Newton & Polly

ENFLAMED

KNIGHTS OF BRETHREN

JODY HEDLUND

NORTHERN LIGHTS PRESS

Enflamed
Northern Lights Press
© 2022 Copyright
Jody Hedlund Print Edition

Jody Hedlund www.jodyhedlund.com

ISBN 979-8-9852649-2-0

Scripture quotations are taken from the King James Version of the Bible.

This is a work of historical reconstruction; the appearances of certain historical figures are accordingly inevitable. All other characters are products of the author's imagination. Any resemblance to actual events or locales or persons, living or dead, is entirely coincidental.

Cover Design by Roseanna White Designs
Cover images from Shutterstock
Interior Map Design by Jenna Hedlund

Chapter 1

ESPEN

IF I HAD TO LISTEN TO MY FRIENDS SPEAK OF THEIR WIVES ONE more second, I was going to heave. And that wouldn't be pretty, because my stomach was stocked to the brim. Since arriving in Vordinberg a fortnight ago, I'd been taking advantage of all the royal kitchen had to offer.

I shoved away from the large round table and stood with the other Knights of Brethren. The meeting room had grown stuffy and sour even with the open window. Torvald was already out the door and well on his way to visiting his bride, Karina. I didn't begrudge him his happiness. He deserved it.

Gunnar was slipping through the door now too, eager to be with his wife, Mikaela. Of course, King Ansgar had an impatient look upon his face—one he oft wore when he wanted to spend time with Queen Lis.

My question to Kris from moments ago lingered in my mind: *"Do you think we'll have the same good fortune as our friends? If they could find true love while on their quests, what are the chances that we will also find love?"*

"Shall we meet with Maxim and Elinor straightaway?" Kris's blue eyes contained a glimmer of irritation—one that told me he was as interested in finding true love as a fish was in finding a net.

Or maybe he was simply jealous, like I was. Aye, I could admit the churning inside my gut had to do more with envy than anything else. My friends were with the women they adored. They could openly and freely express their love. But I'd never been able to do so.

I bit back a sigh at the hopelessness of my situation and loving a woman who could never be mine.

Best to focus on improving myself. That had become my life principle. It helped to take my thoughts off what I couldn't have and put them on what I could gain if I worked hard enough.

I clamped a hand on Kris's shoulder. We were attired alike in our casual garments—surcoats over dark brown tunics and hose, leather belts holding our swords, and calf-length leather boots. "I was hoping we could search together for the holy lamp, but now that we'll be going our separate ways, how about a friendly contest to see who can find the lamp first?"

Kris's shoulder was tense. I knew everything about him, including that he loved challenges. Surely a wager would help improve his mood.

He rubbed at his chin before nodding. "Very well."

"Good then."

"What will you give me when I win?"

"When you win?" I quirked a brow at him. "I intend to win and will require you to pay me with a week's worth of guard duty."

A smile began to work at the corners of his mouth as we made our way toward the door, following the other knights. "The only way you will finish before me is if Maxim and Elinor assign you a closer location in which to search."

The distraction was working, and I allowed myself to relax just a little. "I'll ask them to give me the place farthest away just to prove you wrong."

Now that Gunnar and Torvald had completed their mission to find the sacred chalice, I was relieved that Kris and I would have an opportunity to do something important for king and country. The trouble was that our mission to find the holy lamp was urgent, something we needed to accomplish with all haste since we were on the brink of war with Swaine.

Last autumn, King Canute of Swaine had attacked in the Valley of the Red Dragons, using the fierce Ice Men and their red draco to aid him. Because he had a distant tie to Norvegia's House of Oldenberg royal lineage, he believed the throne belonged to him more so than to Ansgar, who had no royal blood and was a commoner. Of course, Ansgar had freed the Sword of the Magi and proven himself to be worthy of the kingship. In addition, he was married to Queen Lis, who was the niece of the previous Norvegian monarch, King Ulrik.

Nevertheless, Canute wanted the throne and was rallying his forces to take it any way he could. This spring we'd learned that one of our own wise Royal Sages, Rasmus, had gone to Swaine and was now colluding with Canute. We had no doubt he'd suggested using Dark Warriors who hailed from the far northern reaches of Swaine and were known for being able to fight their enemies in the dark of night. No torches, candles, or light could stay lit in their presence . . . except one—the holy lamp.

Even if Kris and I might jest about the lamp, we desperately needed to find it. According to Maxim and Elinor, the light that burned within the holy lamp came from the tomb of Christ himself and couldn't be extinguished. Although Maxim and Elinor didn't know for sure how the holy lamp worked, they believed it would be crucial in saving us from the Dark Warriors.

Now that Kris and I had volunteered to find the sacred relic, we were off to get our itinerary from Maxim and Elinor and would leave as soon as possible.

"I think I'll ask for a slow and lame horse," I added, glancing over my shoulder at Kris with another teasing grin. "Then I'll prove that not only do I have the brawn, but I also have the brains."

"I suppose next you will tell me you also have the beauty."

With my attention still on Kris and walking half backward, I stepped through the open door into the hallway. In the next instant, I found myself smacking into someone.

The person—a woman—gasped and stumbled backward.

I swiveled and grasped hold of her only to find myself looking at Sylvi Prestegard, the woman I loved with all my heart and soul, the very one I could never have. As with every time I saw her, my pulse rammed hard against my chest.

"Espen?" Her vivid blue eyes framed by thick lashes peered up at me with pleasure.

"Aye, 'tis me and none other." I took her in like food to a starving prisoner who'd just been set free from a dungeon. She was as stunningly beautiful as always. Her high-boned cheeks were flushed, and her lush lips curled up into a welcoming smile. She was wearing a fashionable blue gown with a cotehardie over her bodice that showcased her curves to their fullest. A jeweled necklace of sapphires garnished her neck, and her waist-length blond hair was laced with ribbons and more sapphires.

Saint's blood. She was even more exquisite—if that was possible—than I remembered from the last time I'd seen her several months ago.

"What are you doing here in Vordinberg?" I asked.

Her gaze had already darted behind me toward Kris, who was stepping into the hallway beside me, and in the next instant she threw herself upon him. "Kristoffer!"

His eyes widened in surprise, but he opened his arms and gathered Sylvi into a hug, one containing all his affection for his little sister.

She laughed her delight—likely at having surprised us both with her presence. As she pulled back, she surveyed Kris from his head to his toes. "You are well?"

"I am as well as always." He smiled down at the vivacious maiden. "And you?"

With their blond hair and blue eyes, the family resemblance between siblings had been plain since the first time I'd met them, when I'd been but a lad of ten. Kris had been eleven and Sylvi eight, too young at the time to understand or care about the differences in our stations in life.

Instead, we'd formed fast and solid friendships that had endured the test of time. Kris was still my closest friend. And Sylvi . . . well, she was still my friend too. But somewhere over the years as we'd grown older, she'd become more than just my friend. And she'd become more than just my best friend's little sister. She'd become my everything.

Inwardly, I sighed at the dilemma I faced every time I saw her, which was only a few times a year now that Kris and I were a part of the king's elite group of Knights of Brethren. I was immensely attracted to her, but I had to shove my feelings into a chest and lock them up where neither she nor Kris nor anyone else could ever see them.

As she released Kris, she turned again to me. Although she didn't examine me the same way she had her brother, she held out her arms just like she always did before launching herself against me and hugging me with equal enthusiasm.

The smartest thing for me to do was to lightly pat her, then break the embrace. But the instant her body pressed against mine, my arms reacted with a brain of their own. They circled around her, drawing her as close as humanly possible. My nose hadn't gotten the notification she was off-limits either. I found myself bending my face into her hair and breathing deeply of her rosewater scent.

She broke away, and as much as I was tempted to linger, I released her and put the appropriate foot of distance between us as friends. I'd already figured out over previous visits that friends could stand closer than strangers but if I drew in any nearer than one foot, my position looked conspicuously cozy and intimate.

Maybe I'd harbored hope last autumn, when the law had changed to allow nobility to marry commoners. Maybe I'd entertained the notion that I could finally say something to Sylvi about how much I cared for her. But it hadn't taken long to realize that, though the law may have changed, people like Lord Prestegard had not. He still had high expectations for Sylvi's marriage partner.

Lord Prestegard had always had grand plans for Sylvi, praised as the most beautiful woman in Norvegia. When

Sylvi turned eighteen two years ago, Lord Prestegard had matched her with Rolfe Solberg, a wealthy nobleman with an enormous ship-building business. Though Rolfe had been a widower with several children, Sylvi had willingly accepted the arrangement since Rolfe had been handsome and charming. They would have married last autumn, but Rolfe died unexpectedly just weeks before the wedding.

Lord Prestegard had allowed for the customary grieving period, but recently I'd heard he'd begun making new plans for her.

The truth was, law or no law, a future with Sylvi was completely and entirely beyond my wildest aspirations. I was nothing but a fisherman's son and wasn't wealthy or prestigious enough to ever be considered a serious match for a maiden like her.

If I did express my interest, I'd lose the trust and respect of Lord Prestegard. I'd jeopardize my friendship with Kris. And I'd compromise my standing among the other nobility who accepted me into their midst even though I wasn't nobly born.

Most of all, if I let my attraction show, I'd scare Sylvi away. I'd heard enough of her lamenting over recent years to know she was easily repelled by men who paid too much attention to her beauty.

"And how do you fare, Espen?" she asked.

I wanted to say I was faring superbly now that she was here. It was an answer I would have given any other maiden. Ironically, I could speak the words when I least meant them but couldn't say them now when they were true.

Instead, I scrambled to find a response that would cover up my longing for her. "I'll be doing well once I beat

Kris in the race to find the holy lamp." I gave him a playful shove.

He nudged me back. "You wish."

The sconces on the wall flickered brightly and illuminated a familiar spark in Sylvi's eyes—one that said she was interested in what we were up to, one that reminded me of all the times she'd wanted to be involved in Kris's and my escapades when we were children. She'd tagged along all too oft, much to the chagrin of her mother.

"No, you may not join us in our race," Kris said, clearly thinking the same thing I was.

"Oh, please." She clutched his arm. "I am in sore need of an adventure."

Kris shook his head. "This is no adventure for a lady."

Sylvi turned her big eyes upon me along with her pleading expression, which was much too pretty to resist. There was also a flash of desperation there—one I didn't recognize, one that I wanted to pick apart and analyze. But she blinked, and it was gone.

The word *yes* settled on the tip of my tongue. Sylvi knew she could get me to agree to anything. Whenever Kris resisted, she needed only to come to me, and I would give her whatever she wished for. I'd never been able to say no to her.

As though sensing my acquiescence, Kris slanted me a warning look. "Espen is not giving in to your whims this time."

Sylvi pushed out her bottom lip in a playful pout. A kissable bottom lip. Not that I'd know about kissing her. I'd never even come close to it. But her lips . . . they were perfectly full and perfectly pink.

Fie upon me. I jerked my gaze away from her mouth

and glanced down the passageway leading away from our meeting room. The other Brethren had gone their separate ways, and no doubt Torvald, Gunnar, and Ansgar were even now kissing their wives on their perfectly kissable lips.

My eyes nearly twitched with the need to look at Sylvi's lips again. But I forced myself not to. "We were just now going to visit Maxim and Princess Elinor to discover where each of us will need to travel for our searches."

"This is an urgent mission for the king," Kris added gently. "And I regret that we must be off with all haste and shall not have time to spend with you during your stay here."

"No time at all?" Her gaze bounced between us, and I could see her mind at work.

"Not much." I guessed, like Kris, that our quest would begin today or on the morrow at the latest.

Her delicate brows furrowed, and once again I glimpsed a desperation in her expression that had never been there before.

Something was amiss. I only needed to be with her a few minutes to know it.

"Will you not allow me to go with you to your meeting?" She held my gaze, unrelenting in her determination to sway me. "At the very least, you can let me live vicariously through your adventures."

"Of course, you can come," I said.

"No, I'm sorry, Sylvi." Kris spoke at the same time as me.

Sylvi ignored Kris and focused pleading eyes upon me.

"There's no harm in her joining our meeting, is there?" I tried to keep my tone as casual as possible so that Kris wouldn't read anything into my request. "Sylvi has missed

9

us and wants to spend as much time as possible with us before we have to leave. Right, Sylvi?"

"Yes. Since you are leaving so soon, you must give me every moment possible." She linked one arm through Kris's and then her other through mine so that she was in the middle.

As her fingers tightened around my bicep, warmth coursed through my muscles. Her touch always did this to me—turned me into a crackling ball of flames.

"Don't be a dolt, Kris." I raised my brows, daring Kris to let her come along.

"Fine." Kris peered down at Sylvi fondly before pressing a kiss to her head. "You can accompany us to the meeting. But behave yourself."

"I always behave myself." Sylvi's lips turned impish and melted my heart into the puddle that already contained the rest of my body.

Though I was sad our reunion would be short, I couldn't deny I was relieved I wouldn't have to keep up pretenses for too many days. Acting as though I didn't love Sylvi was getting harder each time I saw her. I was afraid that one of these visits, I wouldn't be able to hold myself back and that I'd make a horrible mess of everything.

I couldn't let myself do that. I loved her too much to hurt her in any way.

Chapter 2

Sylvi

I had to find a way to escape the marriage being arranged for me. The thought had tapped a dreaded rhythm over the past few days as I'd traveled to the capital city, until now it gonged in my head unrelentingly.

It was so loud I could hardly pay heed to the many details Maxim and Princess Elinor had given to Kristoffer and Espen regarding their upcoming mission for the holy lamp.

"Essentially," Maxim said, dragging his finger over the map spread out on a cluttered writing table, "Kristoffer will visit several sites in the east, and Espen will go north."

"Good then." Espen dropped his pointer finger to a spot on the map in the Hundreds, the dozens upon dozens of islands that provided a natural buffer to Norvegia's western coastline. "I'm familiar with the north as Pollock, my family's fishing village, is here."

I took a closer look at the islands to the south of

Finnmark. "Then your family lives close to Gullk-ronnen?"

Espen paused but didn't meet my gaze.

"Do you not remember?" Kristoffer continued to study the map. "'Tis how Father came across Espen. One summer on his way to Gullkronnen, he stopped in the village. While there, he saw Espen in a mock swordfight with his friends and recognized his talent."

I did remember some details, but it had been long ago, and he was so much a part of our family now that he was like a second brother to me. If ever I needed something, Espen was the one I turned to. Not that Kristoffer wouldn't come to my aid if I asked him. But he was sterner, more logical, and needed to think through every option before giving in to me.

Not Espen. He was even-tempered and agreeable. He didn't have to evaluate everything from a hundred different angles before making his decision.

As footsteps echoed in the hallway outside the room that Maxim and Princess Elinor used for their study, I glanced toward the door, half expecting Father to poke his head inside and tell me it was time to finalize the marriage plans.

I couldn't hold back a shudder.

Espen quickly shrugged out of his surcoat. Then before I knew what he was doing, he draped it over my shoulders.

"Are you cold, my lady?" Princess Elinor asked from where she stood beside Maxim in a long black robe, watching me with her keen green eyes.

"Just a little, Your Highness."

The princess waved toward a servant and gave instructions to add more fuel to the low fire burning upon the hearth. Apparently, the room had once belonged to Maxim's father, Rasmus. Floor-to-ceiling bookshelves lined the walls, filled with scrolls and leather-bound books as well as numerous other containers and relics. Two writing tables faced each other, one for Elinor and the other for Maxim as they worked together to advise the king in matters of the greatest importance, including now the search for the holy lamp.

The warmth of Espen's body lingered in his coat. It contained the scent that was uniquely his, an earthy mixture of sage and sea. Espen loved spending his spare time fishing, boating, or swimming. It was almost as if the sea was part of his blood. Now, as I hugged his coat around my nearly bare shoulders, I wished for those simpler times when we were all children and could cast our troubles aside by running off to the water's edge to frolic in foamy waves and wet sand.

Why did life have to become so complicated as one grew older?

I didn't realize I'd sighed until I felt Espen's gaze upon me. His brows lifted in his usual manner with an unspoken question, asking if something was amiss.

The window shutters were opened wide, allowing in the bright sunshine from the summer afternoon. The light seemed to reflect in the blue-green of Espen's eyes. The color like that of the sea glass I collected, a swirling mixture of the clear and calm coastal waters that bordered our family's summer estate in Gullkronnen.

I'd always loved Espen's eyes. But over recent years, he rarely looked at me directly or for long. He, like Kristoffer, had important duties as a Knight of

Brethren and didn't have much time to spare for a maiden such as myself.

Yet now, with Espen watching me and silently seeing into my soul as he always seemed to do, I let the tension ease from my body. I was with Espen, and he would help me.

So would Kristoffer. It just took my brother longer to put the clues together than it did Espen. But once Kristoffer understood my fears, he'd do all he could to convince my father and uncle to see reason.

Though Father and Uncle hadn't informed me of the true nature of our trip to the capital city, I knew why we'd come. They'd picked my match. There could be no other reason for traveling two days from Karlstadt, drawing closer to the threat of war instead of farther away.

The problem was, I'd heard rumors regarding their list of potential marriage partners. And none of the men were suitable. When I'd voiced my concern before leaving, Father had listened to me tenderly. But then he'd patted my hand, as though I were a child instead of a grown woman, and he'd told me not to worry, that any man would be very lucky to have me and would treat me like a queen.

I didn't need to be treated like a queen. But I did want a match with someone who would love me for who I was inside and not simply for my outward beauty.

Espen dropped his attention back to the map.

I studied his profile. He wore his light-brown hair tied back with a leather strip. Although his hair was a shade darker than mine, it would soak in the sun during the summer months and would turn a golden brown. In our younger years, when his hair had been naturally fairer, many people had assumed he was a relative, a cousin, because of our similar coloring.

As he'd grown, he'd become stockier than Kristoffer, wider in girth, and broader in his shoulders, though he and Kristoffer were both about the same height. Even Espen's face was squarer, with a wide forehead and nose, deep-set eyes, and thick brows. He had a heavy layer of scruff over his jaw and chin that lent him a maturity and air of authority that he wore well.

Espen had turned into a handsome man. And my friends always gushed over him and Kristoffer and vied for their attention whenever the two came home to visit.

I sidled closer to Espen, hoping the meeting would end soon so that I might speak with him and Kristoffer of my plight. As my shoulder brushed against Espen's arm, he stiffened.

Espen didn't like to be touched. I hadn't noticed that quality about him when we'd been younger. But I'd recognized the stiffening and pulling away more oft now that we were older. Sometimes, I sensed that even my hugs made him uncomfortable. But I hadn't let his awkwardness stop me from treating him like I did Kristoffer.

In fact, I pressed against Espen again, wanting to prove to myself and to him that our friendship was as solid now as in the past.

At the contact, he paused mid-sentence, and the muscles in his arm flexed against mine.

Princess Elinor's sharp gaze shifted between Espen and me, as though she was attempting to solve a riddle.

Surely she didn't think Espen and I were attracted to each other. Even if she was the most intelligent woman in the land, she was wrong on that score. Espen regarded me as a friend and nothing more. He'd made that clear ad nauseum over the years.

I could admit that at one point in my girlish dreaming, I'd concocted a future where the dashing and handsome Espen swept me off my feet and carried me away into the sunset. Yes, I'd been fascinated with him—and half in love with him . . . until he and Kristoffer had grown up and gone off to war. It was hard not to care about Espen. He was sweet and sensitive and sympathetic. And he was funny, winsome, and amiable. He had no enemies. Everyone loved him.

Alas, when it had finally been my turn to grow up, I'd realized Espen was right—that we were just friends. I'd understood what I hadn't earlier in my life. To my family, my appearance was my greatest asset. I'd been groomed by my beautiful mother to be just as beautiful, if not more so, for the purpose of making an advantageous match.

My marriage to Rolfe would have brought my family much wealth and prestige. Now my father and uncle were scheming again. They dangled me like a prize to be won to the man who offered them the most.

No matter what Princess Elinor might think about my relationship with Espen, I'd long past put aside my feelings for him. I'd matured enough to know that Espen was not and never would be a candidate for my husband. While Father cared for Espen in a fatherly way, Espen couldn't ever measure up to the rich and powerful noblemen my father was considering.

I was better off if I didn't jeopardize the camaraderie, the sharing, the trust, and everything else I held dear about him over an infatuation I still felt once in a while.

"A sennight?" Maxim was saying. "Maybe a fortnight at the most."

"'Tis not much time for the mission." Kristoffer stood back from the writing desk, rolling on his heels, the sign he was anxious to be on his way. "If finding the sacred chalice took Gunnar and Torvald months, how do you propose Espen and I locate the holy lamp in a week or two?"

Maxim's intense dark blue eyes bored into Kristoffer. A tall and thin man with ebony hair, he had a scholarly aura but also a hard, foreboding edge. He was a brilliant man. Some claimed he was even brighter than his father, Rasmus. "'Twill not be hidden as carefully as the chalice. But, yes, the task is an urgent one. You must not let anything or anyone distract you from finding it."

"Then I suppose we must forgo finding our true loves on the mission." Espen cracked a teasing smile at Kristoffer. "I know how much you were looking forward to coming back with a wife just like the others. But I'm afraid you'll need to refrain."

I'd heard rumors that both Gunnar and Torvald had recently taken wives, but I'd yet to learn the details. Now that I was in Vordinberg, I had no doubt I'd hear everything soon enough.

Even so, a strange unease pricked me at the prospect that Espen and Kristoffer might return from their quests with wives the same way Gunnar and

Torvald had. Kristoffer was too practical and level-headed to fall in love in a week or two. Moreover, he was too loyal to his family to consider anyone except the maiden Father and Uncle would arrange for him to marry.

But Espen? He had no constraints and could marry whomever he pleased.

Maxim narrowed his eyes upon both Kristoffer and Espen. "I'm afraid both of you must refrain from *finding your true loves.*"

"You needn't worry about me." Espen released a chuckle. "I'm content to continue enjoying as many women as I please."

I cringed at Espen's admission. I'd heard the tales about his womanizing, and I didn't like to think about him consorting with his adoring fans.

"But Kris, on the other hand," Espen continued, "now, he's the one we need to keep an eye on."

Kristoffer just shook his head at Espen's exaggeration.

"No, Espen," I said grasping his arm. "If anyone can charm a woman in a sennight, you have the skills to do so more than Kristoffer."

Espen glanced down at my fingers on his arm, and his smile faltered.

Maxim's narrowed gaze shot to me, to Espen, then back.

Surely he didn't assume, as Princess Elinor had, that I cared about Espen beyond friendship. I quickly made a show of prodding Kristoffer too. But as I attempted to keep the interaction light and platonic, I could feel Maxim studying me again.

Even though I had nothing to hide, I refused to meet his gaze.

Chapter 3

Sylvi

"I must be off today," Kristoffer said as we exited Maxim and Elinor's study. He was already striding down the passageway toward a set of stairs that would take him to the wing of the castle where the Knights of Brethren resided.

Espen didn't move to follow him. But as he lingered beside me, I could sense he didn't want Kristoffer to rush off without him.

My hope was deflating with each passing moment. The two had to leave on an urgent mission for the security of our country and couldn't delay on account of my woes.

"Kris, wait," Espen called, a note of distress in his tone.

My brother halted, clearly hearing the distress too. He lifted one of his fair brows, his impatience radiating from every muscle.

Espen never let Kristoffer's attitudes deter him from speaking out. "Don't you think we should hear

Sylvi's concern before we leave?"

Though I hadn't mentioned I had a concern, it was just like Espen to realize that I had one.

Kristoffer glanced at me, almost as if he'd forgotten I was there. His eyes gentled. "I beg you to forgive me, Sylvi. I know you only just arrived, and I would like to visit with you. But I have a long, hard ride ahead of me, and I cannot waste a single moment."

"I understand—"

"You can spend one hour with Sylvi, can you not?" Espen's tone chastised.

"You heard Maxim." Kristoffer stood tall and regal, reminding me of my father. "The matter is of the utmost urgency."

"'Tis alright, Espen." I reached out to lay a steadying hand upon his arm but then just as rapidly let it drop. "I understand that you must both be off as soon as possible."

"You're important too." Espen nodded encouragingly at Kristoffer. "And if you have a problem, then we want to hear it. Isn't that right, Kris?"

"Of course." He started back toward me, although hesitantly.

My worries over my impending match paled in concern to the welfare of the nation. "No, you must both go. I shall manage my own affairs."

Kristoffer halted. "Are you certain?"

"I would not like to be the cause of the fall of our country." I waved him off, trying for a breezy air. "Go, and I will see you when you return."

Kristoffer exchanged a glance with Espen, as though attempting to gauge what Espen would do.

Espen didn't budge. "I doubt I'll find a ship willing

to leave Vordinberg so late in the afternoon. Most likely I'll depart on the morrow before dawn."

"Very well," Kristoffer said. "Then you will attend to whatever Sylvi needs during the remainder of your time here in Vordinberg."

"Aye, you know I will."

Kristoffer nodded his thanks. Then he strode toward me, wrapped me in a hug, and said his farewells. A moment later, he was gone, and I stood beside Espen alone in the dimly lit passageway.

He rubbed a hand over the back of his neck, kneading it as though trying to ease his tension. Was he as anxious to be rid of me as Kristoffer?

A sliver of hurt pricked my heart. "Do not feel obligated to stay with me, Espen. I need a friend, not a nursemaid."

"Fie, Sylvi." He met my gaze, and his eyes were warm and full of his usual kindness. "I know you don't need a nursemaid. And I would put aside my plans if I could." The note of earnestness in his tone eased some of the sting.

"I would never expect you to."

He glanced to the opaque round window at the far end of the hallway. Though it didn't allow in much light, it afforded enough to know that there was still time before the evening activities demanded our attention. "I must go down to the wharf and secure my passage on a ship. Perhaps you can ride along, and we'll talk then?"

"I would like that."

"Good then."

I didn't know what Espen could do to change my circumstances. But at least in telling him my fears, I would have a listening and caring ear.

The trip down to the waterfront along Ostby Sound was an easy and quick ride from the royal castle. The road wasn't busy at the late afternoon hour. As we drew near the wharf, the scent of fish and brine wafted in from the sea. The breeze was warm and filled with the promise of summer. The deep water, protected by a barrier of islands, glistened with sunshine.

The beauty of it reminded me a little of our summer home in Gullkronnen. If war broke out the way everyone predicted it would, then Father intended to send Mother and me to Gullkronnen so that we'd be far away from the fighting.

If only he'd send us away now. Then I wouldn't have to face the prospect of a loveless marriage to a man of questionable character.

As I finished sharing my concerns with Espen, his brow was furrowed. "I can't understand why your father and uncle have brought you here for a betrothal when our country is on the cusp of war."

"They have not specifically said they are planning my betrothal, but why else would they insist that I accompany them to the capital?"

Espen stared ahead at the myriad of ships and boats in the harbor. Only a few still had sails aloft, and I selfishly prayed that didn't mean they were leaving yet tonight. I wanted a few hours with Espen at least. Was that too much to wish for?

Even as he rested his hand casually on his thigh, his jaw tightened, the muscles working up and down and radiating displeasure.

Was he unhappy to hear the news of my upcoming match?

I mentally slapped myself. Why was I always thinking that Espen's moods and emotions revolved around me? I had to cease from such foolishness. "I know a match is inevitable. And I understand Father and Uncle have given me more than enough time to grieve for Rolfe. But I do not like any of the candidates they have arranged for me this time."

"Do you know who they are?"

"I have heard them speak of certain men as possibilities. But I was not sure of their list until I arrived this afternoon and learned which other guests have joined us here in Vordinberg and will be attending the feast tonight for the Noble Council."

My stomach cinched again at the thought of the three top prospects, and I wanted nothing more than to flee.

Espen reined in his horse and shifted in his saddle. His handsome face contained a wariness that gave me hope he would come to my rescue. Even if his word didn't hold as much influence as Kristoffer's, surely my father would listen to Espen pleading on my behalf. "Their names?"

"I shall not know for certain until the meal this eve. But from everything I have gathered thus far, I have concluded they have chosen Lord Sletten, Lord Grimsrud, and Lord Jorstadt."

Espen released a snort of disgust.

The sound added to my hope.

"The only decent one is Sletten." He spat the name. "But he's three times your age, old enough to be your grandfather, and has been married four times already."

"I have never met him, but my friends have told me he looks as old as his age. Not that I am concerned about physical appearance." I added the last sentence hastily. I resented when people made much ado over my physical attributes, and I had no wish to do the same to others. Even so, I didn't want to marry a man so advanced in years.

Espen muttered under his breath something about Sletten having one foot in the grave and one foot out. Then he spoke more forcefully. "The king has heard rumors that Grimsrud and Jorstadt are behind the roving gangs that have plagued the Richlande Lowlands these past years."

"I have heard such rumors too. Surely Father and Uncle have as well. Why would they consider such men?"

Espen returned his troubled gaze to the waterfront and the seagulls flying low and squealing out their desire for the fish loaded in barrels upon the wharf. "These cannot be the men your father has picked for you. Not only are Grimsrud and Jorstadt of questionable character but they're brutes."

I'd given back Espen's surcoat and had donned my cloak. Now I pulled it tighter to ward off a chill. "Believe me, Espen. The tales abound of their coarse behavior—drunkenness, brawls, and thievery."

"Why is your father considering them?" Espen's question was hard. "They aren't rich and powerful like Rolfe was."

"I suppose they provide some sort of advantage to Father and Uncle, though I cannot understand what."

Around us, the waterfront was busy with fishermen

cleaning their nets, sailors washing decks, and tradesmen unloading wares. Although a few men had stopped to watch Espen with interest, no one had approached us.

"Choosing so poorly is out of character for your father. Even if he has always sought to align you with a marriage that would be for his gain, I never believed he'd neglect your safety and happiness."

"I have never believed he would do so either." My father had always treated me with a measure of kindness, even if he had focused on my outward appearance above all else. So why now would he put me in a perilous marriage arrangement, one that would likely bring me great unhappiness?

Espen heaved a breath of frustration.

"You will speak to him, Espen, will you not? And share your concerns?"

"Aye. I'll do what I can. But your father would listen to Kris better than he would to me."

"He respects you too. And if you tell him all you know about Lord Grimsrud and Lord Jorstadt, then he will have to reconsider his plans."

"Or he'll just marry you off to the ancient Sletten."

My heart plummeted. I wished I was smart enough to speak to my father and voice my concerns. But Kristoffer was the one who'd inherited the intelligence in our family. "Is there anyone else you can suggest to him? Someone who would prove to be an advantageous match?"

Espen remained silent for a long moment—so long I began to think he wouldn't answer.

"Surely you know of a good man," I persisted.

"I cannot think of anyone immediately. But I'll

ponder the dilemma."

"Thank you, Espen. You are a good friend. The best, as a matter of fact."

He nodded curtly, then guided his horse toward the closest cargo ship. I followed, suspecting that even if Espen offered a hundred names of eligible men, my father and uncle wouldn't be swayed. They'd already plotted and planned and had likely considered every man from the mountains to the seas and in between.

Even so, I'd pray Espen could convince them to change their minds.

Chapter 4

ESPEN

I WAITED OUTSIDE THE DOORS OF THE GREAT HALL WHERE THE Noble Council and their guests had convened for their feasting. I'd been pacing for the past hour, and I was running out of time. The ship I'd arranged to take me and my squires to the Hundreds was setting sail during high tide in the early hours of the morn, and I still had much to do before leaving.

I stalked back to the door and peeked inside toward the table where Sylvi sat between her father and uncle. Sure enough, the three men she'd mentioned were supping at the table with her. And the men had been ogling her the whole time I'd been waiting.

Of course, she was hard not to ogle. Attired in a flowing crimson gown, she was breathtaking, especially with her golden hair curled and piled upon her head like a crown.

Even though I was keenly aware of every curve of her body, every flush of her skin, and every nuance of her facial expressions, I couldn't focus on her beauty tonight, not when my anger paced inside me like a caged cougar.

My muscles were coiled tight, my stomach hard, and my hands fisted with the need to charge in and pounce upon the men who were vying for her attention. I wanted to snarl at them to abandon their efforts and never look at Sylvi again.

But I had no right to do so. In fact, if I did, I'd likely be pulled off, thrown in a dungeon, and pronounced a raving lunatic.

I couldn't bring trouble upon myself tonight, not on the cusp of so urgent a mission. As aggravated as I was, I had to handle the situation with maturity. And I had to remember that even though I wanted to rescue Sylvi, there was only so much I could do. There was only so much Kris could do too. Her father had every right to marry her to the man of his choosing no matter how much we might protest.

It's just that I'd always assumed Lord Prestegard would find Sylvi another suitable match, one like Rolfe. I'd never expected this . . .

I studied Hemming Grimsrud. He was a good ten years older than I was. I could see the aging in the lines of his face. He wasn't a man of much importance. But over the past few years, he'd slowly been building an army of retainers, mostly thieves and thugs, who preyed upon the weak.

Whenever he interacted with Sylvi, his eyes were cold and his smile calculated. I had no doubt Sylvi could see past his façade since her smile was forced and the light gone from her eyes.

If only Lord Prestegard would finish his meal so that I might speak with him. I'd already sent a servant to let him know I needed a moment of his time. The servant had returned with the message that Lord Prestegard could not be disturbed until after the meal.

From what I could tell, he was done eating and was avoiding me. Did I dare walk into the hall and address him in front of everyone? Doing so would embarrass Sylvi and Lord Prestegard. But what choice was he leaving me? I couldn't sail away without trying to help Sylvi.

I drew in a fortifying breath and stepped into the doorway.

Sylvi's gaze darted to me, and her eyes rounded, seeming to beckon me to rescue her.

If only I could offer her the prospect of a husband who would make her truly happy. But I feared that even if I helped her avert an unfortunate match tonight, I wouldn't be able to prevent or postpone an unhappy union the next time her father chose someone she didn't like.

As her attention stayed upon me, the others at the table began to follow her gaze, until at last, Lord Prestegard did likewise. At the sight of me, he frowned and then pushed up from his spot.

He approached Lord Klepp, who was hosting the feast. As a prominent member of the Noble Council, Lord Klepp kept an estate within the city walls, a regal home that rivaled the royal palace in its size. I'd been to it before as an honored guest, never as an outsider awaiting recognition.

But even now, as Lord Prestegard spoke to Lord Klepp and several other noblemen, they frowned at me, and I sensed this was my lot in life, to always be standing on the outside looking in, respected but never completely accepted.

Aye, this was an awkward situation, and I was making a fool of myself. But I'd go to the ends of the earth and back for Sylvi. I'd even do it crawling on my hands and knees over hot coals.

As Lord Prestegard advanced toward me, Sylvi rose and trailed after him. She was never one to sit back and let others do the work for her, and she never lacked courage.

But in this case, I wanted to speak with Lord Prestegard without having to mince words. And I wasn't sure I'd be able to do so with Sylvi present.

"Espen." The man who had been like a father to me for many years strode toward me. He maintained a youthful look about his face, his blue eyes and blond hair the same as Kris's. Always in the past, he'd welcomed me warmly, treating me like a second son. But tonight his expression took on an edge I hadn't seen there before.

He stepped into the hallway after me, and I gave him a slight bow of respect. "It's good to see you, my lord."

Before he could respond, Sylvi glided through the door and came to stand beside me. Much to my dismay, she tucked her hand into the crook of my arm. The touch seared me just as it always did, making every nerve perk up and tune in to her. I needed to slip her hand out and step away, but I suspected doing so would make me look guilty, as if I was trying to hide something from Lord Prestegard.

"Can this not wait, Espen?" Lord Prestegard didn't look at Sylvi, apparently thought nothing of his daughter holding my arm.

"I apologize for disturbing you, my lord. But I'm heading out on a mission for the king within the next few hours. So I must speak now or live with regrets."

I owed Lord Prestegard much for bringing me into his home. He'd bestowed upon me many privileges, turned me into one of the top swordsmen in the country, and provided opportunities I wouldn't have had otherwise.

Lord Prestegard glanced at Sylvi and then at me before expelling a tired sigh. "Does this have to do with Sylvi's match?"

I hesitated. Could he still so easily read me? He'd always had an uncanny knack for seeing my inner workings.

"Go on, then." His voice held a note of irritation.

"My lord, there are no favorable words circulating through the king's court about Grimsrud and Jorstadt."

Sylvi was watching her father with her keen blue eyes filled with hope—a hope I prayed Lord Prestegard wouldn't crush.

I pressed forward with what I needed to say. "I advise you to stay away from any connection with the two men."

Lord Prestegard lifted one brow. "And who gave you license to advise me on who I may or may not associate with?"

"I don't presume to have such license. But I wanted you to be aware that the king doesn't highly regard either of the men."

Sylvi grasped my arm more firmly. I guessed she meant to encourage me to keep going, but I could do naught less than stare at her slender fingers circling my arm. I didn't want my traitorous eyes to linger over her hand and then make a trail up her arm to her neck, cheek, and forehead, but with Sylvi I never knew when I'd lose control of my faculties and turn into a simpering fool.

"What is this really about, Espen?" Lord Prestegard's tone hardened.

I jerked my attention back to his face to find him

looking between Sylvi and me intently. Surely he didn't think I was asking him to put off picking Sylvi's match because I had aspirations for her myself. I understood my place in the social order and had never tried to gain any prestige, was content to live in Kris's shadow. Lord Prestegard knew that. My easy acceptance of the differences and my humility had kept me in his good graces over the years.

But now, in approaching him this way and asserting myself, I was upsetting the equilibrium that had always existed.

As though sensing her father's rising anger, Sylvi lifted her other hand to my arm and clung to me more fiercely. In the process, her shoulder pressed into me. Suddenly, I was all too conscious of the length of her arm and legs so near mine—but a hair away. Just like earlier, when we'd been in Maxim and Elinor's study and she'd brushed up against me.

"I can see what is occurring." Lord Prestegard's gaze bored into me.

Fie. With how I was reacting to Sylvi, I was giving Lord Prestegard the wrong impression. I needed to set him straight. "My lord, I assure you my concern has only to do with the nature of the candidates and my desire to see Sylvi happily married."

From the iron in Lord Prestegard's eyes, I knew I hadn't convinced him. In fact, all I'd done in this interaction was cast suspicion upon myself.

"Sometimes duty comes before happiness," he said in a condescending tone. "And Sylvi knows that, do you not, my dear?"

The hint of a smile and the hope in her eyes faded. "I liked Rolfe so much better—"

"This is all beyond your capacity to understand, Sylvi." He softened his tone like one would to a young child. "Your duty is to be your lovely self. And mine is to orchestrate what is best for our family."

"I know I do not have the understanding, but—"

"That is precisely why you must trust that whatever I do is for our family's advancement. You surely want to play a part in that, do you not?"

She bowed her head in acquiescence, but not before I saw the despair in her expression. No doubt she'd loathed every minute of the meal with the men and had anticipated her father having some compassion. Instead, he'd treated her as though she couldn't think for herself.

My muscles had grown increasingly tense, and now they felt as though they would snap.

"Please return to the feasting, Sylvi." Her father bestowed upon her a gentle smile. "I would like a final word with Espen alone."

Sylvi nodded and released me. Although she lifted her head and glided gracefully to the door, I could see the stiffness in her back and sensed her hurt.

I wished there was more I could do for her, but what could a simple man like myself accomplish against a powerful nobleman like Lord Prestegard?

At the door, she paused, her eyes shadowed. "Farewell, Espen. I wish you every blessing on your mission for the king."

"My thanks, Sylvi." I bowed my head in her direction, and when I raised it, she was gone.

Lord Prestegard studied me a moment, and for the first time in my interactions with him, I felt no warmth, only frostiness. I'd beheld him level his frigid wrath upon others but had never imagined it being directed at me.

Since he was already angry with me, why not say more? "My lord, you cannot give Sylvi to old men and criminals—"

"She will never be yours, Espen."

At the directness of his statement, the rest of my reply fled.

He stepped closer so that his chest nearly touched mine. "You have overstepped yourself."

I needed to apologize, grovel, maybe even use humor to lighten the situation. But I couldn't make myself do what I needed to. Instead, I lifted my chin and held his gaze. "I know my place, and I have never aspired after Sylvi." My words came out calmer and more firmly than I'd expected. "If only you could see past her outward beauty, then perhaps you would do more to protect the real beauty that lies within."

This time his response stalled. He closed his lips and pressed them in a tight line.

Even if I was indeed overstepping myself, the words needed to be spoken—were, in fact, overdue.

"Remember where your loyalty should lie." Lord Prestegard's whisper was harsh. "You would not be here at court with the king if not for me. Do not forget that."

Then without giving me a chance to say more, he strode away.

I watched him retreat until he disappeared into the great hall. Sylvi had been counting on me to help her, and I'd failed her miserably. I'd done nothing but make Lord Prestegard aware of my affection for Sylvi. And after hiding my feelings for so long, I hadn't wanted him to learn of them in this manner, as if I were a jealous lover bent on trying to keep her from other men.

As laughter and conversation spilled into the hallway, I

started toward the dining room door again. I had to do something. While I could stomp in and use physical force to say more, I didn't want to cause Sylvi additional trouble or embarrassment.

Only feet away from the door, I halted, helplessness settling over me so heavily that I wasn't sure I could sail away from Vordinberg and leave her behind. But what choice did I have? What choice had I ever had when it came to Sylvi?

I'd run out of time to do anything for her tonight. But before I left, I'd write her a note and assure her I would find a way to help her when I returned.

Chapter 5

Sylvi

My temples pounded with the coming of a headache. Each step away from the great hall only made the pressure worse.

I needed my bed.

Even if Father had been callous during the conversation with Espen a short while ago, at least he'd had the decency to excuse me to withdraw to my room. He was well aware of the headaches I experienced from time to time. I'd inherited the malady from my mother, and so he knew I must rest before the aching worsened.

I suspected the debilitating pain had to do with my distress over the matchmaking. From what I'd been able to tell, most of my headaches started during the times when I was feeling the most duress.

Whatever the case, I was glad to be away from the stares of the men in attendance. All eve, I'd felt like a rare jewel my father had put on display, one he was willing to sell to the man who could give him what he most wanted.

What did the noblemen have that Father wanted?

During the courses and conversations, I hadn't been able to discern what it was, even though I'd certainly tried.

As I halted in front of my guest room, I nodded toward the guard who had accompanied me. "Thank you. As I will retire for the night, you may return to your other duties."

He bowed and began to retreat the way we'd come.

I didn't travel to Vordinberg oft with Father, but the few times I had, we'd stayed with Lord Klepp, who'd been friends with Father for many years. His home was situated near the royal residence, close enough that I could spend time with Kristoffer and Espen to my heart's content.

Not this visit.

Letting my shoulders slump, I entered the simply-furnished chamber. I hadn't been able to bring any of my servants with me on this trip, but Lord Klepp had been kind enough to assign a woman to my care.

She wasn't in the room at the moment, and I guessed she hadn't expected me to return until much later.

A single sconce on the wall illuminated the room and revealed a simple folded piece of parchment beneath my feet. From what I could surmise, someone had slipped it under my door.

A missive for me?

Anticipation bubbled within my chest as I retrieved the note, tore open the wax seal, and unfolded it.

A glance at the name scrawled at the bottom read:

"Your friend, Espen."

The bubbles inside turned warm. Espen was so thoughtful. Even though he was in a hurry to begin his mission, he'd gone out of his way to stop by Lord Klepp's and had attempted to speak to Father.

Espen hadn't been able to get Father to change his mind tonight. But hopefully, he'd given Father something to think about.

I stepped closer to the light and read the note: "Dear Sylvi, I regret I was not able to help you. When I return, I shall do more. Until then, do whatever you must to stall your father's schemes and avoid his matches."

Do whatever you must.

I leaned against the door, my headache forgotten. What could I do to stall my father's schemes and avoid his matches?

Did I dare come up with an excuse and return to Karlstadt? Perhaps leave on the morrow without telling him?

I shook my head. No, he'd only send his men after me and force me to come back. Or he'd bring his three choices to Karlstadt to finalize the plans there.

Was there someplace else I could go? Perhaps to stay with friends?

I shook my head again. I couldn't involve them, didn't want to chance exposing them to my father's ill will.

Who could I impose upon? Was there anyone who would shelter and hide me away until Espen or Kristoffer returned and could help me? I needed someone strong enough to withstand the danger I might bring. Someone loyal enough to shield me without giving away my location. And someone caring enough to take me in even though I couldn't repay them.

Who would do such a thing for me?

I could think of no one . . . no one but Espen.

My thoughts spun with the information I'd gleaned at the waterfront earlier in the day. He'd chosen a medium-sized cog ship, one that was returning to the Hundreds after delivering loads of salted and dried fish. I knew exactly where it was moored on the wharf, flying a blue flag with the emblem of an eagle on the quarterdeck.

What if I went with Espen?

My pulse tumbled to a halt. Was such a plan feasible? I'd never been good at plotting, had always just gone along with Kristoffer's and Espen's ideas. But surely this could work.

Espen said I should do whatever I must to stall Father's schemes and avoid his matches. Traveling to the Hundreds would certainly qualify. I'd buy myself a week or two away from Father. And perhaps Espen and I could devise alternate options during the hours of traveling when he wasn't busy looking for the holy lamp.

Yes. My pulse kicked forward again, this time racing. From what I'd gathered when Espen had been speaking to the ship's captain, they were departing at high tide, which would be an hour or two before dawn, according to the captain.

I had plenty of time to get ready and make my way to the wharf. And surely I'd have no trouble leaving Lord Klepp's estate. It wasn't walled or guarded the same way the king's castle was. After the maidservant finished assisting me out of my gown, I could send her away, letting her know I'd be fine without her. Then I would get dressed, sneak out a side door, and make my way down to the wharf.

No one would realize I was gone until morn. By then I would be far out to sea.

I started toward my bag sitting atop the trunk in the corner. What would Espen say when I made my appearance at the waterfront? He would be glad to see me, would he not?

I pictured his face when he'd been standing in the hallway speaking with Father. His handsome features had regarded Father with loyalty and respect, even when Father had been curt with him. I knew how much Espen appreciated Father, how much he looked up to him. He'd already risked putting a rift in his relationship with Father on account of me. Taking me with him to the Hundreds would cause him to fall from Father's good graces altogether.

I lowered myself onto the edge of the trunk.

I couldn't involve Espen in my escape. I didn't want the blame of my running away to fall on his shoulders. Perhaps I needed to put the plan out of my mind completely.

For long seconds, I tapped at my lip. I needed another option. But the longer I tapped and tried to force myself to think of other plans, the more my excitement mounted at the prospect of sailing away with Espen. It would be an adventure like those we'd had as children. Perhaps I could even aid him in searching for the lamp. And it would certainly be satisfying to spend time with him. After all, I'd relished the opportunity to be with him today, and our time together had ended much too soon.

I dropped my hand from my lip and sighed. If only I could accompany him in a way that wouldn't earn him my father's ire.

I plucked at the drawstring on my bag, pulling it open. If I hid on the ship and then revealed my presence after we were well away from Vordinberg, then no one could blame Espen for my coming along. I would heap the culpability upon myself so that Father could only be angry at me and not Espen.

The maidservant had taken out my gowns and hung them in the wardrobe in order to air them and smooth out the wrinkles. Only a few items remained in the bag, including the boy's tunic, leggings, and cap I sometimes donned when I hiked along the water's edge to find sea glass.

I tugged the garments out along with a hat that covered my hair. I'd found the disguise necessary to keep from drawing unwanted attention during my hiking, and it allowed me more freedom. Boys could go many more places and do many more things than a noblewoman.

In fact, I'd found myself using the attire more and more, so much that I'd stuffed it to the bottom of my bag, hoping I'd find some time to comb the beaches while in Vordinberg. The sea glass along the southern coast of Norvegia was ofttimes clearer and lighter than that in the west, glistening in shades of pale gold and green and blue. And I loved having diverse colors to work with in the artistic designs I created.

I could easily put on my disguise, and no one would recognize me, not even Espen. I smiled at the prospect of fooling him. When I revealed myself, we would share a good laugh.

Less than an hour later, I exited through a servant's door with my bag in hand and made my way past the stables to a side gate. At the sound of voices near the exit, I halted and crouched behind a shrub.

I pulled my cap down to hide my face. My hair was coiled underneath, and not a strand was visible. Even so, the half-moon was bright, and I didn't want to chance anyone seeing my face.

The voices belonged to two men. I couldn't see them, but at the mention of my father's name, I listened more intently.

"Lord Prestegard has finally agreed to it." It was Lord Grimsrud. Just the thought of the man sent a shiver up my spine. All throughout the eve, he'd stared at me relentlessly. Of the three suitors, he was the youngest and most attractive, with long dark hair, olive skin, and inky eyes. But he was also the one I'd liked the least. His comments had been cutting and coarse, his bearing arrogant, and his interactions condescending.

As uncomfortable as he'd made me, I'd learned to ignore unwanted attention from men. I'd perfected the skill shortly after I'd blossomed into a young woman, when I'd first begun to receive notice from men everywhere I went. Mother had also instructed me on how to play coy and use my womanly wiles to my advantage. She'd informed me that my beauty was my greatest asset and that I needed to wield it for my advantage.

So far, I'd failed to do so. And instead, my father was wielding it.

"Then he's chosen you after all?" came the second

voice, one I didn't recognize.

"I'm the only man who can produce the number of signatures they require."

I stopped breathing to make sure I could hear the conversation correctly. Was Lord Grimsrud insinuating that my father had chosen him to be my spouse?

"How soon before you can wed her?"

"I have asked to take her home with me at week's end," Lord Grimsrud answered. "As my wife."

"And has Lord Prestegard agreed?"

"If I guarantee him one hundred more men and instruct them to convene at Endressen."

The other man released a low whistle.

I had to cup a hand over my mouth to hold back my surprise. Father was intending to marry me off and send me away already?

"You must go and secure the loyalty of the men anon." Lord Grimsrud's voice dropped so low I almost didn't hear him. "When you have their names and signatures, return to me at once."

"Very well, my lord."

"If you fail me, he may very well give her to someone else, and I cannot abide the thought of any other man but me having the most beautiful woman in Norvegia."

"If he has promised you, then she is yours."

"I will not rest until we speak our vows and she is in my bed."

A gurgle of disgust pressed for release, but I swallowed it back. I flattened myself, suddenly afraid of having either man locate me. What would they do if they learned I'd overheard their conversation? I didn't want to find out. I needed to escape now more than ever.

Even as the panic began to build inside my chest, I remained motionless. A few moments later, footsteps passed by, thankfully without slowing. I made myself count to fifty before rising and heading toward the gate.

As I exited and glanced both ways up and down the side street, no one was in sight. I hovered close to the buildings in order to stay in the shadows and prayed I'd make it to the waterfront and the ship before it was too late.

My father was using me callously and coldly. That was now evident from the deal he'd orchestrated with Lord Grimsrud. If I'd had any reservations about hurting him by leaving so secretly, I no longer cared. And if my departure interfered with whatever he was hoping to gain from my union, it served him right.

One thing was very clear. I was going away, and I didn't intend to come back.

Chapter 6

Sylvi

I treaded water near the hull, waiting for another cloud to cross in front of the moon. I still had time. The cog remained moored, and sailors and passengers were still coming and going on the plank that connected the boat to the wharf.

After I'd arrived at the waterfront, I'd considered trying to sneak across the plank when no one was looking, but surely someone would notice my approach and question why a lone boy was boarding, would perhaps demand to know if I'd paid for passage.

Instead, I'd decided to swim circuitously to the boat, hide in the water, and climb up one of the ropes dangling over the side.

Though it was June, Ostby Sound, like most northern bodies of water, still retained the chill from the winter months. My feet were turning numb, as were my legs. But I was a good swimmer, had become as proficient as Kristoffer and Espen from the many years of swimming in the fjord, tributaries, and lakes that surrounded our summer home.

I strained to hear any commotion near the quarterdeck. It was mostly quiet, except for the lapping of the water against the thick oak panels. With a glance to the moon as it began to disappear behind a cloud, I grabbed on to the rope above me and heaved myself upward. I lunged for the next knot, wiggling to free myself from the grasp of the sea.

With each inch I scaled, I whispered grateful prayers that not only had I learned to swim from Kristoffer and Espen but I'd also had plenty of practice in climbing. There wasn't a single place they'd gone that I hadn't followed—or at least attempted to follow.

As my fingers reached the top of the deck rail, I paused and listened again. Boisterous voices rose into the crisp night air, hopefully far enough away that no one would notice me slipping over onto the deck.

The clouds would soon slide past the moon. I had to act now.

With a last heave, I mounted the final distance. For one second, I was straddling the rail, out in the open for anyone to see. Even in the dark, if someone had been looking in my direction, they would have noticed my outline.

My heart pounded with both anticipation and anxiety. And before I lost my courage, I swiveled and lowered myself slowly and silently, knowing I still needed to be careful until I was safely hidden.

As soon as my boots touched the deck, I darted for the opening that led to the cargo hold. During the return trip to the Hundreds, the ship would carry mostly empty barrels and crates that would be distributed amongst the fishing villages and filled with more of the pollock, mackerel, haddock, and halibut now that the cod fishing season was over.

If this ship held any cargo in addition to the empty containers, it had been loaded during the daylight hours, and now no one was paying any heed to the opening. I slipped inside and crawled on my hands and knees. The blackness was overwhelming, and I bumped into a barrel. As I felt my way along, I finally found what seemed to be a secure place behind several crates.

Shivering now from my wet and cold clothes, I leaned against the wall and pulled my knees in tight for warmth. How many hours would I need to hide before I could safely make an appearance? No, the real question was how long could I survive being cold without needing to show myself to Espen and ask for a blanket?

I rubbed at my arms, then rested my head against my knees. Even though I knew Espen wouldn't be upset that I'd made my way aboard the cog, I didn't want to chance anyone deciding I couldn't come, turning the ship around, and taking me back to my father.

"Father, how could you?" My whisper was drowned out by the waves lapping against the ship, the creak of the boards, as well as the unhurried footsteps overhead. Even if my words were lost, the hurt inside wouldn't go away.

Yes, it was time for me to be married. I was of marriageable age, and I'd resigned myself to my father finding me another suitable man. However, I'd expected him to once again take my wishes into consideration and to make sure I was agreeable to the union.

Why hadn't he done so this time? Why hadn't he listened to my reservations? Had he stopped loving me?

Tears pricked my eyes, but I blinked them back. I needed to stay angry with him and not allow myself to feel the misery over this break in our relationship. I was a strong woman, and if he refused to provide a safe and happy future for me, then I would take matters into my own hands and forge my own way.

Chapter 7

ESPEN

I STOOD IN THE BOW LETTING THE WIND PUMMEL ME. IT WAS COLD, but the thrashing wasn't punishment enough for my failure to disentangle Sylvi from the terrible matches Lord Prestegard had arranged.

I'd tried to sleep over the past few hours since weighing anchor and sailing out of Ostby Sound. Though the hammocks in the sterncastle were comfortable enough, I'd only tossed restlessly, the image of Sylvi's sad face etched into my mind.

Even now, as I breathed in the fresh air that was laden with sea spray, I willed myself to stop thinking about her, to appreciate the vastness of the open waters now that we were past the Cimbrian Strait. Especially the horizon where the pinkish-gray clouds touched the waves.

"Looks like we have a stowaway, fellows!" one of the sailors shouted from the stern.

"No, I am not a stowaway." The voice was calm and womanly and belonged to . . .

I spun so fast I almost tripped over my feet. There,

standing in front of the opening to the cargo hold, was a thin lad in a long tunic and leggings. The sailor had ahold of the back of the boy's neck and was pinching him.

The stowaway struggled to get free. "I demand that you take me to Espen at once."

My heart sped and shoved against my chest. "Here I am."

The lad whipped his head around, and I found myself staring into Sylvi's pretty blue eyes, rounded and begging for help.

As the soldier continued to pinch her neck, rage welled up within me. With a growl, I strode forward, my sword out even though I didn't remember unsheathing it. At the sight of me bearing down upon him, the sailor let go of Sylvi and staggered backward, his eyes wide.

Upon reaching Sylvi, I drew her to my side. In the same motion, I swept my sword in a wide arc, taking in the rest of the sailors and passengers who were present, including several merchants and my squires. "Do not lay a hand on her again. Unless you want to lose it."

I didn't care that my tone was ominous or that I was coming across as a brute. This was Sylvi, and I wouldn't stand for anyone touching her, much less hurting her.

The sailor was staring at Sylvi as though she'd grown a second head. He clearly was just now realizing he'd discovered a woman instead of a boy.

I wanted to shout out at him that he was an idiot. Even in a hat and boy's clothing, it was obvious Sylvi was a woman—a very beautiful woman.

She huddled closer to me, brushing against me.

Suddenly I became aware that she was shaking. Was she afraid? Or cold?

I glanced down to find that her skin was pale, her lips

blue, and her clothing damp. "Fie, Sylvi. You're wet. And freezing."

She tried for a smile, but her teeth were chattering too hard to form one.

Biting back several choice words, I jammed my sword in my sheath. Then I swept her off her feet, cradling her to my chest. With a frown, I stalked across the deck toward the sterncastle.

Everyone moved out of my path, and no one spoke a word. As I kicked against the captain's cabin, the door opened into the chamber that was only, at most, eight feet long by six feet wide. The captain wasn't present. But even if he had been, I would have asked him to leave.

As I lowered Sylvi to the room's lone chair, I beckoned outside to one of my squires. "Do your best to find Lady Sylvi a change of clothing."

I didn't wait for his response and instead grabbed the blankets covering the captain's bed. I draped them around her, wrapping her as tightly as I could.

"Thank you, Espen," she managed even as she continued to shiver. "I didn't realize I'd grown so cold."

I rubbed her arms through the blankets. What in the name of holy saints was Sylvi doing aboard this ship? The question clamored for an answer, but I needed to get her warmed up first.

I glanced over my shoulder out the open door again to my other squire. "Bring me a bowl of whatever is cooking."

A short while ago, one of the sailors had stoked the embers in the firebox and had started a pot of something. It didn't matter what she ate, as long as it was warm.

As I focused on her again, this time her lips turned up into a genuine smile. "I shall be fine in a few minutes,

Espen. You have no need to fret."

No need to fret? She clearly didn't realize the power she had over me—that I'd always worried about her and always would. In fact, if my squire didn't track down another outfit for her, I'd strip down to my braies and give her my own clothing. "Are you feeling warmer?"

She tilted her head to one side in that adorable way she did from time to time. "My head is cold. 'Tis likely from my wet hair. Perhaps if you take off my hat and unwind the braid?"

"I can do that." But could I really? Tentatively I lifted her cap and placed it on the bed. Her plait was coiled into a high knot.

"You will need to remove the pins first."

I squinted down at the knot, seeing the ends of several pins. "How many are there?"

"I did not keep count, Espen." A note of humor graced her voice. "If the task is too difficult for you, then free me from my cocoon, and I shall do the deed for myself."

"No." I rubbed at her arms again. "I'll do it."

As I studied the knot from all angles, all I could think about was dropping the pins one by one, letting her hair ripple down, then digging my fingers in until they were lost in the thick depths.

Balling my fists against the temptation, I swallowed hard. No, I couldn't do this. It was much too intimate. Maybe I needed to let her remove her own pins.

Her body gave a huge shudder, and she huddled deeper into the blankets.

Saint's blood. She was freezing. I had to stop thinking about myself and do this for her. I lifted my hand, but then let it hover above her hair.

"Espen." Her tone contained chastisement. "You can

wield any weapon placed in your hand more expertly than most men in the kingdom. Surely you can manage removing a few tiny pins from my hair."

"Aye, I can handle it just fine." Gingerly I touched one of the pins. "I'm just figuring out my strategy."

"Strategy?"

"Aye, so that I don't cause any tangles." I gave myself an imaginary pat on the back for coming up with an excuse so quickly to hide my fascination with her hair.

"Tangles are inevitable. Hopefully you have a comb? While I brought a few necessities along, I could not pack everything I shall need for the duration of the trip."

"So, you have a bag and extra clothing?"

"'Tis in the cargo hold, but the contents are likely wet since I had to swim to reach the boat."

"Where exactly are you going?"

"If you allow it, I shall accompany you wherever your journey takes you."

With my fingers on the pin, my thoughts raced in a dozen different directions. If I allowed Sylvi to come with me, the repercussions would be severe. What if people assumed that I'd abducted her? Even if my squires and others realized she was fleeing from her father's marriage arrangement, they would expect me to return her. In fact, having her along would damage her reputation and tarnish mine. I would lose whatever respect I had left with Lord Prestegard and possibly ruin my friendship with Kris.

Aye, letting her accompany me was a bad idea.

But I would do it anyway. I could do naught less, no matter the consequences.

I jiggled out the first pin without touching her hair and expelled a pent-up breath as I placed the offending item on the bed next to her hat. As I carefully removed the rest of the pins, she regaled me with the tale of how she'd crept along the wharf, found a secluded area, and slipped soundlessly into the water before swimming to the cog, climbing aboard, and crawling into the cargo hold.

"No one noticed me until one of the sailors came down for food and drink and discovered me asleep."

The coil had unwound, and now her braid hung down her back. The bottom was already unraveling. Surely it wouldn't be too hard to finish loosening the strands so that her hair was free of constraints and could dry.

I touched the end, the damp pieces brushing my fingers and sending an unbidden thrill through my blood.

"I was not expecting him to be so rough," she continued, oblivious to the effect she had on me—somehow always turning my world upside down.

I untwisted a part of the strand but then hesitated. What was I doing? I was playing with fire, that's what.

"I was half afraid he intended to throw me overboard as fish bait." She released a soft laugh—one that only warmed my blood even more.

I had to think of something else besides her. But what? Whenever I was with her, she was all I could think about. "More likely he would have pressed you into service and then put you to work scrubbing the deck or emptying chamber pots."

"Oh my. Then 'tis a very good thing I boarded the correct ship. I admit, I was slightly disoriented after swimming."

I paused as the danger of all she'd done barreled into me. "Aye, there were several cogs. You're lucky you made it to the right one."

Even with hearing about all she'd risked, the conversation wasn't distracting me from my attraction to her the way I'd hoped it would. With each slow unraveling of her braid, my body seemed to be unraveling at the same time.

Maybe if I finished the deed as fast as I could, then I'd be able to step away and put the appropriate one foot of distance between us.

Sucking in a breath, I let my fingers fly over her braid. As more and more hair came loose and began to flow around my fingers, I couldn't avoid having it spill over my hands and wrists and even my arm.

By the time I reached the plaited section near her neck, I was completely undone. As I combed through the final few crisscrosses, I knew I needed to pull away, that I'd done enough. But another part rationalized that I was a friend helping a friend.

I dug in and, as the last of the twists came loose, I let my fingers slide in deeper. Even though her hair was damp, the thick silk closed around me and wouldn't let me go.

At some point, she'd fallen silent. What did she think of my boldness? Surely if she didn't like it, she would speak up and tell me to stop.

I combed down, letting the damp strands caress my hand. A groan pushed at the back of my throat, and a strange burning need clawed at my chest.

She still said nothing, and held herself still, as if aware of something happening between us. How could she not be conscious of it? Especially with the heat that was rolling in waves off my body? She would soon have no need to change. My flames would dry her.

I untangled my fingers, but then before I could stop myself, I slid them in again. This time, I was too close to her neck, and the tips grazed the spot right behind her ear.

She stiffened.

I battled a sudden and swift urge to pull aside the curtain of her hair, bare her neck, and press a kiss there.

What was I doing? I'd been with her for less than ten minutes and was already making a fool of myself over her. I had to stop. There was too much at stake—namely, our friendship. I didn't want to lose her and our ease of relating. And I didn't want her to lump me with all the other men who lusted over her.

With an extreme amount of self-control, I extricated my hand and stepped away from her. I cleared my throat to make sure I sounded casual. "There. I did it. No tangles."

"Good." Was her voice slightly breathless? Clearly she was sensing something. Or mayhap I was scaring her.

After she'd risked her life to make her way onto this ship, I didn't want her to fear me. She'd come because she expected me to keep her safe, and I couldn't break her trust. Not for any reason—especially not because I lacked control of my own raging attraction to her.

Thankfully, my squire chose that moment to step into the doorway, a small stack of clothing in his possession. "I was able to find these, sire, though I'm not sure if they'll fit the lady."

Sylvi rose, let the blankets fall away, and took the garments before I could figure out what to do. "Yes, they will suffice for the time being. Thank you. Now if you will both be so kind as to step out, I shall don them."

She didn't have to ask me twice. At the merest thought of her undressing, I couldn't exit the captain's cabin fast enough. As the door closed behind me, the burning low inside my gut only fanned hotter.

I needed to dive into the sea and drench every spark that was flaring. But I feared no amount of dousing would ever extinguish what I felt for her.

Chapter 8

Sylvi

I'd done it. I was safe with Espen and away from my father's scheming.

My relief made me almost giddy as I donned the warm woolen leggings and the dry tunic. They were much too big and not entirely clean, but I managed to roll and tie them into a semblance of decency. After I put on the heavy cloak and covered the ill-fitting garments, I opened the door to the sight of Espen's broad back. His feet were spread and arms crossed as though standing guard.

I had the strangest urge to glide my hand up his back to his neck and dig my fingers into his hair just as he had mine.

Oh my. Every move of his hands in my hair had tightened my muscles with a pleasure I couldn't explain. And I could still feel the warmth of his touch against my neck, the soft graze of his fingers. Had he lingered for an extra second, or had I merely imagined it?

"Are you decent?" he asked still facing away from me.

"And if I say no, what will you do?" I couldn't keep from teasing him.

"You'll force me to lock you away until we reach our destination." Thankfully, his voice contained a note of mirth.

As he peeked over his shoulder at me with a smile, I allowed myself to relax. Everything would go back to normal between us as it should. Our friendship would be the same as always. And we wouldn't need to worry about any awkwardness settling in.

He turned and was holding out a steaming bowl of what appeared to be pottage. "Eat this. It will warm you."

Before I could argue, he steered me to the chair in the captain's cabin. As I lowered myself and took the bowl from him, I caught him looking at my hair, which was still unbound and falling around me in disarray.

I gathered a handful and wrangled it back. I must look a fright attired in men's clothing and with my hair so unruly. "If only Lord Grimsrud could see me in my current state, he'd no longer think me the most beautiful woman in Norvegia."

Espen dropped his head as if to hide his reaction.

"'Tis truly horrible, then?" I took a small bite of the pottage and let the warmth fill my mouth.

Espen peeked up, and something in his eyes sent more of the strange pleasure coiling through my middle. That something wasn't the kind of bold wanting I was accustomed to seeing in the eyes of men. Instead, it was a banked flame, one that was hot enough to sear but closely guarded.

He let his lashes fall and dipped his head again.

This time my stomach dipped with him—a strange motion, almost as if the ship had crested and fallen over a large wave. Rather than leaving me seasick, I felt light, almost dizzy with the contentment of being with him.

"Well?" I couldn't keep the note of happiness from my voice.

He visibly drew in a breath, then rose so that he was looking straight at me. Whatever had been in his eyes before was gone, replaced with the usual friendliness. "Aye, Sylvi, I'm sorry to say, you couldn't look horrible even if you rolled around in fish guts."

I smiled around the next bite of pottage. "What about fish guts and chicken feathers? I would surely look horrible then."

"Not even then."

He wasn't exactly flattering me. He was simply being his usual sweet self. Even so, I loved knowing he accepted me even when I was at my worst—that I didn't have to be perfect for him to think I was pretty.

His attitude was a refreshing change, an encouragement I didn't receive even amongst my family, who had always expected me to look and dress the part of Norvegia's most beautiful woman.

Attired in mail and a cloak held closed by his golden sword pin given to him by the king, he leaned against the open door casually, but something in his movements was carefully controlled. Had Espen always been so measured around me, as though he was holding himself back?

"So, are you ready to tell me why you chose to join me on my quest to find the holy lamp?" His question was as nonchalant as usual too, but somehow today, at this moment, I could feel an undercurrent between us. Of what, I did not know. But it was there and tugged at me, keeping my insides taut.

Suddenly breathless, I swirled my spoon in the pottage. "And what if I came because I wanted to be with you? Is that not reason enough?" I tried for a teasing tone and hoped it came across that way.

He folded his arms, his thick biceps growing more pronounced. "Of course, I am irresistible to most women." His grin cocked up on one side so that he looked roguish, especially with strands of his long light-brown hair blowing in the wind and his unshaven face scruffier than usual.

"And that is exactly why I chased after you." I loved our banter, but this time I couldn't seem to gain the upper hand, couldn't seem to gather my wits, couldn't seem to find my footing in the continuing dizziness of our exchange.

I took another bite of the pottage, trying to make sense of this interaction I was having with Espen. What had changed between us? Why was I feeling this new thrum of excitement and anticipation with him?

He glanced behind him, then lowered his voice. "Did something happen, Sylvi?"

At the gravity in his tone, I let my spoon grow idle.

He crossed toward me and dropped to one knee in front of me. "Did someone harm you?"

"No." The seriousness of my predicament fell over me now too. "But I overheard Lord Grimsrud, and Father already gave him his word that he could marry me by the end of the week."

Espen's blue-green eyes darkened into a stormy

sea. As I shared with him my tale of discovering his note in my chamber and deciding to leave, I spared no detail, including the conversation I'd overheard between Lord Grimsrud and his servant.

"Names and signatures." Espen stared at a spot behind me, his mind clearly trying to solve this new riddle.

"What do you think he meant?" I licked the last drops of pottage from my spoon, my belly now warm and full.

"I think your father is conspiring somehow."

"Conspiring against whom?"

Espen's eyes narrowed. "I don't know. But he's clearly trying to gather support. From the sounds of it, he's been using your three candidates to do so, promising you to the one who provides him the most names and signatures."

None of it made sense. "Lord Grimsrud sent his servant out to gather one hundred more signatures and said he will not rest until our vows are pledged and I am in his bed."

Espen bolted upward and strode to the door. He faced outside, kneading the back of his neck as though he wanted to tear it off.

"Something is just not right with Father," I said softly. "I sensed it even before I overheard Lord Grimsrud and his servant."

Espen turned, his expression tortured. "Something's definitely not right."

"Then you are not angry with me for coming with you?"

"Of course not. I cannot abide the thought of that crook taking you home."

"I cannot abide it either, which is why I shall not return to Vordinberg when you take the lamp back." I hadn't thought too much about the future yet. So far, I'd been intent upon escaping and surviving. But now, at the prospect of my father and Lord Grimsrud awaiting my return, I didn't want to go anywhere near the capital, not until they were gone.

Espen began to pace the length of the tiny cabin. "I'll think of a way to keep you from having to marry Lord Grimsrud. I vow it."

But how? I didn't speak the question aloud. It was the same question we'd faced outside the great hall when we'd spoken to my father last night. "If my father is indeed hosting a challenge among the three contenders, then he will not be willing to change his terms of the agreement, not after already gaining their cooperation."

"Then we'll have to find another man—a good and worthy man—for you to wed." Espen was still pacing. "And you'll need to marry him this week before your father locates you."

"Where will we find a good and worthy man?"

Espen stopped and pinned his serious eyes upon me. "Is there someone you care about? A man you've met that you know you could marry?"

I started to shake my head. I hadn't entertained thoughts of any other man since Rolfe's passing. Not that I'd loved Rolfe. But I'd liked him well enough that I'd looked forward to our future together.

"There has to be someone, Sylvi," Espen persisted. "Maybe you won't have a heart match, but if he's kind and brings you happiness, then you must marry him."

The crashing of waves and the raucous talking of

the sailors filtered into the chamber as I let my mind wander back through the noblemen I'd met over the past year. Each one had been too overcome with my outward beauty to take me seriously and value me for who I was and not merely for how I looked.

"If we narrow down the man," Espen said, "then on our return voyage, we can make arrangements to travel to his home and see you wed."

He rattled off the names of several noblemen who were also a part of the Knights of Brethren. I shook my head at the suggestions even though they were respectable men. He proceeded to list some of the noblemen who came to court from time to time, men of good character. But, again, I found something negative about each one.

"You're being difficult." His tone was laced with exasperation.

"I cannot narrow down a man when I harbor affection for no one."

"No one?" His brows rose. "Come now, Sylvi. Surely there is one man you can tolerate. Even as a friend."

I smiled. "There is you."

"Be serious."

"You are the only man I can tolerate."

"As flattering as your compliment is"—his voice turned sarcastic—"I'm not a viable candidate."

I laughed lightly. "You're very viable."

He rolled his eyes. "Since you're not in the frame of mind to take this seriously right now, we'll address the matter later."

What if marrying Espen was my best option?

I sat forward, letting my mirth fall away. I studied

him with all seriousness. Was this my answer? Did I dare consider marrying Espen?

He was shaking his head and glancing out at the deck, his eyes averted. With one boot hooked back against the door frame, he outwardly appeared relaxed. But I could see the tension etched into every muscle.

As though sensing my scrutiny, he cast a glance my way before staring out of the room again. "Don't even think about it, Sylvi."

"Why ever not?"

"Because I'm not of the nobility, for one thing."

"You know that does not matter to me."

"It matters to your family."

"I no longer care what my family wants."

"Your father will loathe me."

"He will loathe me more." I didn't want to jeopardize Espen's relationship with my father or my family. I knew how much he admired my father. And my father cared for him as a son. But already, in siding with me, Espen had drawn Father's censure. I regretted that I'd put him in this trouble, but surely his connection with the king would keep him from any reprisals from my father.

"Already, by having you here with me, I'm endangering my friendship with Kris. If we marry, I would lose all hope of his forgiveness."

"Kristoffer will thank you for rescuing me from a very bad match."

"If I make you my wife, he'll slit my throat in my sleep the first chance he has."

"He will do no such thing, and you know it."

"He won't support us being together. He's always made it clear that I'm not to regard you as anything more than a sister and friend."

"He has?"

"Aye. And I agree with him. You're off limits. You always have been and always will be."

So that was why Espen had never shown any interest in me, not even in those early years when I'd attempted to draw his attention. He'd built an unscalable wall between us and didn't plan to tear it down.

I understood he was an honorable man and lived by high standards. He didn't want to do anything to compromise who he was and what he stood for, and I didn't want him to do so either. But in this case, wasn't saving me the most chivalrous thing he could do?

I had to find a way to break through his defenses and excuses. "My family will already be displeased with me for running away. They will likely disown me for this. So that means I am free to live the way I choose."

"They won't disown you." He cast a glance my way. In that instant I glimpsed stark desire in his eyes. I'd seen that look enough in other men to know what it was.

I stood, my body suddenly thrumming. Espen did like me. Maybe it wasn't the same way other men did, but an attraction existed, even if just a little. Maybe I liked him too, just a little. And maybe that's why we'd experienced sparks when he'd unbraided my hair earlier.

We could explore the attraction, could we not?

I started toward him slowly.

He dropped his boot and straightened. "Hold on, Sylvi."

I didn't stop.

He held out a hand as though that could keep me from approaching.

It wouldn't. He should know by now that I wasn't so easily swayed. I captured his hand and wrapped my fingers around his. At the contact, his attention shifted to our interlocked hands. His nostrils flared just slightly. No one else would have noticed. In the past, I wouldn't have paid attention either. But this time, I was looking for clues that he desired me more than he would admit.

If he longed for me the way other men did, then why wouldn't he be willing to at least consider taking me as his wife?

Maybe he wouldn't be able to give me the life of luxury I was accustomed to, but what had such a life ever given me in return? It hadn't satisfied me. It certainly wasn't offering me a happy future. Instead, in some ways, it had left me weak and empty and wishing for more.

He stared at our hands before finally lifting his gaze. The yearning from moments ago was gone. In fact, it was so completely absent that I faltered, nearly took a step back. Had I just imagined the desire there?

"We're friends and friends alone," he said softly, as though speaking to an errant child.

I shrugged as nonchalantly as I could manage. "Friendship is the foundation of all good marriages, is it not?"

"Mayhap. But I don't want to risk ruining our friendship."

"I do not wish to ruin that either."

"Good then." He squeezed my hand platonically

before letting go, as if the matter was settled.

It wasn't settled for me. In fact, the idea of the two of us being together was only growing in appeal with each passing moment. I just needed to discover Espen's truest feelings for me. I didn't want to coerce or seduce him into something he didn't want. I couldn't risk him loathing me for causing him to abandon his principles.

But I had to at least explore the possibility of us becoming more than friends. While I might not be proficient at much, I was very skilled at using my beauty to allure. And it was time to focus the full force of my womanliness upon Espen.

Chapter 9

ESPEN

EXQUISITE TORTURE. THAT'S WHAT SYLVI'S PROXIMITY WAS TO me.

In the fading light of eventide, she rested her head against my arm as we sat together by the deck rail. "So, we shall reach your family's fishing village late in the afternoon on the morrow?" Her question held a hint of something that told me she was still plotting all the ways she could weaken my resolve.

She'd employed the tactic all day, had hardly left my side since our morning discussion about finding a new husband she could marry this week.

My heart thundered every time I considered her idea that the two of us get married. It was preposterous, unfathomable, and completely irrational. I wasn't considering it in the least, no matter how hard she was trying to convince me it was a good plan.

"Aye. My family will welcome us and open their home for as long as we have need." I tore off a hunk of the dried fish on my trencher and stuffed it in my mouth.

I was considering leaving Sylvi with them while I forged ahead with my squires. We would need to borrow a rowboat to reach the Chapel Cliff where Maxim and Princess Elinor believed the holy lamp may have once been stored. I'd never been there before, even though I'd witnessed the light during my days as a fisherman. The place was built on the outer banks of the Hundreds on a tall cliff-like rock that rose out of the water and soared high above the islands. A chapel at the top housed a light that the keeper maintained and burned at all times to guide the many ships navigating the dangerous waters.

Sylvi and I had discussed the place at length today, especially its history during the days when Norvegia had been raided by seafarers from Uthelande. Treasures and riches had oft been kept in the chapel because the imposing height and steepness of the cliffs made the climb to the top treacherous. Not many could scale the cliff without aid from the keeper, who provided a rope ladder only to those he deemed worthy enough to ascend.

Sylvi shifted, her leg bumping against mine. My body was much too in tune with each contact point—the brush of her arm, the touch of her hip, and now her leg. Most of all, I was keenly aware of her face near mine—so close I could almost rest my chin on her head. I'd wanted to, but I'd refrained, just as I'd refrained numerous other times throughout the day.

Her trencher on her lap was untouched. "What will they think of me?"

"They'll think you don't eat enough."

She laughed and twisted at the piece of brown goat's cheese on her plate. "I shall let you eat for the both of us."

I paused in breaking off another piece of fish. The year

her father had brought me to their summer home had been a season when the waters off the Hundreds had become overfished, and my father and other fishermen had needed to row much farther out into the Dark Sea to have any success at fishing. Even then, the nets hadn't been nearly as full, and we'd faced the dangerous storms that arose out of nothing.

That summer as a ten-year-old, I'd been growing rapidly and hungry all the time anyway. With the scarcity of fish, I'd been ravenous those first days when I'd lived with the Prestegards. Sylvi, always sensitive, had been quick to offer me her food then, even though she hadn't needed to. And she was doing so again.

"You need to eat too, Sylvi," I said gently, the same way I had all those years ago.

She picked up the wedge of cheese, nibbled off a bite, and then returned it to her trencher. "Tell me another tale from your childhood and your fishing days."

Around us on the deck, none of the other passengers were paying us any heed. Though we'd garnered some raised brows early in the day, a few well-placed glares had warned everyone to accept that Sylvi was with me.

I hadn't felt the need to explain who she was and why she was here to anyone but the captain. Nevertheless, from the admiring sidelong glances cast her way, it was obvious everyone had figured out who she was— Norvegia's most beautiful maiden.

Of course, my squires were aware of my friendship with Sylvi. If they were wondering why I hadn't yet turned the ship around to send her home, they'd kept it to themselves. Now they were sprawled out near the stern, a rowdy game of dice keeping them occupied. A few of the sailors who weren't on duty had joined them.

Thankfully, for the duration of the day, we'd had calm weather, the wind filling the single sail and moving us along at a decent pace. I would have preferred a stronger gale to push us faster. But we were still making good time and would be within the skerry channels by morn.

The skerries were small rocky islands with minimal vegetation that weren't habitable by people but were home to seals, walruses, and sea birds. The rocky islands were usually found in clusters and ran parallel to the coast. Because they stretched for many miles, they afforded protected channels for safer traveling.

During the summer months, sailing the Dark Sea was never without risks, but it was much easier and smoother than in the winter, when the gales were fierce and the waves rough. Nevertheless, I would rest easier once we made it to the skerry channels.

As I finished my last piece of fish, Sylvi took my trencher and placed hers on my lap instead. I started to push it back, but she stopped me by laying her hand over mine. "Eat it, Espen. Please. My stomach is still adjusting to the sea."

At the intimate pressure, I hardly comprehended her words—was instead too conscious of the feel of her soft skin.

She squeezed gently.

Summoning up my reserve of steel, I disentangled my hand from hers as I'd done the rest of the day whenever she'd made a not-so-secret effort to draw me into her marriage plan. As I filled both of mine with food, I could hear her exasperated sigh.

Even if I wasn't falling prey to her ploys, I had to give her credit for trying. She was determined and persistent.

I stuffed in a chunk of cheese, never one to turn down

food since I was nearly always hungry. I searched my memory for another story I could tell her, a new one to entertain her. Since I'd spent my early years on the fishing boat with my father, I'd had many adventures, some dangerous.

I'd already told her the most exciting tales—those involving storms, whales, sea monsters, and death-defying danger. I'd experienced it all and had always loved fishing and the sea. During those first weeks away from it, I'd been sorely homesick, not only for my kin but for the sea.

My family had missed me too, but my father had been proud of what I'd become and boasted of me tirelessly. My steady income and the spoils I'd earned after battles provided for my kin so that over recent years, they'd never been in want. Someday, when I finished my work as a Knight of Brethren, I had every intention of returning and fishing alongside my father again.

"I don't know," I said after swallowing my bite. "I don't think there's anything more I can tell you that you haven't already heard."

She leaned in. This time she lifted slightly so that her mouth was near my ear. At the warmth of her breath in the hollow, I clenched my fingers into a fist to keep from reaching for her.

"There is one thing you can tell me that I haven't heard." Her voice was as thick as honey.

"What one thing?" My question came out somewhat husky, much to my embarrassment.

"Admit that you want me." In the next instant, her lips brushed my earlobe.

At the contact, heat charged through my blood. Her mouth, her lips, her breath. Saint's blood. She was so near.

I felt almost frantic with the longing to turn and lay claim to her. But once I did, I wouldn't be able to stop myself from doing so again.

I gritted my teeth against the need. "I know what you're doing, Sylvi. And it's not working."

"What am I doing?" She whispered in the hollow of my ear again.

This time as the heat surged, I scrambled to my feet, letting the trencher fall to the deck with a clatter.

She stood just as quickly.

At the attention we were drawing, I spun to face the sea, drawing in a steadying breath and focusing on the rolling waves that hid the dark depths underneath.

Fie. Resisting Sylvi was a sore trial. But I had to do it. If I let myself give in to my desire for her, I'd only bring trouble upon us both, wouldn't I?

I'd had all day to think about her reasoning for being together. I could admit that I was relieved she wasn't interested in any of the choices of men I'd offered. And I could admit that I was thrilled I was the only man she wanted to be with. At least for the time being.

Regardless, she didn't need to settle for me, her very last option. Given plenty of time and the right occasions, she'd meet someone exceptional. The trouble was, we didn't have time or occasions. We had to find her a spouse this week, as soon as possible, before her father could get ahold of her and force her to comply with his unscrupulous matchmaking.

She stepped beside me, and I could feel her hesitation, almost as if she realized she'd taken her plotting too far this time. She remained silent, and from the corner of my eye I could see her staring out at the sea, her brows furrowed, her lips pursed.

I wanted to say something to smooth things over between us, but my thoughts were crashing into one another with the punishing rhythm of the waves, and I couldn't make sense of what I needed to do.

A part of me knew I ought to resist my attraction to her, just as I'd always done. But another part wanted to throw caution away and give in to this plan of hers. Aye, in doing so, I'd put a deep wedge between myself and Kris as well as Lord Prestegard. But Sylvi's happiness was worth any rifts or repercussions.

I opened my mouth, knowing I had to say something, but she spoke first. "Forgive me, Espen. I am losing everyone and everything else in my life. And I cannot abide losing you and our friendship too."

"You won't lose me or our friendship—"

"Yes, I am pushing you away with something you do not want."

The problem was that I wanted her too much, but how did I go about telling her that?

"So, because I value our friendship more than anything else, I shall cease my wooing you and resume our normal interactions."

Wooing me? Was that what she thought she was doing? I almost snorted. She had no need to woo any man. I would fall at her feet in adoration without her encouraging it. So would most men.

"Since I am clearly irritating you more than anything, I shall retire to my cabin for the night and give you the peace you are seeking." With that, she turned and began to make her way across the deck toward the captain's cabin, which he'd graciously given over to her for the remainder of the voyage since she was the only female aboard.

I watched her, frustration welling up within me. She hadn't done anything wrong, and yet by the slump of her shoulders and in the drag of her steps, I sensed her regret. I opened my mouth to call out to her to wait, to come back so that we could talk some more. But what would I say?

Even if this was hard for both of us, the best thing to do in this situation was to let her go. And then maybe on the morrow, I'd have more clarity regarding what to do.

Chapter 10

Sylvi

I was going to die.

The ship rose then fell with such force that I would have tumbled out of my narrow bed, except I was clutching the wooden bedframe with one hand and a pot in the other.

The blackness of the night swirled around me. I could see nothing, not even the pot in front of me. As nausea rose again with the swell of another wave, I heaved. Nothing more came out, since I'd already emptied the contents of my stomach long ago when the pounding of the storm had wakened me from a deep slumber.

Ever since, I'd been sitting on my bed in the tiny chamber, praying our ship wouldn't sink, that the storm would end, and that my misery would cease.

Once in a while above the roar of the wind and the crashing of waves, I could hear the shout of one of the men. Each time I thought of them, I felt worse, knowing I was in this tiny room sheltered from the battering of the rain and waves while everyone else was being pummeled as they fought to empty the excess water from the hull and cargo hold to keep the vessel afloat.

As the nausea passed, I breathed hard, trying to calm my racing pulse. And at the same time, I whispered a prayer for the men, especially for Espen, that Providence would keep them safe. I was anxious for news on how he fared, but I knew even without him uttering instructions that he would want me to remain here on my bed in this cabin. I also knew if I was in immediate danger, he would come get me.

Not because he was attracted to me and couldn't get enough of me. He'd proven all of yesterday that he was immune to my wiles in a way no other man was. In fact, I'd gone as far as practically placing a kiss on his ear to get some kind of reaction from him, and all I'd done with my bold move was push him away.

I'd been mortified with myself for my brazenness. And after closing the door on his confused stare last eve, I'd crawled into bed and pulled the covers over my head. I didn't know how I could ever look him in the eyes again.

The simple fact was, Espen wouldn't go against his principles and have a relationship with me that went beyond mere friendship. A part of me admired him for his strength. But another part couldn't keep the disappointment at bay. It felt strangely similar to when I'd liked him as a young girl only to have him spurn me then too.

I was also embarrassed to admit, I'd never once considered whether he had a maiden he already cared about, someone he'd made a pledge to. What if he was simply trying to remain faithful to her?

The ship rolled again. And so did my stomach. I tried to maintain my equilibrium and hold myself still, but my body wouldn't cooperate, and in the next instant, I was heaving again.

When I finished, I closed my eyes. As the ship righted, it tossed me against the wall, and my head smacked painfully. The blackness of oblivion hovered just out of reach. A moment later, it swallowed me and took me there.

Gentle hands shook me. "Sylvi." Espen's voice rose above the crashing and clanking.

My head throbbed, and my stomach clenched. I opened my eyes to darkness and tried to push myself up, but I fell back, too weak.

The ship was still rocking with rough waves, but the movement wasn't as extreme. Had we come through the worst of the storm?

His hands glided over me as though he sensed I was injured. As the fingers came into contact with my head, I cried out at the sharp pain.

"You're bleeding."

I was overcome with dizziness. Before I could formulate words, the blackness engulfed me once more.

The next time I awoke, a soft light penetrated the darkness of the cabin. Espen was bent over me, his face etched with determination. One of his squires stood beside him. They were both dripping wet. I could feel the pressure of a bandage wrapped around my head and guessed they'd worked together to tend my wound.

As with the last time I'd awoken, I could feel the waves still pressing hard against the ship, so much that my stomach revolted. The moment I tried to push up, I fell unconscious again.

Chapter 11

ESPEN

"I NEED TO STAY WITH HER," I TOLD MY SQUIRE.

As the lantern cast a low glow across Sylvi's pale face, my chest pinched with anxiety. I should have checked on her much sooner, to see how she was faring.

But I'd tied myself to the deck like everyone else to avoid being swept out to sea. And I'd worked feverishly to keep the ship afloat. With each crash of the waves, the vessel had taken on too much water, and we'd needed all hands to bail.

When the roughest part of the storm had passed, I'd made my way first to Sylvi's cabin. From the moment I'd found her injured with a gash on her head and unconscious, I hadn't stopped berating myself.

"Would you like me to stay too, sire?" My squire asked the question timidly, all the while staring at the door.

Was he insinuating that my being alone with Sylvi would be improper? I tossed him a dark glare. "She's injured and unconscious. I hardly think a chaperone is necessary."

"Very well, sire."

Once the door closed behind him, I made quick work of shedding my wet garments and donning something from the captain's trunk. Thankfully, other than the water rushing under the door and flooding the floor, nothing else in the room had gotten wet. As far as I could tell, Sylvi was dry and so was the bed.

I lowered myself to the chair and brushed my hand across her smooth, high cheek. "I'm sorry, Sylvi."

She shifted but didn't wake.

For someone like me, who'd grown up on the sea, the rough waters and storm were nothing more than an inconvenience. But my two squires had been sick in their hammocks for much of the storm. No doubt Sylvi had been ill too, although her pot was tipped over on the floor, the contents likely washed away from the water that had been rushing in and out of the cabin.

Her eyes fluttered open, and she groaned.

I leaned forward, wanting to do something to ease her pain. "I'm here now. Tell me what you need."

Her eyes rounded, and she cupped a hand over her mouth. She was sick to her stomach again, except she had nothing to expel. As she ceased her heaving, she flopped back into the bed, listless and weak.

If I could but hold her still and keep her from feeling the rolling of the ship, that would ease her discomfort. I stood and hesitated beside her bed. With a glance at the door, I considered asking my squire to return and sit in the chair as a chaperone after all.

But, blowing out a tense breath, I lowered myself onto the bed and gathered Sylvi into my arms. I stretched out against the wall and pulled her close, wrapping both my arms around her and sheltering her in the curve of my body so that she was tightly ensconced.

Without herbal remedies to prevent her queasiness, my holding her was the next best means of helping her. I'd seen the method work oft enough during my days at sea. My steadiness would keep her from feeling the sway of the ship so severely, would lessen her being tossed around, and would diminish the dizziness and discomfort.

As I drew her in even more, I closed my eyes at how right it felt to be taking care of her. Being with her, at her side, and ensuring she was safe—was there anything else in life that compared to that mission?

I couldn't imagine anyone else with her helping her the way I was. In fact, the very thought of another man doing this made my blood run cold, the same way it had always run cold whenever I'd pictured her with Rolfe Solberg. During those months of her betrothal to the wealthy nobleman, I'd stayed away from Karlstadt as much as possible so that I wouldn't have to see the two together. But even when I'd been absent, my dreams had been tortured with images of Rolfe holding her the way I was right now.

Of course, I'd tried to ignore those dreams, tried to resign myself to Sylvi being with another man, but always in the back of my mind I'd been unsettled.

Until now. I pressed my nose against her hair and breathed her in. Holding her was like gaining entrance to paradise.

I'd told myself that I could never have her. Never. But what if I'd been wrong? What if this was my chance to be with her as I'd always wanted? I couldn't let this opportunity slip through my fingers, could I?

If I did, surely I'd be miserable the rest of my life.

As a heavy wave slammed into the ship, I held her

tightly, bracing her, letting myself take the battering.

Aye, this was exactly where I wanted Sylvi. The only place I wanted her. Right here in my arms, in my embrace, where she would always be safe.

I awoke with a start. Although I'd learned to get by on a meager amount of sleep, somehow during the early hours of the morn, I'd dozed.

As my eyes flew open, I could see from the level of oil in the lantern that I hadn't slumbered for long. Maybe an hour.

At Sylvi's movement against me, I pulled her nearer, that same need from earlier in the night driving me to protect and shield her.

Instead of her listlessness in response, this time she pressed in, burying her face against my chest and releasing a sigh.

I could sense her beginning to awaken, but she wasn't fully alert. I gently touched the bandage on her head. It was dry, which hopefully meant the bleeding had stopped. The gash at her hairline hadn't been large enough to require stitches, but I'd covered it in a healing salve that had been among the sparse items in the medical box under the bed.

From the quiet outside the cabin and the faint light coming from under the door, I guessed dawn had arrived and chased away the storm. It was time to release Sylvi and put the proper distance between us.

But even as I willed my hands to let go of her, they shifted and found her hair instead. It was bound in a braid, and my thoughts turned immediately to my unraveling of her braid just yesterday.

I ran my fingers along the length of the plait, the smoothness and silkiness stirring the memory of combing my fingers through the strands. I wanted to loosen her hair and dig my fingers in again. In fact, I wanted to wake up every morn like this, holding her tight.

She released a sleepy sigh and stretched her legs. "Espen?"

"Hmmm . . .?" I dropped my hand away from her hair, guilt shimmying through me at my forwardness. What would she think when she found us in the tiny bed, lying together as close to one another as humanly possible?

"Is the storm over?" she whispered.

"Aye."

"Good." She made no move to extricate herself from me. I guessed she was still half slumbering. Or perhaps she intended to use this situation to woo me.

She'd said last night that she would cease and resume our normal interaction as friends. Did I want her to try to woo me again?

I gave myself a stern inward shake. As perfect as this situation was for forcing something to happen between us, I wouldn't take advantage of her. And I didn't want her to have to resort to flaunting herself to convince me to help her.

If she truly wanted to marry me to avoid her father's matches, then I needed to do that for her . . . as her friend. Because that's what friends did. They helped each other without reservation or recompense.

"Sylvi?" I loosened my hold and pulled back enough that I could see her face.

Her lashes fluttered up, and her sleep-filled eyes met

mine. Even pale and sick and with a bandage, her beauty stunned me. But as always, I tamped down my desires. She was more than just a beautiful woman, so much more. With as much focus as everyone else put on her physical appearance, I wanted to be one person who saw past that to her truest self.

She wiggled slightly, freed her arm, then lifted her hand to my cheek. Her palm flattened against the scruff on my jaw, sending jolts of awareness rippling along every nerve-ending, reminding me just how close she was, how soft and warm and curvy.

She'd never touched my face before, not even yesterday in all the contacts she'd initiated. What did she mean by it?

Her lashes dropped slightly, shadowing her eyes, making them darker. With desire?

Nay. I was imagining things. Either that or she was utilizing the situation to stir me up again to get me to do her bidding. And I didn't want her to show affection to me like this in pretense. I would rather her do it genuinely or not at all.

"I'm sorry I made you feel as though you had to woo me in order to gain my help."

"And I am sorry for bothering you with my wooing." She didn't remove her hand.

I reached up and gently tucked her hand back against my chest. "As my friend, you shouldn't have to work at gaining my cooperation."

She cocked her head, studying my face.

"If you need my help, I'll give it to you freely, without you needing to earn it."

"I do not understand."

I swallowed all the objections, all the excuses, all the

warnings for why I shouldn't assist her in this way. "I'll marry you, Sylvi."

Her eyes rounded. "You will?"

"Aye."

The blue was as clear as a wellspring in the dawn light. I wanted to drink her in and quench my thirst for her. But I scooted back as far as I could go, flattening myself against the wall. On the narrow bed, it wasn't much, but it put another inch between us.

"Do you want to marry me, Espen?" She made no move to touch me, thankfully. I wasn't sure how well I'd resist if she laid on her charm at this moment. "I do not want you to do it if you will come to regret it. For doing so will surely have consequences for you."

"I'm aware of the consequences."

"I have no wish to harm your friendship with Kristoffer. He is important to you."

"You're my friend and important to me too."

"And my father? This will anger him."

"Aye. I'm aware of that too."

She kept her gaze locked with mine as though she needed to see inside to the truth. I wished I could tell her how much I loved her, that she was more important to me than Kris, her father, or any other consequence I might have to face as a result of marrying her. But I'd only scare her and perhaps even send her running away again.

"I'll do this for you, Sylvi, and if in a few months you don't need my protection through marriage, I can petition for an annulment, freeing you from the union, if that's what you wish."

I wouldn't wish it for myself, but I knew I had to offer it.

Chapter
12

Sylvi

An annulment? *"Then you only see marriage to me as a* short-term solution? You do not wish it to be permanent?"

"Mayhap."

His expression was guarded, keeping me from seeing how he truly felt. Did he want to marry me, or was it too much trouble, a headache he didn't want? Or perhaps he wanted to free himself eventually to marry someone else.

"I would not wish to keep you from another maiden," I said hurriedly. "Someone you have thought about having as your wife—"

"There is no one else."

"But a day or so ago you admitted you enjoy chasing after women."

He started to shake his head, his brows furrowing.

"Yes, when we were with Maxim and Princess Elinor and discussing finding true love, you said that you were content to continue enjoying as many women as you pleased."

"If we wed, I vow I'll never look at another woman again." His tone was earnest, and I believed him. He was a man of integrity and would honor his marriage vows.

"Even so, I cannot force you into a union when you value your freedom."

"I don't value it as much as I value you."

"But you will soon regret all you have sacrificed."

"I'll never regret helping you, Sylvi."

I allowed myself another moment to examine his face, the strong, sturdy lines, the broadness of his features, the tanned skin, the scar on his chin from where he'd slit it open the time he'd rescued me, stranded on a rock at high tide because I'd been searching for sea glass and had sat down to sort out my collection without paying attention to the changing water levels.

He was so good to me and always came to my rescue. "I do not want to take advantage of you or our friendship. And I feel as though I am asking too much."

"You know you could ask me for the whole world, and I would give it to you." Though his words were serious and stirred something in me I couldn't name, he followed his statement with a smile, one that was light and mirthful.

"Very well." I tried for humor too. "If you will give me the whole world, I shall indeed be left with no choice but to marry you."

"Then it's settled."

"Only if you are certain."

He hesitated to respond, which told me more than his words, that this concession wasn't easy for him.

"Aye, 'tis the best solution."

"Thank you, Espen. I vow to give you back your freedom whenever you wish for it."

"And I vow likewise to you."

I nibbled at my bottom lip, wanting to reassure him more, but not certain what else would.

His attention dropped to my mouth and my nibbling. Something changed in his expression, but he glanced beyond me to the door, shuttering his eyes to half-mast. He cleared his throat, then spoke. "If we are to keep these vows, then we must remain chaste."

"Chaste?"

He squirmed and cleared his throat again. "Aye. No sharing of physical—affections."

"Oh my." At his insinuation, I could feel my face flushing. "Of course not."

"Friends only," he added with more emphasis.

"I agree." But did I? I fended off the disappointment I'd experienced with him before. Disappointment that he didn't see me as anything more than a friend. Even if I were his wife. "I shall try to respect your wishes. After all, you have never liked when I touch you."

"Never liked?"

"You have always pulled away or stiffened at the slightest contact."

"You believe I pull away from you because I don't like your touch?" He gave a mirthless laugh. "The truth is . . . I pull away because I like it too much."

His confession sent my insides into a wild tumble. "I did not realize . . ."

"I didn't want you to know."

"'Twas part of your efforts to keep me off limits?"

"Aye."

Would he ever give himself permission to break down the barriers? Or would he insist on keeping them there forever?

As though hearing my questions, he pushed himself up and gingerly crawled over me, being careful not to touch me, clearly taking his instructions about being chaste to heart.

Once he was standing, he grabbed the garments he'd draped over the chair. He started to shed his shirt, but then cast me a glance. "I need to get out of the captain's clothing and don my own."

"Very well." I settled myself into the spot he'd just vacated on the bed, relishing the warmth he'd left behind.

He started to tug up his shirt but paused, glancing from the shirt to me and back. "Chaste, Sylvi."

I leveled a stern look at him. "Espen Haakon, I have seen you in nothing but your braies for my entire life." All the times we'd gone swimming, fishing, or cliff-diving, we'd stripped out of our garments down to our undertunics. Had he forgotten?

He angled his chin stubbornly. "The past was different."

We had grown up, and our bodies were different. Even so, it wasn't as if he was intending to bare himself before me.

He waited, watching me, something smoldering in his eyes.

A low flame sparked to life inside my belly. Maybe he was right. Wordlessly, I rolled over until I faced the wall.

A moment later, his shuffling told me he was changing. The whisper of his garments sliding over his skin stirred the heat and sent it to the far corners of my body. I didn't realize I'd stiffened and was holding my breath until he crossed to the door.

I rotated back over and took him in, donned again in his own clothing. Even if it was still damp, he wore it well and made an imposing picture standing with his feet spread, his hand upon the hilt of his sword and his brows furrowed upon me.

"When will we wed?" I asked, not sure why my voice was breathless.

His attention lingered upon me for a second longer than normal before he dipped his head. "We'll wed tonight in my parent's village."

"Tonight?"

He rubbed at the back of his neck. "Once your father learns where you are, he'll send his men to retrieve you. 'Twill be safest for you if we seal a union before I leave on my mission."

"You are right, of course." At the prospect of becoming a married woman this very night, my stomach fluttered with strange anticipation.

"On the morrow, I must begone to find the holy lamp."

"I want to sail out to Chapel Cliff with you."

He shook his head.

I hastened to reassure him. "I promise I shall not slow you down."

"You can't promise me that."

"Then you think I will be a burden?"

"Nay—"

"Please?" I scrambled for any excuse I could find. "If my father's men come, I shall be safer with you, shall I not?"

He pressed his lips together.

I smiled, as if that could work some kind of persuasive magic over him.

He released a sigh. "Alright."

My smile widened. "I love being with you on this adventure, Espen."

He took in my smile, and his eyes lit with genuine happiness. "I'm glad you're here too."

Chapter 13

Espen

My father's burly frame enveloped me, and he slapped my back affectionately.

Before I was out of his arms, my mother grabbed me into a hug. "Welcome home, son." Her embrace was just as fierce and loving. As she pulled back, she held onto both of my arms and scanned me up and down just as she always did. "Are you getting enough to eat?"

I smiled and patted my stomach. "Aye, to be sure."

"You look too thin."

Surrounded by my many siblings, my parents stood side by side, sturdy but weathered by the wind and sea, their thick skin leathery, their wiry hair speckled with gray, their smiles the proof that a hard life didn't have to lead to a joyless life.

As our cog had sailed into view of the island and the fishing boats moored along the shore, the few fishermen still cleaning their nets after the long day out at sea had paused to watch our approach. At the sight of me standing in the bow, they'd shouted excitedly, calling to others until people began pouring from their homes, leaving their evening meals behind.

By the time we drew abreast of the wharf, most of the clan of Pollock had gathered on the rocky ledges to welcome me. To them, I was a hero for becoming a Knight of Brethren and being friends with the king. I'd had adventures and experiences they couldn't even begin to imagine.

I regretted that I was only able to visit once or twice a year. But every time I came home, I realized how much I missed my big, loving family and the many friends whose families had lived on the island as fishermen for generations.

It would be a busy eve ahead. Everyone would gather at the town center for feasting and dancing. The villagers never passed up an opportunity to celebrate any occasion.

But first, before I let the people sweep me away . . . I turned and extended my hand to Sylvi, who was standing with my squires, watching the exchanges with wide eyes. She'd never met my kin before. In all the years I'd spent with the Prestegards, Kris had come home with me on a couple of occasions, but most of the time I'd returned alone.

"Everyone," I said, raising my voice above the rhythmic lap of waves as well as the hubbub. "I'd like to introduce you to my bride-to-be."

At my pronouncement, a hush fell over the gathering. All eyes shifted to Sylvi. She'd discarded the bandage on her head earlier, and now in the fresh air, the cut was healing nicely, and hardly noticeable amidst her wind-tossed hair. Even though she was wearing boy's clothing, nothing could hide her beauty. Behind her on the western horizon, the sky seemed to choose that moment to showcase her, giving a backdrop of pinks and oranges. The sea was mostly calm and glassy, reflecting the colors of the sky above.

She held herself with the composure of a graceful noblewoman, but as she placed her hand in mine, her fingers shook just a little.

I squeezed her hand, hoping she'd sense my assurance that everyone would love and accept her. I'd already told her so a dozen times.

She tentatively drew to my side, and I had the strange need to show everyone she really was mine. I slipped my arm around her. When she casually wrapped her arm around my waist, I relished how she fit and the naturalness of holding her this way.

"Everyone," I said again. "This is Sylvi."

My father had stepped forward with an enormous grin, ready to draw Sylvi into an embrace. But at the mention of her name, he halted, and his smile disappeared as fast as the sun behind winter clouds.

My mother, taking her cue from my father, hesitated, her smile wobbling.

"Sylvi?" Father boomed, his voice loud from perpetually speaking above the crashing of the waves day after day. "As in Sylvi Prestegard?"

"Aye." I tightened my grip.

My father glanced from my face to Sylvi's. I knew what he was thinking without him saying a word. 'Twas what most people would wonder tonight: how a man of my lowly position had gained permission to marry a woman like Sylvi. They would hear the truth soon enough about how she was only marrying me to escape an awful match her father had arranged.

But I didn't want to ruin the occasion with the dismal truth.

"We're planning to get married tonight, here, in the chapel." I met my father's gaze with a serious one, hoping he'd understand that I would explain everything to him later privately. But for now, I needed his support and help.

A flicker of concern passed like a fleeting shadow across his face, but then in the next instant, he grinned widely. "Do you hear that, folks? My son is getting married! And we get to celebrate with the happy couple!"

My father's enthusiasm was always contagious, and within seconds the whole village was abuzz with the news of my impending marriage. My mother began calling out instructions to the other women, and my father shouted commands to my younger siblings, most of whom I didn't know well and who were shy around me. Even so, I still took a few moments to introduce Sylvi to the dozen or so brothers and sisters I had.

As the crowd moved us along away from the waterfront, I kept my arm around Sylvi, making sure she stayed close. She hovered nigh but didn't seem frightened, merely overwhelmed at the outpouring of affection and goodwill and the conversation directed our way.

We headed up an incline to the town, which was built upon fertile land and allowed for growing crops and maintaining livestock. Most of the villagers escorted us to the door of my family's dwelling, one of the many tall, colorfully painted townhouses that lined the main thoroughfare. As I paused with Sylvi just inside, I leaned down to my sister Terese, a few years younger than Sylvi, and whispered a request in her ear.

Terese wore her hair coiled in braids as was the

tradition of most women in our fishing clan. She was a pretty, young woman, and I guessed it wouldn't be long ere she was married.

She smiled at me in excitement. "Aye, I can help."

As we moved farther inside the house, I bent in and whispered in Sylvi's ear, "Terese will help you change garments for the wedding."

One of Sylvi's brows quirked, making her look both sassy and adorable. "You do not wish to marry me in men's clothing?"

"I'd marry you in anything." The confession was out before I realized what I was saying. As her brows lifted higher, I quickly tried to cover my sincerity with mirth. "But my family and friends would refuse to feed me if I didn't provide you proper wedding attire."

I could see my father watching our interaction intently, likely deducing my truest feelings for Sylvi in a single glance. In fact, I wouldn't be surprised if he'd known for years about my attraction to Sylvi.

Terese led Sylvi up a narrow stairway, and my father pushed me down into the nearest chair as my siblings and cousins and uncles and other family friends continued to pour into the main living area—a large room with a trestle table and benches at the center taking up most of the space. A couple of wooden chairs sat near the hearth, where a large pot was bubbling, and flat dark bread was warming on a baking stone.

Instead of taking the place of honor at the head of the table, I shifted and deferred to my father, moving to my usual spot to the left of him. I wanted the opportunity to talk with him privately, but I hardly had a chance to breathe as the questions were fired my way.

Everyone wanted to know about the recent events in

Hardanger Forest with the jotunn and the sacred chalice. I gave them the brief version of Gunnar and Torvald locating the chalice, facing danger, and then getting married. And of course, they were anxious to know more about the rumors of war and what was happening with King Canute of Swaine. I told as much as I was able but spared certain details.

After a short while, Father pushed up from his spot and sliced a hand in the air. "Enough. We'll have plenty of time to talk later after the wedding. For now, Espen must get ready for his bride."

I glanced down at my garments. They'd long since dried from the soaking of the storm, but I smelled of the sea, and likely looked like I'd nearly drowned. Aye, I needed to groom myself for Sylvi. She deserved the very best. And though I wasn't able to give her the type of wedding and feasting her family could, I would do all I could to make the eve special for her.

My father led me out into the alley behind the house, a narrow path between rows of townhouses that contained privies and garbage barrels. A washing bucket filled with rainwater hung on a poker near the back door.

Father chatted about local news while I lathered up and rinsed off. When he held out the towel, his expression turned grave. "She's in trouble, is she?" He'd dropped his voice several decibels so that anyone lingering in their doorways or windows nearby wouldn't hear our conversation.

"Aye."

"She's wanting you to marry her to help her out."

"Aye."

My father stroked his beard. "And you don't have Lord Prestegard's blessing."

"He won't approve, if that's what you're asking."

"But you're doing it anyway."

"Aye."

He continued stroking his beard, only faster. Finally, as I donned the clean tunic he'd provided, he spoke again. "I fear you may be putting yourself into mortal danger in going through with this wedding."

I wrapped my belt around my waist. "Lord Prestegard will be angry with me, to be sure. But I don't think he'll bring harm to either Sylvi or me."

"If you've thwarted him badly, he might want you out of the way."

"I'm a Knight of Brethren. He wouldn't endeavor to slay me. Besides, he's not a violent man."

My father made a noise in the back of his throat as though he disagreed with me.

"He's always been kind—"

"Because you've always done as he's asked. But now he'll see this as an affront not only to his authority but to all the privileges he's provided you over the years."

I ran my fingers through my damp hair, combing it back. By going through with the wedding, I'd ruin whatever goodwill I had left with Lord Prestegard, but I was relying heavily upon my association with the king to keep from suffering harsh repercussions.

The alley was growing darker, but as far as I could tell in the lengthening shadows, we were still alone.

"You've always had a soft spot for Lady Sylvi," my father said.

"She's been a good friend, just like Kris."

Father crossed his arms, his lips quirking up into one of his easy grins. "It's easy to see that you love her."

I paused in tying my hair back with a leather strip. Was

it really that obvious? And if my father had guessed I loved Sylvi, had she?

I'd vowed to set her free from the marriage whenever she wanted. That meant I needed to keep a better guard on my love and the emotions that being close to her day after day was sure to generate. Even the wedding itself would elicit feelings.

"She doesn't yet feel the same?" my father asked.

I wanted to lie and tell him she did, but I shook my head.

"Have no fear, she'll love you soon enough." My father's voice rose a notch and filled with anticipation. "All she needs is a little encouragement."

"Mayhap—"

"And I'd be happy to help her along." My father winked. "If you know what I mean."

My stomach gave a lurch at the prospect of his interfering. The nature of my relationship with Sylvi was already precarious, and I didn't want anything to drive her away. "We're fine and need no help."

"Not to worry." My father's grin widened, and his eyes began to dance, the sure sign I did need to worry.

"Please don't say anything to her about my feelings."

My father chuckled and squeezed my shoulder. "Of course not."

Somehow his words didn't reassure me.

Chapter 14

Sylvi

"Espen will think you're beautiful," Terese said as she drew some of my long loose hair over my shoulder so that it was hanging in front of me in silky waves and covering the gash at my hairline, which now stung only a little.

Espen's sister as well as a couple of cousins her age had primped and preened over me more than any of my maids had ever done. I was attired in a simple but pretty gown that Espen's married sisters had worn for their weddings. Even so, I didn't think Espen would find me beautiful. He wasn't like other men and was determined to avoid any physical attraction between us.

"You have all done a wonderful job of transforming me." I smiled at each of the young women in turn, the low lantern light in the dormer room illuminating their excitement at being a part of my bridal preparations.

I'd learned Terese, at seventeen years, was the oldest daughter living at home. She shared Espen's stockier build and light-brown hair. While she was sturdy and strong, she had lovely features that radiated with kindness.

"Ready?" Espen's mother called up the stairs. "Espen is at the chapel door, and everyone is here waiting for Lady Sylvi."

Terese had already informed me of their marriage customs, that friends and family would escort me to the church where Espen would be waiting. The priest would perform the ceremony on the chapel doorstep in front of the crowd, acting as witnesses. Then the newly married couple would go inside for a simple mass before returning and being pronounced man and wife.

It was less formal than the wedding ceremonies of the nobility, but I liked the simplicity as well as the way it was a community affair. It wasn't how I'd pictured myself getting married, but it seemed entirely fitting and perfect.

As I descended from the dormer, Espen's mother gasped at the sight of me, and tears sprang to her eyes. When I reached the last step, she drew me into her arms, squeezing me long and hard. "You're just the right woman for Espen, and I know you'll make him very happy."

Dusk had fallen for the short walk to the church, and many carried lanterns or torches, lighting the way, their laughter and songs filling the balmy summer air. All the while, Espen's mother's words resounded in my head. *I know you'll make him very happy.*

Would I make him happy?

I wanted to. But how?

As we drew nearer to the chapel at the center of

the village green, I glimpsed Espen on the doorstep. Lanterns hanging on either side of the arched doorway highlighted him, showing that he'd changed too. Though he wasn't wearing anything fancy—a plain brown doublet over his tunic and leggings—the sight of him made my heart patter faster.

He was a fine, fine-looking man. There was no reason to deny it—not that I ever had. In fact, now that we were getting married, maybe I could allow myself to truly enjoy his fineness.

Yes, I'd agreed to Espen's rule about remaining chaste and not allowing physical affection between us. But that didn't mean I couldn't admire him openly the way a bride should.

As the crowd around the chapel parted and created a path for the last of the distance to Espen, a tender sense of joy pulsed through me. When his eyes locked on me, his gaze glittered with such raw appreciation that I couldn't contain my smile.

At my approach, he held out a hand to me. His eyes narrowed and seemed to ask if I was sure I wanted to do this. I knew what he was telling me, that now was my chance to put an end to our arrangement if I'd changed my mind.

I didn't hesitate. I slipped my fingers into his, feeling as though that's where they belonged, as if with him I was home.

He gave me a nod, then assisted me up onto the step beside him.

Espen's parents and family stood the closest with the entire village behind them.

As the priest moved from inside the chapel into the open door, a leather-bound prayer book in his hand, a reverent hush fell over the gathering. The glow of the recently set sun and the ever-present ebb and flow of the waves added to the beauty of the night.

"Dearly beloved friends," the priest began to read from the book, "we are gathered together here in the sight of God and in the face of His congregation, to join together this man and this woman in holy matrimony."

As Espen's eyes settled upon mine, I was lost. I only half listened to what the priest was saying, too mesmerized by the swirling of blue and green in Espen's eyes, like a changing tide, rushing in and out.

"Wilt thou have this woman to be thy wedded wife, to live together after God's ordinance in the holy estate of matrimony? Wilt thou love her, comfort her, honor and keep her, in sickness and in health? And forsaking all others, keep thee only to her, so long as you both shall live?"

"I will." The low rumble of Espen's response shot straight through me, stirring warmth deep inside.

The priest shifted to look at me. "Wilt thou have this man to be thy wedded husband, to live together after God's ordinance in the holy estate of matrimony? Wilt thou love him, comfort him, honor and keep him, in sickness and in health? And forsaking all others, keep thee only to him, so long as you both shall live?"

What about our bargain, that we would give each other an annulment if we wanted to separate? How could I reconcile that vow to this one being asked of me right now?

I hesitated.

Espen's gaze remained unswerving, as though perhaps he'd expected me to have second thoughts in this moment. It wasn't for the reason he believed. I hadn't changed my mind about marrying him. But I was changing my mind about giving each other the option to separate. I wanted our vows to last for as long as we both lived.

The priest whispered through his teeth. "You must say the words, my lady."

"Of course." I lifted my chin as though daring Espen to defy me. "I shall take Espen to be my husband for as long as we both shall live and not a day shorter."

At my improvised declaration, I loved watching his eyes round. And when his nostrils flared just slightly, I knew I'd pleased him, even if he'd never admit it.

A few minutes later, the priest led us inside the chapel. The simple sanctuary was lit with several sconces and a shining candelabra on the altar. Hand in hand, Espen and I approached the front prayer rail, where we knelt. The priest prayed over us, offered us the sacraments, and then prayed again.

When we rose and turned, I was surprised to find the back of the chapel full of Espen's family, all of them smiling broadly at us. As we waited for them to hasten outside, Espen traced the empty spot on my ring finger.

My skin tingled where he touched me.

"I'm sorry I don't have a ring to give you yet."

I shrugged. "We have a hundred or more witnesses to our marriage and have no need for a ring."

"I want you to have one."

His tone was so earnest that I didn't dare hold his gaze a moment longer lest I melt like tallow into the woodwork. Before I could think of a reply, the priest waved us forward toward the door.

As we crossed the distance and stepped outside

into the night, the villagers ceased their chattering and focused upon us. The priest stood behind us, his voice ringing out loudly and clearly: "As much as Sir Espen and Lady Sylvi have consented together in holy wedlock and have witnessed the same before God and this company, and thereto have given and pledged their troth either to the other, I pronounce that they be man and wife together. In the name of the Father, of the Son, and of the Holy Ghost. Amen."

"Amen!" came the calls from the villagers, along with clapping and cheering.

I smiled up at Espen, trying to grasp the reality that I was married to him.

For an unguarded moment, his expression seemed filled with happiness, as though he truly wanted our union and wasn't doing it out of duty to me. And when his lips curved up into a handsome grin, it contained a measure of satisfaction, as if he'd just attained something significant.

"Let the celebration begin," someone in the crowd shouted.

"Hold on!" Espen's father boomed above the commotion. "Since Espen has no ring yet to seal this union, I suggest he seal the union with a kiss."

The words were met with a cheering clamor that could have beaten back advancing forces.

Espen stiffened, and even though he kept his smile in place, it took on a forced quality. As he met his father's gaze, he narrowed his eyes, even as his father winked.

For myself, I didn't quite know what to think of the suggestion. I'd never contemplated kissing Espen before. The kiss to his ear while aboard the ship didn't count. It had been more of a simple graze of my lips than a kiss.

Did I dare rise to the occasion now and allow him to kiss me? Even if I'd wanted to refuse—which I didn't—I could foresee no way out of it. Not with the way the crowd was carrying on.

"Go on now!" Espen's father was the loudest of everyone, and he grinned proudly at Espen. "Show these folks how a Haakon man kisses his woman."

Espen remained as rigid as a mast. I had no doubt he was replaying his words about remaining chaste and not allowing physical affection to spring up between us. He was a man of his word and took his vows seriously.

Yet, what harm could come of sharing one little kiss? On our wedding night? In fact, kissing in front of all these people would certainly help solidify proof of my marriage should my father question it.

"Come on now, Espen!" His father shouted louder and more eagerly than anyone else.

Espen's hand tightened within mine, and his brows began to dip into a scowl.

Without waiting for Espen to act, I stood on my toes and lifted my face to him. I was giving him permission to follow the directives of the crowd.

His gaze dropped to my mouth. I could tell he was thinking about it.

My stomach began to flutter like a flag in the wind, one lowered in surrender.

He didn't move.

I rose just a little higher and pressed in, feeling the long, broad length of him.

"We can't." His whisper was tight, almost strangled.

"We must," I whispered in return. "Now stop worrying."

Finally he bent, his mouth hovering just above mine.

I closed the last of the distance, letting my lips touch his. The connection was soft, light, but sent shivers of anticipation over my skin.

The cheering around us escalated again.

With a sigh of pure delight, I lowered myself back to my heels. I'd kissed Espen. I'd really kissed him.

Before I could separate entirely from Espen, his father called out again. "Oh, come on, Espen. That wasn't a kiss. Give her a real one."

Others began to call out the same thing.

I started to shift, to smile, to show everyone the kiss had been sufficient, at least for me. But in the next instant, Espen's hands slid to my cheeks. He swiftly and decisively pulled me back toward him. Then, before I realized what he was doing, his hold turned firm, and he swept down, capturing my mouth with his.

Espen's father was right. The previous gentle brush couldn't be classified as a kiss, not compared to this. Espen's mouth came against mine with a power that took my breath away. It took away my consciousness of everything and everyone else too, except him. He was all that existed in my universe.

His lips meshed with mine hungrily, stirring something inside me I hadn't known existed—a hunger of my own. I pressed myself into him, tangling my lips with his, following his lead and tasting of him with the same fervor he tasted me.

"There you have it!" Espen's father called. "That's

how we do it!"

Good-natured laughter filled the air.

Espen broke the kiss and guided my head against his chest, almost as if he needed to hide my mouth lest he be tempted to kiss me again.

I wanted to lift my head and my lips and allow him to kiss me as long as he wanted. But I was too weak to do anything but grasp his tunic to keep myself from crumbling into a heap. His kiss had enflamed me, started a fire, and now was consuming me, so that all I wanted was more of his kisses.

As I rested against his chest, the rapid thudding of his heartbeat echoed in my ear. His chest rose and fell in quick succession, matching mine. The kiss had clearly affected him as much as it had me.

A spark burned between us. We could try to deny it all we wanted, but it was there, and it didn't seem to be going away.

The good-natured teasing was relentless, even after Espen began lobbing comments back about his skill and expertise and how they all needed to learn from him. When he released his hold of me, he was still jesting with some of his family.

Before I could protest or find a way to hold his hand again, I found myself being ushered away with the women, and Espen was surrounded by the men. We were guided a short distance to a blazing bonfire and tables laden with all manner of food.

Soon we were eating and drinking, the women monopolizing my attention the same way the men were eager to speak with Espen. All the while I tried to eat the fare, my stomach quavered with need. But it wasn't a craving for food. Instead, it was a craving for

Espen, to be with him, to have him hold my hand, and to experience another one of his kisses.

I didn't realize how oft I glanced his way until his mother hugged me and mentioned it. "I see you can't take your eyes off him."

He chose that moment to look up. As our gazes connected over the sparking fire, the air sizzled between us.

My breath snagged in my chest. Oh my. Whatever this was happening between us, it was new and exciting, and I didn't want it to end.

Someone spoke to him, drawing his attention away from me.

I hadn't needed another kiss to set me on fire again. One look had been enough. Was this what he'd hoped to prevent by remaining chaste? Setting a blaze that couldn't be extinguished?

Chapter 15

ESPEN

I'D KISSED SYLVI. THE KISS HAD CONSUMED ME FOR THE PAST HOUR of feasting. And I still could think of nothing else.

If only I hadn't allowed my father to goad me . . .

When my father had started calling for a kiss, I'd wanted to step away from the chapel, punch him in the shoulder, and tell him to stop. But with everyone watching and cheering, I'd had no choice, which was exactly what my father intended.

Now that I'd officially kissed the woman I loved, I'd never be the same. The moment I'd tasted the sweetness of her lips, I'd lost awareness of where I was and what was happening around me. I could have gone on endlessly . . . if not for my father's voice breaking through the pleasurable haze.

Thankfully, he'd jolted me back to the reality of what I'd pledged to Sylvi—that I'd married her to keep her safe. I was her only option, and under normal circumstances she wouldn't have considered a man like me. Thus, if I allowed myself to get carried away with her, I'd be taking advantage of her during this vulnerable time when she needed me most.

The truth was, I had to stay strong so that I could give her an annulment. But I wouldn't be able to if I kept kissing her.

Even now, every time I looked at her across the village green, I wanted to stride over, sweep her into my arms, and kiss her senseless. She was already irresistible enough with her bright eyes, big smile, and the vivaciousness with which she moved and talked.

As a willow flute started up a traditional dance tune, the tables were lifted away to make room for dancing.

"Fie," I muttered against the rim of my ale, even as I tore my gaze from her. I had to focus on our friendship and remind myself that I didn't want anything to come between us. Especially not my desire for her. I'd kept that locked away and under control for plenty of years. I could surely continue.

"Let Lady Sylvi and Sir Espen have the first dance!" The call echoed around the bonfire. With good-natured shoving, I soon found myself face to face with Sylvi.

Her cheeks were flushed and her laugh breathless as she took hold of my hands. I was glad she was happy, even if a battle was raging inside me and tearing me up.

We started the folk dance, and soon the other couples joined us. As much as I tried to keep up my guard and not let her nearness affect me, her excitement and enjoyment of the eve tore down my defenses. Though I forced myself to banter and talk like we always had, there was a new undercurrent I couldn't so easily deny.

The hours passed quickly until mothers began to gather their sleeping children. Young and old alike were yawning. Sunrise would arrive all too soon, and with it the summons of the sea.

I'd arranged for rooms above the tavern, since my family's dwelling was already full enough. And as we made our way there, a jovial group of young people joined us, teasing and singing and laughing.

I was half afraid that, when we arrived at the tavern, the revelers would decide they needed to accompany Sylvi and me to our bedchamber and into our bed. But much to my relief, the last of the crowd dispersed, leaving only my squires.

As we ascended to the dormer, I tried to sort out how to tell Sylvi I intended to give her the smaller room while I slept with my squires across the hallway, although I wasn't sure how I'd explain to my squires why I wasn't spending my wedding night with my bride.

Even as Sylvi entered the chamber, I held back in the hallway.

She was talking fast, the sign that she was nervous. But I didn't blame her. The situation was awkward.

Finally, she stopped at the bed. An oil lamp had been lit on the bedside table and illuminated her as she traced a hand over the coverlet before peeking over her shoulder at me. "Are you coming in, or are you planning to stand there all night?"

I didn't budge, and I didn't reply. I could only swallow hard, trying desperately to push down everything I felt for this maiden, who was now my wife.

My wife.

I took another step back.

"No," Sylvi whispered almost angrily. "You cannot leave."

I halted. "I won't break our agreement to remain chaste."

She released an exasperated sigh. Then she stalked over, tugged me into the room, and closed the door behind me.

I fought the urge to throw it open, run to the sea, and jump in for a night swim. Maybe doing so would cool me off and douse my yearnings.

Sylvi planted herself in the middle of the room, her eyes fiery. "If you stay in a separate room, then everyone will talk. And if my father questions anyone, he will learn our marriage is a farce."

I could only watch her, letting her reasoning break through my reservations. "You're right." Of course we had to continue the charade. What had I been thinking? The truth was, I hadn't been thinking. I'd been too distracted by her. "I'm sorry. I'll try to do better."

At my apology, some of the stiffness in her shoulders seemed to dissipate. For long seconds, she was quiet, staring at the door behind me. When she spoke, her voice was gentler. "I understand marrying me is not what you wanted, Espen. So I thank you for making this sacrifice for me."

"No, it's not like that." I did want her. I always had. But what I wanted and what I could have were two different things. How could I explain that to her?

She cocked her head to the side, waiting for me to say more.

"I could ask for no better woman to be my wife," I started, searching for honest words, needing to reassure her that none of this was her fault. "You are everything a man could ever want. Truly."

"But . . . ?"

But she was made for better? But she deserved more than the life I could give her? "At this point, we don't know what the future will bring, so it's best if we keep things uncomplicated between us."

"Uncomplicated?"

The tension inside me mounted, and I grabbed the back of my neck and began rubbing it, trying to alleviate some of the pressure. A part of me wanted to throw away all caution and embrace this woman fully as my wife. Her resistance was down, and I'd be able to win her over. Yet at the same time, if I gained her in her weakest moments, I'd always wonder if she truly wanted to be with me.

If—when—I won her, I wanted her to be strong and able to give herself to me because she was free to do so, and not because the circumstances coerced her into it.

"Please, Sylvi." My tone dropped to a plea. "I think 'tis best if we remain only friends for now."

Her shoulders deflated a little more. And this time I sensed my words discouraged her.

"It's not that I don't find you attractive," I whispered, afraid that my regular voice would betray me with the depth of my feelings. "It's obvious we have something between us."

She nodded, a flush working into her cheeks.

I felt a measure of satisfaction in knowing I wasn't the only one feeling the heat. Nevertheless, I had to keep control of those feelings. "Just because something is there doesn't mean we should nurture it. At least, not right now."

"Are you saying that perhaps there is a future for us?"

The word *aye* rushed to the tip of my tongue, but I knew I couldn't give her false hope. "Before today, I never would have believed I'd be standing in this room as your husband. So I suppose anything is possible. But to be completely honest with you, Sylvi, I feel as though it will take a miracle for us to have a future together."

Any hope or excitement remaining in her eyes from the eve flickered out. Her expression turned grave.

This dousing was for the best. In my heart, I knew it. But at the moment, I was all too tempted to stalk over to her, gather her in my arms, and whisper my love into her ear.

As the silence dragged out, I clenched my hands into fists and forced my feet to stay where they were.

Finally, she sighed, almost wearily. "I guess we should slumber. Morn will be here soon enough."

I nodded and turned to the door. "I'll step out so you can ready yourself for bed."

"Thank you." Her response was quiet and resigned.

Less than a quarter of an hour later, I lay on the ground as far from her as I could get. Sylvi had been abed when I'd returned, and now I could hear her shuffling and knew she was still awake.

I held myself motionless, hardly daring to breathe, almost as if in making one wrong move, I'd crack into pieces that couldn't be put back together. Though I hadn't slept much the night before because of the storm, I wasn't tired. Instead, energy hummed in my veins.

"Espen?" Her soft whisper carried across the room like a caress.

I closed my eyes and tried to block out images of her, especially the one of her in bed, her hair spread out over her pillow and her dreamy eyes upon me.

"Are you awake?"

As tempted as I was to close my eyes and pretend to slumber, avoiding Sylvi in the past had never worked to diminish my desire for her, and it would work even less now. "Aye."

She sighed sleepily. "I have no friend truer than you."

"I would have it no other way."

She paused, then spoke in a rush. "I shall do my best to be a true friend to you in return."

"My thanks." Her statement should have made me happy. This was what I'd been pushing for since the start of our voyage together and the mention of marriage. But somehow, her declaration made me feel cold, like a hearth fire that had been stomped out, leaving only ashes behind.

Chapter 16

Sylvi

I clung to the sides of the rowboat in the bow, my stomach growing queasier as we moved into the open sea. I tried to keep my focus off the churning waves and on the cliff-like rock formation that was growing larger with each stroke of the oars.

From a distance, I hadn't noticed the single jagged square cliff rising from the water. But now, as we left the skerry channels behind and faced the western edge of the Hundreds, it was more distinct, standing like a tall lone sentinel a hundred or more yards from the imposing cliffs of the nearest island.

Chapel Cliff looked as if it had once been part of an island but had been sliced away by a giant axe, like a block of kindling chopped from a log. The colorful rock was mostly granite with bright splotches of sienna, thick veins of black, and gleaming crystals of white.

As the cliff rose out of the water, it gradually widened until it formed a flat plateau. From a distance,

I couldn't yet see the stone dwellings that had been built on the level ground at the top, but from what I'd heard, a chapel and a cottage existed for the lightkeeper and his family. Apparently, a small plot of land had also been created for a vegetable garden so that the residents could grow their own food and sustain livestock.

Our boat crested the swell of a bigger wave, and I cupped my hand to my mouth, afraid of being seasick.

Rowing directly behind me, Espen paused and handed me a cloth. "Eat the ginger and press the cloth to your nose."

I took it to find a cut of ginger root wrapped in the cloth. Even though my stomach revolted at the prospect of chewing and swallowing anything, I followed Espen's instructions, and within minutes the roiling inside subsided. As I held the cloth against my nose, I breathed in the tangy-spicy scent of ginger oil, letting it soothe me further.

I glanced over my shoulder at Espen. His arms strained against the oars as he dug them in and out of the water with a practiced rhythm. His squires had come with us and were also aiding with the rowing but weren't as strong or proficient as Espen.

He was staring at Chapel Cliff, but his gaze shifted to me, concern etching a line in his forehead. "Feeling better?"

"Yes, thank you. I am grateful I shall not need to meet the lightkeeper and his wife smelling of the stench of my vomit."

He didn't break his pace in his dipping and lifting as he spoke. "I have heard it said that the lightkeeper only allows one visitor at a time."

"We can ask him if you may bring me. Surely he shall not think your wife is a threat." *Wife.* The word rolled off my tongue naturally, and I liked the sound of it.

"Mayhap not. But 'tis a difficult climb to the top. And dangerous."

"I have climbed many dangerous cliffs with you and Kristoffer and shall not be afraid."

Espen nodded at my outfit. "So that's why you donned the boy's garments again today? You were confident you could convince me to let you go up with me?"

"And have I convinced you?"

"Have I ever once said no to you?" His brow rose, revealing the twinkle in his eyes.

I smiled, a strange sense of relief sifting through me. After the awkwardness of sleeping together in the same room last night, I'd been afraid we'd lose our easy camaraderie. I was glad to see that we could carry on as usual. Or mostly as usual. Ever since our conversation in the bedroom above the tavern, I'd resolved to show Espen I could respect his wishes to maintain our friendship.

"Since you love saying yes to me, we shall visit the chapel together." I faced forward again, holding the ginger-scented cloth against my nose.

"Just because I can't say no to your whims doesn't mean I love saying yes."

"I think you do love it."

He snorted.

My smile widened, and I lifted my face to the sunshine. Even though the wind swirling from the open Dark Sea was cold and made me glad for a cloak, the June sun was promising a warm day ahead. The splash of water glistened with each downward plunge of the boat, and a mist sprayed against my face.

"Look," Espen called.

I followed the direction he was pointing to the island we were passing. Soaring with wings outstretched was an enormous bird of prey. It circled lazily in the sky, as if it didn't have a care in the world. Oh, to be so free . . .

"See the white tail feathers? It's a sea eagle."

"'Tis majestic."

"Aye, to be sure. It probably has a nest in the cliffs nearby."

It soared lower, then with outstretched legs, it skimmed the waves before rising with a fish in its talons and flapping upward, its powerful wings pushing it hard.

"Do you see that?" I asked, suddenly remembering all the reasons I'd loved traveling every summer to our family's home in the Hundreds.

"Aye. I see it."

At the wistfulness of Espen's tone, I glanced at him again. He was still rowing without slowing his pace, but his eyes were on the eagle, following its movements as it soared and then flew toward the cliffs.

"Do you miss living here in the Hundreds?" I asked.

"I suppose I do."

"You suppose?"

"At times like this." The reflection of the sea made his blue-green eyes even brighter. "You've heard it said that you can take the boy away from the sea, but you can't take the sea out of the boy."

Now, after meeting his family and seeing his childhood home, I could only imagine how hard the parting had been when he'd come to live with us. What had it been like for him? I turned on my bench so that I was facing him instead of forward. "When my father first brought you to our home, was it strange?"

He rowed several strokes before giving a slight shrug. "Mayhap, but I adjusted soon enough."

"In all the years you lived with us and trained with Kristoffer to become a knight, did my father let you go back home?"

"He wanted me to break away from my kin, thought it would be for the best if I severed my ties. And he kept me busy, affording me no time or means for returning."

"I am truly sorry, Espen. Your family is lovely, and you must have sorely missed them."

"Aye. I did." He met my gaze frankly. Although he didn't say the words, I could tell he appreciated my acknowledgement of the difficulty he'd once experienced.

His gaze shifted to Chapel Cliff ahead.

I was content to watch him instead—the way the sunlight warmed the lighter brown in his hair, turning it to sandstone; the way the wind roughened his cheeks, making them ruddy; the way the sea brought out a confidence in each movement he made.

"'Twas not all bad though," he said. "If not for leaving my kin, I wouldn't have met you and Kris."

"That truly would have been a loss," I bantered.

"I'm serious. You both became my kin."

"After meeting your family, I see that mine was no replacement." They'd never interacted with me so freely or openly or with such unreserved acceptance as Espen's parents had.

"Your parents show their love differently but no less."

"Are you certain?" I couldn't keep the skepticism from my tone. "My own father is willing to give me to the man who best serves his interest. And my mother concerned herself with making me into the kind of maiden my father could use. How is that love?"

"I have always loathed that your parents groomed you to better their own means."

I sat up straighter, his words taking me by surprise. "You have?"

"Aye." He kept his attention focused ahead, as if he was embarrassed to look me in the eyes as he revealed his secret. "After your coming-of-age ball, I had to stay away from Karlstadt and the sight of you with other men."

"I noticed you rarely visited after that. Was it really because you did not like seeing me with my suitors?"

"I'm not jesting."

I couldn't keep from beaming. The thought of Espen's jealousy made me ridiculously happy.

"After you were betrothed to Rolfe, I wanted to do him bodily harm."

I chuckled. "Why? Rolfe was a kind and caring man."

"He had you. And I resented him for it."

"You need not have worried. He was only half the man you are." I meant to tease, but somehow sincerity made its way into my tone.

"Did you love him?" Espen's voice was light, but I sensed my answer was important to him.

"I surely tried to love him as best I could. And he was a kind man. But no, I never felt—" What I'd felt with Espen?

He prompted me. "You never felt . . .?"

"Love. But perhaps I would have learned to love him eventually."

"Doubtful."

"I suppose you wanted me instead and believe you are the only one I can love?"

"Aye." The one word was serious, so serious that my humor fell away.

I studied his face, tenderness for this friend swelling so powerfully that I wanted to throw off all the restraints and simply hug him. But I held back, knowing that standing up and launching myself at him would rock the boat and endanger us. It would also break the parameters I'd agreed to last night in maintaining friendship only.

"I have always believed you viewed me as an annoying little sister, a nuisance."

"That's true too." A grin tugged at the corners of his lips.

I wanted him to keep talking, to tell me more secrets from his past, but I suspected I'd reached the limit he was willing to share for this one day.

We were drawing near to Chapel Cliff, and I twisted on my bench to take in the massive stone ledge that grew up out of the water and rose into the sky. Now that we were nigh upon it, I craned my neck to get a better view of the plateau.

The underside of the flat rock above was covered in moss and lichen, likely making it slippery and difficult to navigate for anyone who might try to climb up the rock base. The kings of old had been wise to see the value of the chapel high above and to use it as a place to store their greatest treasures.

I prayed Espen would indeed find the holy lamp there and that he would be honored and revered as a result of the discovery. And I hoped I could be by his side both now and when he presented it to the king.

But I was afraid that someday soon, he would realize the hardship and heartache I'd brought him, and he'd regret binding himself to me.

Chapter
17

∽⧼⧽∾

ESPEN

I RANG THE BELL AT THE BASE OF THE CLIFF AGAIN, BUT AS THE wind carried away the clank, only silence filled its place.

"Perhaps no one lives there anymore." Sylvi stared at the stone platform high above us.

"The lightkeeper always appoints someone new to take his place when he is no longer able to serve. Usually his son."

I'd expected a boat to be moored to the iron links in the cliff wall—one that the keeper used to travel for supplies and news. Perhaps he'd gone away for the day. Or perhaps something was amiss.

My squires had their shields at the ready, as did I. Ready for what, I didn't know. But I wouldn't allow a volley of arrows or a shower of stones or anything to fall from the top and harm Sylvi.

Sylvi's forehead creased, and her nose wrinkled adorably as she waited, like me, for a response from the lightkeeper.

I'd been ringing the bell for a while to no avail. As it

was now past midday, I didn't want to tarry much longer before beginning our return voyage to Pollock, since the afternoon and eve oft brought the possibility of storms and rougher water.

I'd eyed the sides of the cliffs from all angles, trying to decide if I dared to climb them. I could see areas where footholds had been carved out of the rock, as if many had already attempted the feat. But I suspected few people had ever succeeded.

Maxim and Princess Elinor had given me as much information as they knew about Chapel Cliff, and I'd put it together with the legends I'd heard while growing up. As far as I knew, the lightkeeper had always remained in control of who could come and go from the cliff, lowering the rope ladder to those he deemed to be unthreatening. In fact, I'd heard stories of lightkeepers severing the rope and sending everyone climbing it into the frigid depths below.

They took their task seriously to protect the light and keep it burning. As far as I knew, it had never once gone out and always shone brightly, especially during the long dark nights of the winter months.

Although no one knew with certainty if the holy lamp was kept among other precious items in the safe confines of Chapel Cliff, I needed to find out one way or another.

"What shall we do?" Sylvi asked.

I lowered myself to my bench, unable to quell the unease as well as my disappointment. I couldn't let King Ansgar or my country down, had to find a way to explore Chapel Cliff. But such a task was apparently going to be more difficult than I'd anticipated.

"Unfortunately, without the lightkeeper providing a way for us to ascend, there isn't much more we can do today. We don't have the time or the equipment to attempt to climb up on our own."

"Then we shall come back again on the morrow?"

"Aye."

"Very well. I shall relish another eve with your family." Sylvi settled back in her spot. I loved that she was easy to please and went along with whatever plans came our way. She'd been that way as a child too—had to be to keep up with Kris and me.

As I prepared my oars, a scuffing came from far above, followed by the cascade of pebbles. I jolted forward, lifting my shield above Sylvi, but knowing I'd throw my very body across hers to save her if need be.

"What is it?" Sylvi tried to peek out.

In the next instant, something came plunging down from the top of the cliff. Before it could hit the shield, it halted and dangled above us.

"'Tis the rope ladder." Sylvi pushed out into the open, stood, and tried to grab on to the bottom rung.

I took hold of her wrist and gently lowered her arm. "I'll be going up first since we don't know what awaits us at the top."

At the gravity of my warning, she backed up a step and wobbled.

I reached out to steady her, fitting my hands on her hips. She wasn't truly in danger, and I could admit I was taking advantage of an occasion to touch her. Her eyes were large and luminous, and I couldn't keep my gaze from dropping to her lips. Aye, I'd thought about our kiss all night and all day, even though I'd told myself not to. And now, the memory of our mouths meshing sent a burst of heat through my gut.

Did I dare claim another kiss? I was possibly climbing

into a dangerous situation. What if something happened to me, and I never saw her again?

As though sensing the direction of my thoughts, her lips parted just slightly, those lips that had kissed mine in return and had fit so well.

No. I tore my gaze away and gave myself a mental shake like I oft did before heading into battle. I would be fine. I was a skilled fighter, one of the best in the land. I could proficiently manage anything that came my way. I didn't need to worry, would see Sylvi again, had to stop making excuses to kiss her.

I released my hold of her, then jumped and latched onto the bottom of the rope. Peering up, I waited a moment for someone to look down on me from above and ask me questions about the nature of my visit or give me instructions about the climb up. At the very least, I hoped the lightkeeper would show his face, assuring me that he was a decent fellow and meant us no harm.

But nothing happened.

"Hello?" I called. Only silence filtered down, so I reached for the next rung, then paused, waiting again for an invitation to climb.

I made my way cautiously up a few more before looking down at Sylvi and my squires.

Sylvi's expression contained a barely concealed excitement. "Should I still wait until you reach the top before beginning my climb?"

"Aye, don't come up until you hear from me." I made eye contact with my squires and nodded. We'd privately discussed the possibility that I might need to stay at the top for an extended length. If so, they were to find a shelter at one of the nearby islands for the night. They also knew without my saying so that if any peril befell me, they were to take Sylvi and flee to safety.

I began climbing again and could feel the ladder swaying in the wind. I studied the top half where the thick rope fell flush against the cliff. Who had tossed the ladder over the edge, and why hadn't he shown himself to us yet?

I'd waited long enough, had given the person at the top time to halt my progression. There was no reason to hold back any longer. I picked up my pace, and the next time I looked down, Sylvi and my squires were several tall tree lengths behind me, their gazes riveted to me.

When I reached the halfway point, I peered out over the sea, the immensity of Chapel Cliff settling over me and filling me with awe. 'Twas truly a wonder that anyone lived in such an isolated place. What kind of person would choose such a life?

As I climbed the final distance, I braced myself, knowing I might face aggression of some kind. Mayhap I was heading into a trap. Mayhap I'd be chained and made a prisoner the moment I appeared.

Whatever might come, I was trained to fight. This was my duty. And after Gunnar and Torvald had completed their mission for the king successfully, I wanted to do something now, too, no matter the danger.

The trouble was, I also had Sylvi to think about. If something happened to me, who would protect her? What would stop her father from taking her and bending her to his will?

My steps faltered as I neared the last rung.

I wasn't ready to die today—couldn't die.

My pulse pounded with steadily mounting anticipation and readiness. With one hand holding the rope, I used the other to unsheathe my knife. Then cautiously, I pulled myself up until my line of vision was level with the plateau.

Long blades of grass were blowing in the wind, bending over a man who was lying face down and motionless, his arm outstretched and fist open. His fingers were thin and venous with knobby knuckles, the kind of hand that belonged to an older person.

Seeing no immediate threat, no one hovering and waiting to attack me, I scrambled over the ledge the rest of the way until I was kneeling beside the man.

I surveyed the plateau, taking in several low stone buildings with roofs made of sturdy slate, a large garden behind one, fruit trees in blossom, at least a dozen chickens, some goats, and a pig. A metal pipe stuck out of the roof of a narrow shack, which I assumed was a smokehouse for preserving game and fish for the winter.

On the edge closest to the sea stood the chapel. It was a one-room structure with but a simple cross adorning it. The open windows on three sides revealed a light burning from within. While the glow was dull at midday in the bright sunshine, I'd witnessed its power at night—a light so brilliant that sailing vessels for miles out could see it and were guided safely to shore by following it.

Everything was too quiet. Too peaceful. And I unsheathed my sword, half expecting a horde of Swainians to rush out of the buildings to attack me. I watched and waited a moment longer before dropping my attention back to the man in front of me.

Next to him was a large stake that seemed to be anchored beneath the grass into the stone plateau. The rope ladder was attached to it. From what I could surmise, this man must have heard the ringing of the bell below, come out to lower the ladder, perhaps had struggled to do so but had somehow managed it.

I pressed my fingers to the pulse in his neck and felt the steady beat. He wasn't dead.

Carefully, I shifted him until he was on his back. Indeed, he was an older man with the thick leathery face of someone who'd been branded by both sea and wind. White hair peeked out from underneath his cap. His cheeks were sallow and his body thin with age. But he didn't appear to have the telltale signs of someone ill or diseased.

His tunic and leggings were threadbare, patched and resewn in a dozen places, stained with time . . . and blood, which was seeping through his tunic above his belt.

With a start, I tugged up the long garment to find linen wrapped around his middle. Bright red saturated the cloth.

What had happened? Had he sustained an injury while tending to the light? Or perhaps in making repairs to one of the buildings?

I glanced around again, taking in more details—a hoe left abandoned in the long grass near the garden, sprawling weeds crowding out the new plants, a smashed bucket beside the well, broken fishing gear tossed aside by the open doorway of the dwelling.

A shiver crept up my spine. It appeared as though the place and the man had been attacked in recent days or weeks.

I unwound the bandage wrapped around his waist until, at last, I peeled it away to reveal a raw, oozing injury. I'd seen enough wounds in battle to recognize this one. He'd been stabbed by a knife.

Though the puncture looked deep, I didn't see evidence that his internal organs had suffered. If so, he likely would have died by now. My guess was that this wound was painful and needed tending, but that it wasn't mortal.

I searched him further and found another wound on the back of his leg in his calf—a deep gash that was seeping blood and pus. Perhaps it made walking difficult, which would account for why it had taken him so long to reach the edge and lower the rope ladder.

I didn't know what this man had available to help doctor his injuries, but I would task my squires with gathering and bringing back medical provisions on the morrow when they returned for me.

In the meantime, I needed to do what I could. And as long as the danger wasn't lurking in the shadows of this cliff-top hideaway, then I'd summon Sylvi up to assist me with the wounds. Like most women, she knew enough about the medicinal properties of herbs to concoct basic salves and decoctions when necessary.

Hastily, I made my way across the open grass to the dwellings, scanning the interior of each one until I was assured the only other person at the top of the cliff was this man—likely the lightkeeper.

As I returned to the edge, I peered over to find that Sylvi and my squires were staring up, waiting for me.

Even from a far distance, I could see the worry etching Sylvi's face. At the sight of me, she dropped her hands away from her heart where she'd been clutching them and let her shoulders relax.

"The lightkeeper is injured and in desperate need of medicines," I called down to my squires. "Sylvi can climb up and help me tend to him while the two of you return to my family's village, gather supplies, and return on the morrow."

Sylvi wasted no time in hopping up and grasping the rope. My squires assisted her as she started climbing, holding the rope secure at the bottom while I did the best I could to steady it from the top.

Nevertheless, the wind battered her as she ascended. My heart plummeted each time she struggled to move higher. I nearly lost all rationale when her foot slipped from the rung. But she quickly righted herself and flew up the last of the distance as if she'd been climbing up rope ladders most of her life.

When she neared the top and I could grasp her arms, I pulled her up into the grass beside me. Not until she was kneeling and staring around at the dwellings did I allow myself a full breath.

As I worked to calm both my breathing and my heartbeat, the older man on the ground groaned, and his eyelids flickered open. He took me in first, then Sylvi before he gave the ghost of a smile. "Praise be. God has answered my prayers. The two of you will be the new lightkeepers."

Chapter
18

Sylvi

"The poultice is packed into your wound." *I finished* wrapping a clean strip of cloth around Orvik's leg. "'Twill hopefully take away some of your discomfort."

"You're an angel, child." The old lightkeeper smiled up at me from the bed where Espen had carried him. Wrinkles formed deep grooves on his weathered face, especially at the corners of his eyes. But they were kind eyes regarding me with gratefulness.

Espen and I had located a few herbs in the hand-hewn cabinet where Orvik had indicated they would be. I'd quickly made up a poultice while Espen rinsed and cleansed the wounds. Now as I smoothed a hand over the fresh bandages, I prayed the injuries would heal.

"Drink some of this." Espen approached the bed with a steaming mug. He'd added a few medicinal herbs to the pot already warming over the hearth, brought the mixture to a simmering boil, and now the aroma of cloves and feverfew wafted in the air.

"You're an angel too." Orvik's voice was as weak as his body. But his spirit was strong, and I sensed this wasn't the first trial he'd faced here at Chapel Cliff.

As Espen assisted Orvik into a sitting position, I perched on the bedframe and held the mug to his lips. He drank several sips before his eyes closed and weariness again filled his face.

During the course of being tended, Orvik had passed in and out of consciousness, so that we'd only been able to piece together limited knowledge of what had happened—that a visitor had arrived a fortnight ago, pretended to be in need of protection, but then had proceeded to kill Orvik's wife and harm Orvik, leaving him for dead.

Upon learning of the attack, I could sense from the tightness in Espen's expression that he was anxious to question Orvik and discover more, but he also was waiting for the lightkeeper to feel better and be more alert.

I silently willed Orvik to stay awake so that I could give him more to drink. But when his eyes remained shut, I placed the mug on the bedside table, then rose carefully so that my movement wouldn't disturb him.

I'd already explored the house, which was made up of a main area with a fireplace, a simple round table with stools, and a bed. An attached room, which looked as though it had been added on, had two more beds, likely for children, though currently it was being used for storage and contained boxes and bins and barrels of all sorts and sizes.

I loved the artistic creations that added color and character to the homey main quarters—a piece of driftwood carved into a multiple-branch candleholder on the mantel, collages of shells dangling from the windows, thick woven rugs covering the floor, and more. For just a brief moment, I pictured one of my sea-glass mosaics on the wall.

"I pulled up the rope ladder," Espen said as we stepped outside. "So we should be safe for the night."

I allowed myself a closer look at the cozy plot of land. It wasn't large, perhaps the size of the center green of Pollock. But it was clear that the keeper had taken great pride in the maintenance, turning the cliff dwelling into an inviting place to live as well as making it mostly self-sustaining, so that there was enough food.

A breeze blew briskly across the open clifftop, and I could only imagine how rough the wind was in the winter or during storms. But at the moment, it would appear that the weather wasn't the worst enemy.

"Do you think someone set out to intentionally murder Orvik and his wife?" I asked, following Espen as he stepped into the garden.

"I don't imagine Orvik could make an enemy even if he tried." Espen bent and tugged a weed out of the soil. He shook it, dislodging dirt, before casting it on the grass. He pulled up another and another, completing the same task each time.

Rather than stand idly by and do nothing, I moved into the garden and imitated Espen. "If he's been injured these past two weeks, how could he keep the light burning?"

"Perhaps he's used all his fortitude in doing that, leaving none to care for himself."

I wrestled with a weed that was as high as my knee. Poor Orvik—losing his wife, then being left alone and injured with no means to summon help. As I gave a final pull on the weed, I shook my head. "We shall not be able to go away on the morrow. You do realize that, do you not?"

Espen frowned but continued his weeding. "As weak as he is, I don't want to leave him to fend for himself, but my mission for the king and country must take priority."

I straightened and allowed myself the pleasure of watching Espen work, his back rippling underneath his tunic. He'd rolled up his sleeves, revealing the muscles in his bare arms—arms that had held and comforted me, especially that night during the storm on the ship.

My stomach fluttered as it had taken to doing whenever I studied him. His overlong hair and the dark stubble covering his jaw made him much too appealing and caused my thoughts to wander into forbidden territory.

He shot a glance my way, as though he'd sensed my perusal.

I grasped the next weed, pretending to be preoccupied with it. "Have you seen any signs that the holy lamp is here?"

"In my poking around, I haven't noticed it. I'm hoping Orvik merely has it stored away for safekeeping in a place no one knows about but him."

I sensed a frustrated edge to Espen's tone. "Do you think the person who attacked Orvik and his wife sought the holy lamp?"

"I hope not, but 'tis very possible."

We worked in silence for several moments, my mind spinning with the implications that someone else was searching for the holy lamp besides Espen and Kristoffer.

Regardless of what might happen with the holy lamp, I knew what I needed to do. "You must leave on the morrow, but I shall stay here with Orvik until he is healed."

Espen stood abruptly, a weed dangling from each hand. "No, I won't leave you behind."

"You will be able to travel faster to more places without me slowing you down."

His brows furrowed into dark lines. "I don't care if I have to go slower."

I had the urge to cross to him, slide my hands up his chest to his neck, then bend his head down to mine, giving him no choice but to kiss me. But I folded my arms, making myself remain where I was.

He was examining my face, and I guessed he read my desire there when his eyes darkened.

"This is a safe place for me to stay," I continued, my voice containing a breathlessness I didn't understand.

"The lightkeeper's wife was murdered. And that's safe?"

"I won't put the ladder down for anyone unless I know who it is."

Espen's jaw flexed. "I'd feel better if you're with me, so I can protect you if anyone should come after you."

"I understand. But in this case, perhaps this man's well-being is more important than my own."

Espen shook his head curtly, then bent to remove another weed. "I'll send one of my siblings here to help."

He spoke as if the matter were settled, but as the afternoon passed into eve, my desire to remain on Chapel Cliff only strengthened. For a reason I couldn't explain, the plateau dwelling and the simple lifestyle made me feel safe and secure in a way I hadn't known before.

After a late supper, I walked beyond the garden to the western edge of the cliff that overlooked the horizon and the setting sun. Orvik had awoken for a few bites of dried fish and greens before falling asleep again. Espen, having more experience with injuries than I did, said we would let him continue to rest and wake him later to change the poultice and dressings. Espen also needed the opportunity to ask Orvik more questions, particularly about the holy lamp, because even after more searching, he still hadn't come closer to finding it or any of the treasures supposedly hidden on the cliff.

The wind blew against me, wrestling my hair loose and flapping open my cloak as I peered at the foaming waves below, the crimson and orange and pink of the sun's rays turning the sea into a stained-glass masterpiece. 'Twas a sight to behold.

From my vantage point, I felt as though I was on top of the world and in charge of my destiny. After a lifetime of being a game piece in my father's strategizing and my mother's preening, I was finally free. I could be in control of who could and couldn't have access to me.

At a movement beside me, I felt Espen's presence. He didn't say anything and watched the setting sun. I didn't feel the need to fill the silence. For as many times as we could converse without ceasing, there were also times when we were together and had no need to talk.

"You look at peace," he said without taking his gaze

from the horizon.

"I am." For the first time in a long while.

"I don't want to leave you behind on the morrow." At his quiet statement, protest rose swiftly to my tongue, but before I could release it, he spoke again. "But if you want to stay, I won't fight your decision."

I released a huff of breath. "Thank you."

Although I sensed he had more to say, he lapsed into silence.

"You know how much I appreciate that you value my perspective, do you not?"

"'Tis worth valuing." Even though his shoulders were slightly slumped and his thumbs looped through his belt casually, I could feel tension radiating from him.

"You have never viewed me for my beauty the way everyone else has. Instead, you have always listened and respected me for who I am inside."

"That's what friends do."

"I think you are the only one who does not focus on my appearance."

He shrugged.

"Sometimes"—a soft laugh escaped—"I have even wondered if you are blind to my looks. That maybe because we grew up together, you still see me as a girl and not a woman."

"I'm not blind." His voice dropped a notch. "And I do see you as a woman."

"Really?" I shifted so that now I was looking at him completely. "You have never once complimented me on my beauty."

"Only because I know you don't like the emphasis upon it."

"Is that so?"

"'Tis true."

I smiled at his confession, but for a reason I couldn't explain, I wanted to know how he really felt about my outward appearance. "I give you permission this once to focus on my looks and tell me the truth about how you view me."

He shifted from one leg to the other, as though uncomfortable with my request.

My smile faded. Just because other men thought I was beautiful didn't mean Espen would. I turned away from him and faced the setting sun. "Do not concern yourself with the matter. I do not wish to hear your view after all."

"Give me a moment to pull my thoughts together, Sylvi. I do want to tell you."

"No, please refrain. I was foolish to start such a discussion." I turned, needing to put an end to the conversation before I humiliated myself any further.

His hand snagged mine, and he intertwined our fingers. "Wait. Don't go."

I froze, and for several heartbeats, all I could think about was the solidness of our connection. This was more than friendly. This was intimate, the way two people in love might hold hands.

He cleared his throat and then nodded toward the horizon. "See the way the setting sun casts a glow that creates beauty on everything it touches?"

"Yes." I had just been thinking that very thing before he'd joined me.

"That's the way it is with you. You have the kind of beauty that touches everything around you, making more beauty."

Warmth settled over me. His compliment was unlike any I'd ever received before. But I loved it. I relaxed and stared out over the glowing water and the radiant sky. Was that, then, the purpose of beauty, to use it to touch others and bring them beauty?

I moved closer to his side and leaned my head against his arm. "How do you always know just what I need to hear?"

"I'm simply telling you the truth."

"'Tis more than that to me." It was wisdom and encouragement, something he'd always given me. And those gifts were better than anything else I'd ever received.

"Besides, I don't want to flatter you like all the other men."

"Like all the other men?"

"Aye, you need no more flattery. If I had a silver coin for every instance I've heard a man pay you a compliment for your beauty, I'd be very wealthy."

"I do not hear their praise since it means nothing to me."

"Exactly why I don't join in."

"So you *do* think I am ravishing, but you would prefer not to tell me."

"Are you trying to get me to admit that I'm as obsessed with your beauty as everyone else?"

"Are you obsessed?"

His fingers tightened against mine. "Aye."

Shivers of delight coursed through me. "Good."

"You don't mind?"

"I like knowing. In fact, I have always secretly wished for your admiration, but I never thought to gain it."

"Secretly wished?"

"Surely when we were younger you sensed my infatuation with you."

He paused as though thinking back on the past. "I cannot recall you ever treating me any differently than Kris."

"You were oblivious."

He rubbed his thumb over the back of my hand. "This infatuation with me, does it still exist?"

Oh my, did it ever. I captured my lip to keep from saying the words. From the corner of my eyes, I caught Espen looking at me, at my lips, and the delight inside blossomed into a flowerbed of feelings I wanted to explore.

"Come, Sylvi. I've admitted my embarrassing obsession. Now you must tell me how you really feel."

"How I really feel?" The sea breeze cooled my overheated cheeks but couldn't cool the heat inside me.

"Unless, of course, you're no longer infatuated. Then I have no wish to hear your feelings." Even though he spoke playfully, his tone held a note of worry.

"Very well. I am still infatuated."

"Good then." His thumb caressed my hand again, stirring something inside me that was decidedly more than infatuation.

"But I must confess . . ." Did I dare say the truth? That my feelings were growing deeper?

"What?"

Though we'd agreed upon a platonic relationship for the present, I wanted—maybe even needed—him to know that I truly wished to consider a future together. "Maybe when my father is no longer interested in me and the war with Swaine is over, we can allow for more than friendship."

He was contemplative for a moment.

While I appreciated that he took the time to think before answering, I wanted his heartfelt response, not the proper one. But maybe I needed to be honest with him first before he'd be comfortable speaking the truth to me.

What did I really feel? It was much more serious than infatuation. I didn't know for certain if all these strong emotions that were surfacing were a result of the circumstances, or if they'd been lying dormant all along.

"I don't know about the future, Sylvi," he started, his expression turning earnest.

"I think I might be falling in love with you," I blurted before he could deny my request.

He fell silent.

My body tensed. Had I spoken too rashly? Sometimes I had the tendency to speak without thinking. And perhaps this confession of love for Espen was too soon, too much for him, too serious for us both under the dire circumstances.

I slipped my hand from his and took a step away. When he made no move to recapture our hold, coldness drifted into my heart and settled between us.

He hadn't been ready to hear my musings of love.

I wanted to say something to take back my words, to lighten the mood, to diffuse the tension. But I couldn't force anything past the heaviness. Instead, I spun and did the only respectable option left to me. I walked away.

Chapter 19

ESPEN

WHAT KIND OF DOLT WAS I? SYLVI HAD TOLD ME SHE LOVED ME, and I'd let her walk away.

From where I was perched on the stool next to Orvik's bed, I'd been watching her all morn without her realizing I was doing so. At present, she was standing at the table sorting through an enormous basket of sea glass that Orvik had directed her to in the extra bedchamber—apparently, sea glass that his wife Anja had collected over the years.

Sylvi had been excited to discover the treasure and had been occupied with it ever since, ignoring me completely. In fact, since last eve, she'd been ignoring me as much as she could.

I didn't blame her. I should have said something after her declaration. Of course I couldn't simply blurt the truth, that I loved her with everything that was within me, that I always had and always would.

Even if I couldn't be forthright, I could have assured her that I cared about her. And I could have explained my reservations more fully—that ultimately, I wanted her to choose me not because I was a convenient groom but because she truly desired to be with me.

The fact was, after spending so much time together over the past few days, our emotions were aflame. She might feel like she was falling in love with me. But the circumstances that had thrust us into proximity were likely fueling that attraction. Once we were apart, she'd gain perspective, remember the differences in our social standing, and return to viewing me as a friend and nothing more.

I expelled a sigh.

Orvik patted my knee. "It'll work out in the end. You'll see."

As I dropped my attention to him, I realized he was watching Sylvi too. Was he speaking about my relationship with Sylvi or something else?

We'd informed him we were newlyweds, but we hadn't told him much more than that. Had he sensed the tension between us during the few times he'd been awake?

Or was he referring to the need to find the holy lamp? Earlier in the morn, I'd finally been able to have a conversation with him about all that had transpired during his attack. He'd described a lone fisherman ringing the bell, bleeding from an injury to his head and asking for help.

Orvik and his wife had allowed the man to come up and had tended to his wound. All the while, the man had pressed them for information about the holy lamp. When his wound was finally bandaged, he'd asked if he could see the lamp. By that point, Orvik had sensed something sinister about his character and had refused the request.

The man had grabbed Anja and held her at knifepoint, threatening her bodily harm while demanding that Orvik give him the lamp. Of course, Orvik had opened the secret hiding place beneath the stone of the chapel floor and retrieved the ancient relic. But in the end, once in possession of the lamp, the man had slit Anja's throat and stabbed Orvik. He'd also destroyed their boat at the base of the cliff.

Apparently, Orvik had buried his wife at sea, then he'd continued his task of keeping the light burning. But over the days, he'd grown steadily weaker, so that when we'd clanged the bell, he'd hardly had the strength to reach the rope ladder and toss it over the cliff before passing out.

Although Orvik had done his best to describe the fisherman, I couldn't picture him. Though I'd been gone for years, I still was familiar with most of the clans who'd been living on the islands for generations. And the attacker wasn't from any of the nearby villages.

I'd been mulling over the information while I waited for my squires to return. And my conclusion was that perhaps King Canute of Swaine had learned that the holy lamp could act as a detriment to his Dark Warriors. As a result, 'twas possible he'd paid someone to search for it and attempt to confiscate it.

No doubt Rasmus, who was in collusion with Canute, was behind everything and had known the location of the holy lamp. My muscles tightened at the memory of the Royal Sage and the control he'd exerted over the king and court last autumn. He'd led by fear and coercion and threats, causing a darkness to permeate Vordinberg.

If Rasmus and the Dark Warriors were able to make their way across Norvegia without opposition, the blackness would only return to the land. Without the holy light, how would we be able to stop the takeover?

I dreaded returning to Vordinberg and the king with the bad news, but the quicker I did so, the sooner we would be able to come up with another plan to crush our enemies. I could only pray that with Maxim and Princess Elinor's wisdom, along with the advice of the king and the Knights of Brethren, we'd discover how best to combat the Dark Warriors.

Though I loathed the thought of leaving Sylvi behind, I was beginning to conclude that she would be safer staying on Chapel Cliff with Orvik than going back to Vordinberg with me. For the time being, this solitary place would afford her the best protection if her father should seek her out. And with bands of Dark Warriors already spotted crossing the border, Chapel Cliff would keep her out of harm's way.

She'd also insisted on performing the lightkeeper duties the previous eve, following Orvik's simple instruction for fanning the flame. And now she assured Orvik she would tend it until he recovered enough to resume the responsibility.

In truth, I couldn't have asked for a better place to hide Sylvi. Although I would worry about her all the while I was away, I could leave with some semblance of peace.

If only I could repair the damage I'd done to our relationship before I needed to depart.

I cast a glance out the window, gauging the position of the sun in the sky. 'Twould not be long ere the bell tolled, announcing the boat's arrival.

"I regret I was not able to protect the holy lamp and keep it for you," Orvik said quietly, as though he'd been listening to my unspoken thoughts.

"You are not to blame."

Again, Orvik patted my knee. The sorrow in his eyes was evidence for how much the attack against his wife had affected him. In fact, I feared her death had taken away his will to live, but that he hadn't yet succumbed to death because of his duty to the light.

'Twas a strange light, to be sure—almost miraculous, unfueled by anything other than the bellows every eve. I'd tried to understand its workings, but Orvik claimed the flames defied logical explanations.

Whatever the case, I prayed that in the days to come, Sylvi's presence would soothe his heartache and give him purpose again. For surely he would fight to stay alive as long as she was under his charge.

Before I could beseech him to guard her with his whole being, the distant clang of the bell echoed in the wind.

"Don't worry about Sylvi," Orvik said, once again seeming to read my mind. "I'll make sure she is safe until you can return and join her here."

I'd already told Orvik that I was a Knight of Brethren and couldn't take over for him as the next lightkeeper. But clearly he didn't intend to let go of that possibility.

Within minutes, I was at the edge of the plateau and was dropping the rope ladder to the rowboat and my waiting squires. Sylvi stood in the long grass, watching me, her arms hugging her cloak around her as though she was cold. Sunlight streamed over her, highlighting every nuance of her beauty.

As I finished uncoiling the ladder, I straightened and faced her.

"Farewell, Espen." Her voice was as somber as her expression.

Fie. I didn't want to part ways like this, with

unresolved tension between us.

"Sylvi . . ." Did I dare admit my love for her? Even if I couldn't, I had to say something. "I do care for you—"

"Please." She held up a hand. "You need not say something to make me feel better."

"I should have explained myself last night."

"What is there to explain? You do not love me the same way I do you. And I must accept it."

Though I needed to force myself to walk away and leave things the way they were, my chest burned with the need to assure her this was not her fault. Before I could stop myself, I closed the distance between us and snagged her arms.

Her eyes widened, revealing the hurt I'd caused her last eve.

The burning in my chest only fanned hotter, punishing me and driving me to her. "You're right. I don't love you the same way you love me."

At my declaration, she pressed her lips together and tried to take a step back.

I held fast to her. "I don't love you the same way, because I love you more . . . much more. There has never been, nor will there ever be a maiden I love with as much fervor as I love you."

Her struggling ceased, and she watched me with wonder. "Why did you not say so last night?"

"If you want to be with me, you must have the freedom to choose to do so and not be forced into it because you have no other option."

"But I do choose it—"

"You are not yet free to decide. Until the day you are, I would only loathe myself if I unfairly influenced you to care for me more than you would if a more suitable man was available."

"Oh, Espen. There is no one more suitable. You are the only man I want." She stood on her toes and boldly lifted her face to mine.

I took her offering. I could do naught less. I fused our lips and at the same time wrapped my arms around her, needing to feel the length of her, needing to breathe her in, needing to taste of her sweetness. I deepened the kiss and let my fingers slide up into her hair, nearly groaning at the pleasure of touching her. With each move of my mouth against hers, I wanted her to know I loved her with a passion that she couldn't even begin to understand.

But even as I lost myself in the kiss, my conscience rang with the warning that I was breaking my vow to keep her as only a friend. No matter her declaration that I was the man she wanted, I needed to release her and let time and distance determine our fate. If I would have her be mine—if that was truly a possibility—then I had to be patient and do things right.

With an effort that took more strength than I'd ever needed before, I broke our kiss and moved her an arm's length away.

As she stood watching me with swollen lips and glazed eyes, I desperately longed to pull her into my arms again. Instead, I allowed myself one last caress of her cheek. Then I turned from her and maneuvered onto the ladder.

My muscles were weak and my breathing labored with the remnants of our parting. As I descended, I didn't dare look at her, lest I be tempted to climb up and kiss her again.

Only when I reached the last rung of the rope ladder

and dropped into the boat did I allow myself a final glimpse. She was already pulling the rope up. When she had gathered it all, I dipped my oars in and began to row away. I prayed that when we next saw each other, she would be truly free. And that she would still choose me.

Chapter 20

ESPEN

THE ISLAND AND POLLOCK LOOMED AHEAD, BUT THIS TIME, without Sylvi by my side, I couldn't find any enthusiasm for the visit.

Apparently, the villagers didn't find my arrival as exciting this time either. At dusk, the wharf was deserted. Everyone appeared to be tucked away already in their homes, likely enjoying an evening meal.

We would have arrived earlier, but I'd stopped at several other fishing villages on other islands in the channel, hoping I could discover more information about the so-called fisherman who had attacked Orvik.

But as I'd suspected, no one knew that the lightkeeper had been attacked and his wife killed, since the keepers of Chapel Cliff lived an isolated existence and seldom visited the fishing villages. And no one knew of any fisherman who matched Orvik's description of the murderer.

The only information I'd gleaned that was even slightly helpful was that a strange vessel had been sighted in the area nigh a month ago. While no flags had marked the ship, the wider and stouter shape of the vessel resembled those the Swainians used.

I'd also penned a missive and sent it by courier to the east to the third of the sites Kris was exploring for the holy lamp. With how efficient he was, he'd be nearing the end of his search by now. He needed to know as quickly as possible that the mission to find the lamp was in vain, since Swaine had it in their possession.

As we brought the rowboat alongside the wharf, I hopped out and easily secured the boat to the piling with a clove knot. My hope was that on the morrow we'd find a cog sailing south. I'd put out the word at each stop today of my need for passage, but I might have to tarry a day or two before a ship would be in the vicinity.

I'd sail to Vordinberg tonight if I could. The king and my fellow Brethren needed to hear my news, even if it was discouraging. And now we urgently needed to plot another means of defeating the Swainians and the Dark Warriors.

I paused to knead the back of my neck, the knot of tension radiating as I took in the town and the colorful rows of houses. Amber light glowed from windows. Wisps of smoke rose from chimneys. And the waft of fish permeated the air.

As I started up the trail ahead of my squires, a strange sense of unease prodded me. It was the same feeling I'd had the morn we'd arrived at Chapel Cliff when no one had greeted us. Surely one or two men should still be outside. Maybe even a few children yet playing. Or a wife sweeping crumbs out an open door.

But doors were closed, the streets empty, and the town too silent.

I searched the shadows for a sign of trouble, but only a

mangy dog nosed at a heap of fish guts.

"I don't like the feel of things," I whispered to my squires.

Their brows were furrowed, and their hands already upon the hilts of their swords as if they expected an unseen enemy to rush out at us.

Suddenly I was relieved I'd left Sylvi behind. All day, I'd wavered over whether I'd done the right thing. Several times, I'd considered going back for her and insisting that she come along. I didn't like that she was somewhere without me. I wanted her by my side to ensure that I was the one to keep her out of harm's way.

I'd had to remind myself numerous times that Chapel Cliff was the safest place for her—that nothing and no one could touch her there. Including me.

As I'd relived our parting dozens of times, her declaration had echoed in my mind: *There is no one more suitable. You are the only man I want.*

The words sent a thrill through me every time I thought about them. But in the same instance, I couldn't shake the doubt that lingered. The doubt that I wasn't good enough for a maiden like Sylvi.

Upon drawing near to my family's dwelling, I caught sight of a woman peering out of an upstairs dormer window of a nearby shop. I couldn't distinguish who she was, but she seemed to be signing something to me and was pointing at my family's home.

Had something happened to one of my parents? To a sibling?

With a jolt of fresh anxiety, I picked up my pace. As I reached the stoop, I lifted a hand to the latch only to have the door swing open.

"Greetings, Espen." A familiar voice spoke, and then

out of the dimly lit front room, a figure emerged. Lord Prestegard. In a rich blue doublet and cote, he held himself with a dignified air, his blond hair well groomed, his beard and mustache perfectly shaped. Behind him stood his younger brother, Vilhelm.

While I'd always considered Lord Prestegard a hard but fair man, I'd never been fond of Vilhelm. Not only did he have darker hair and eyes, but he seemed to have a darker soul. He hadn't visited oft during the years I'd lived with the Prestegards, but whenever he did, he reeked of both pride and ambition. Now, even as he hung in the shadows of Lord Prestegard, I sensed he was playing a significant role in whatever plot was unfolding.

Lord Prestegard's blue eyes narrowed upon me and were colder than the Tundra Sea in the depths of winter. "I do believe you've taken something that belongs to me."

Taken something? I didn't need him to say more to know why he was here in Pollock. He'd come for Sylvi. "She's not some*thing*. She's some*one*."

I didn't know why I was mincing words with Lord Prestegard. It wasn't as if my doing so would change how he viewed Sylvi. Because she was and always had been an asset to him, and little more.

Lord Prestegard glanced out the door behind me. Only then did I notice that his armed men were exiting from various homes into the street. Likely, Lord Prestegard had his ship deliver them to the island and sail off. Then he and his men had hidden in homes, awaiting my arrival, intending to surround me and prevent me from leaving.

Although my squires had unsheathed their swords and were already standing in a position to defend my back, we were three against three dozen.

I lifted my chin and met Lord Prestegard's gaze

unabashedly. I'd guessed this confrontation would come at some point. I just hadn't counted on it so soon.

"She no longer belongs to you, my lord," I said with as much confidence as I could infuse into my voice. "She is my wife. The entire village was witness to our union, and now I may do with her as I please." I would never be able to do with Sylvi as I pleased. It was the other way around—Sylvi bending my will to hers. But Lord Prestegard wouldn't understand.

He regarded me as he would an errant child. "Very well, Espen. I am disappointed that you did not involve me in your union. But now that it is done, I invite you and Sylvi to be my guests at Gullkronnen. In fact, we shall sail there this eve."

"I regret that I cannot do so." I didn't regret it at all, but if we were going to play at niceties, I'd do my part. "I must be away with all haste to Vordinberg on business for the king."

"Your squires can carry on to Vordinberg and conduct the king's business without you. Surely His Majesty will understand you were delayed with a wedding celebration at the home of your wife's family. He will not deny you an extra day or two."

"With the threat of war, I'm afraid he'll not be so understanding, especially since my business is of an urgent nature."

"If it was not urgent enough to prevent you from marrying my daughter, then it is not urgent enough to keep you from a wedding feast." His tone contained an edge of granite—one that told me I was going with him whether I wanted to or not.

Behind me, Lord Prestegard's men had inched closer. I was a better swordsman than most of them combined, but I couldn't take them all on, and Lord Prestegard knew it. He'd likely counted out exactly how many men he would need to overcome my skills, since he was acquainted with my proficiency better than most.

Vilhelm had also moved directly behind Lord Prestegard, his knife unsheathed, his fingers twitching as though he hoped he might have the chance to use it.

I bowed my head, feigning subservience. "Mayhap I'll go with you for a day and then head south from there." Lord Prestegard wasn't planning to take me to a wedding feast any more than I was planning to allow him to do so. This charade we were enacting was well played so far, but I had the feeling the game wouldn't last much longer.

"Excellent." Lord Prestegard glanced around the still-solemn town. A few more faces peered out windows and some out of doorways, but I suspected he'd ordered the villagers to stay inside so that no one could give me advance warning of his presence.

One of Lord Prestegard's men had made his way to the wharf and now shot a flaming arrow into the darkening sky. The flash of light would signal his ship to return.

"You must fetch Sylvi anon." Lord Prestegard's gaze challenged me to defy him.

Perhaps he didn't yet know I'd left her at Chapel Cliff. Maybe he believed she was on the island, hidden away with someone. Whatever the case, he intended to retrieve her and somehow foil our marriage so that she would be free to do his bidding.

I couldn't let that happen.

"Sylvi is tired and weak from the storm we experienced on our voyage here." I offered the first excuse I could find. "You will need to excuse her from the feast this time. Mayhap we can celebrate with her later in the summer."

"We cannot have a feast without the bride. Once you explain that her family wishes to congratulate her and celebrate her union, she will surely overcome her queasiness to join us."

"I would explain to her if I could, but she isn't here."

"Where is she?" The question was final. This was all Lord Prestegard wanted to know so he could retrieve her and bestow her upon Lord Grimsrud or one of his other candidates. Sylvi had mentioned overhearing Lord Grimsrud speak of getting signatures. From whom? And for what purpose? The signatures were obviously valuable if Lord Prestegard was going to so much trouble to get Sylvi back.

But I would never tell him where she was, not even if he put a sword to my throat and threatened to slice me open. "She is someplace safe, my lord."

His eyes narrowed.

I wanted to add that he could never have her again, that he may as well not even try. But taunting him wouldn't help my cause.

He closed the distance between us and pushed into my face. "You have overstepped yourself once again, Espen. Remember I was the one who gave you the power to better yourself, and I have the power to take it all away."

My muscles tensed for the battle I would very soon need to fight. "You offered me an advantage, but only I have the power to better myself. No one else can do that for me."

His breath carried the scent of spicy mead and a hiss of displeasure. He stared hard at me before cocking his head at Vilhelm.

In the next instant, the blade of Vilhelm's knife pressed against my exposed neck. The prick of the tip against my skin drew blood.

I hadn't been blind to Lord Prestegard's faults while I was living with him, but I'd never taken him for a cruel man—especially one who would approve, possibly orchestrate, my bodily harm.

What had happened? Had he spent too much time with Vilhelm over recent years and allowed his brother's dark ambitions to become his own?

"Hold on now," my father said from somewhere in the room, his heavy stomping drawing near.

"Stay where you are," Vilhelm said, "or I shall put an end to Espen right here."

The footsteps halted. "No need to hurt the boy, your lordship."

I didn't flinch. Instead, I held Lord Prestegard's gaze, letting him know Vilhelm could threaten and torture me all night, and I still wouldn't reveal Sylvi's location.

As if sensing my resolve to die if need be, Lord Prestegard nodded at Vilhelm. The man shoved me away so that I stumbled back a step. Before I could react, Vilhelm grabbed my father and pointed the knife against my father's throat.

My father flinched but then held himself motionless even as blood began to flow from a slice beneath his jaw.

I froze.

"Do not forget that I know your weaknesses better than most." The gleam in Lord Prestegard's blue eyes told me he did indeed know me all too well, especially how loyal I was to those I cared about, including my kin.

All the years I'd trained as a knight, he'd known I

longed to return to the sea and my family, but he'd pressured me to continue with my training, manipulating me with mentions of my family's happiness and security. And now, he clearly aimed to barter my father's life for Sylvi's.

I glanced behind my father to find my mother and siblings huddled together, their eyes wide with fear. How would they survive without a provider? And if Lord Prestegard could so easily eliminate my father if I didn't comply, what would prevent him from harming my mother or one of my siblings next?

Whatever the case, I couldn't put their lives at risk.

"If you release him, I'll tell you where Sylvi is." Surely revealing to Lord Prestegard that she was at Chapel Cliff wouldn't matter. He would never be able to reach her— not without her throwing down the ladder. And she wouldn't do that.

"Tell us first"—Vilhelm pressed the blade deeper into my father's neck—"then we shall decide whether he deserves to live."

My father pinched his eyes closed and gritted his teeth.

My fingers tightened on the hilt of my sword, and I had the sudden burning need to strike Vilhelm down right where he stood.

As though sensing the direction of my thoughts, Lord Prestegard frowned a warning at Vilhelm. Almost reluctantly, Vilhelm loosened the blade.

Even so, the damage was done. My father was bleeding profusely now, and if he didn't get help, he would soon bleed to death.

Desperation set in, and I loathed that I was bringing this harm to my kin. I shouldn't have involved them, and now I needed to leave before they suffered more. "Sylvi is at Chapel Rock. I will take you to her."

My father swayed. Vilhelm released him, and my father would have crumpled to the floor if not for my mother and sister Terese rushing to his side.

Both Lord Prestegard and Vilhelm watched my family hover around my father for a moment.

"The girl?" Vilhelm asked Lord Prestegard with a calculated gleam.

The question sent a frigid shiver through me, and I didn't give either of them time to speak further. I lunged toward Vilhelm. I would allow them to take me their prisoner, but I wouldn't let them touch Terese or anyone else in my family.

Lord Prestegard was quick in swinging his sword, blocking my progress forward with a parry. Although I was a more accomplished swordsman than Lord Prestegard, I also would never injure him. And he likely knew it.

His interference gave Vilhelm the second he needed to grab Terese. And now instead of the blade pressed against my father, Vilhelm wielded it against my sister.

She trembled but held herself still. She was clearly trying to be brave, but at the line of blood now trailing down her throat, she swallowed hard.

"Let her go." I lowered my sword. "I told you I'd take you to Sylvi."

"The girl will come along." Vilhelm tightened his hold on Terese without taking his eyes from me. "After all, someone from amongst your family should be allowed to attend the wedding celebration."

Vilhelm's slight smile told me all I needed to know. They'd already used my father as the lesson of what would happen if I didn't comply. Now he was bringing Terese as insurance that I would do their bidding.

As several of Lord Prestegard's men drew cautiously closer and reached to disarm me and my squires, the cold grip of fear seized my heart.

I didn't resist as they took my sword and knife then began to bind my hands in front of me. I could only silently pray I'd find a way to free Terese and keep Sylvi from falling back into her father's clutches.

Chapter 21

Sylvi

I missed Espen. As much as I relished the peace and control I felt atop the cliff, it wasn't the same without him. In fact, since watching him descend the rope ladder yesterday, I'd felt as though part of me had gone away with him and that I was no longer whole.

"You're thinking about your man again?" Orvik rested in his bed. He'd awoken a short while ago and allowed me to feed him fish soup.

I didn't know how to cook, had never needed to do so. But Orvik had given me instructions, and I'd managed to chop fish and pare turnips and put the ingredients together with several herbs, concocting something not only edible, but even slightly delicious.

"I am sorry, Orvik." I picked up the empty bowl and stood, smoothing a hand over the simple skirt that had been amongst Anja's possessions that Orvik had insisted I use. "I do not wish to bother you with my sorrow."

"You aren't bothering me." His smile was warm and

his eyes bright. Color was beginning to infuse his face, and he was staying awake longer. A short while ago, I'd cleaned his wounds and reapplied a fresh poultice and bandage, and from what I could tell, the injuries were causing him less pain and hopefully beginning to heal.

Even so, he hadn't gotten out of bed since our arrival, and I'd taken over the duty of tending to the flame in the chapel. Made of stone, the chapel had been built, like the other structures, to withstand all kinds of weather and the worst of storms. The light burned at the center of the chapel in a raised circular pit. A flaming ball with brilliant light glowed at all times of the day and night as well as spilling out the windows.

Orvik had given me instructions and had indicated the light was easy to take care of. The only thing required of the keeper was to pump the bellows beneath the flame at sunset. At the application of the air, the conflagration shot high, nearly to the ceiling of the chapel.

Although I'd witnessed the Chapel Cliff light once or twice in my childhood when passing by in a ship, I hadn't considered what created so brilliant a light. But now that I'd gone in to tend it, I had more questions than answers.

I wanted to ask Orvik what fuel kept the flame burning. Was there a special oil? Or charcoal? A source that burned slowly and didn't need to be replenished oft? And if the flame ever went out, what must be done to restart it? What caused it to be so bright? And though it was hot, why didn't it singe or sear my skin when I got near it?

I'd quickly realized the house was positioned in

such a way that every window overlooked the chapel, providing an easy way to keep an eye on the light. Even now, as I glanced out the window, I could see the chapel and the glow from within in spite of the morning sunshine.

"I loved my Anja the way that Espen loves you," Orvik said through a yawn.

"Then you must have loved her very well, for I have never met a man as kind and loving as Espen."

My thoughts returned to Espen's farewell and his declaration of love. *I don't love you the same way because I love you more . . . much more. There has never been, nor will there ever be a maiden I love with as much fervor as I love you.*

Oh, Espen. He loved me, and he'd left me no doubt about it. If his words hadn't been enough, his kiss had confirmed it. Now the longing for him was keen and sweet and deep. He'd be busy with taking the news to the king about the missing holy lamp. Then he'd be away fighting against King Canute's army and the Dark Warriors. I didn't know how I'd be able to wait days—possibly weeks—until he came back for me.

"I'm leaving to be with Anja soon." Orvik's voice, while soft, was filled with happiness.

Placing the soup bowl in a basin of warm water, I turned to face Orvik. "Your wounds are healing well, which means you will be here for a while. At least, if I have anything to say about it, you will be."

Orvik's thin face was flushed, and a small smile played at his lips. "I'm ready, Sylvi. And now that you and Espen have been appointed to take care of the light, I can go in peace."

I crossed back to the bed, noting how frail he

appeared under the covers. After a fortnight of hardly any sustenance, he was weak. I needed to coerce him into eating more. That's all. Once he had time to regain strength, he would surely live many more years.

Even so, I needed to correct him about his misguided assumption that Espen and I planned to become the next lightkeepers.

I sat down on the stool beside him and took his hand in mine. "You are very kind to bequeath this beautiful place and the charge of the light into Espen's and my care. But as Espen has told you, he is not free. He is a Knight of Brethren and cannot so easily sever his work for the king and country."

"I could see in his eyes and the way he moves that he belongs with the sea."

I'd noticed that Espen seemed to be comfortable and happy with his family and on the ship and even here on the cliff. Perhaps this was where he was meant to be.

But was I?

Orvik gave a nod, as if answering my unspoken question. "Espen belongs with the sea, and you belong with Espen."

Even if the marriage to him had started as a ploy to thwart my father, it had turned into so much more. I wanted to be with Espen. In fact, next time we were together I needed to assure him that I was indeed choosing him of my own free will.

"But how can I convince Espen we belong together regardless of the obstacles that might stand between us?"

Orvik chuckled. "I saw the way that young man looked at you. He won't be able to stay away from you no matter how hard he tries."

The old lightkeeper's words warmed my heart. "I hope you are correct, Orvik. I know I shall not be able to stay away from him. I intend to do whatever I can to convince him we belong together."

"I know you will. I could sense your determination to win him."

I cocked my head and studied Orvik more carefully. There was something about this man that brought a fresh calmness to me whenever I was with him, even when he was asleep.

His eyelids were growing heavy, and he would soon slumber again. Although I enjoyed his company and his tales of bygone days, I also wanted him to rest, especially after his dire prediction that he was going soon to be with his wife.

"I sense my time is short, Sylvi." His fingers groped for mine.

I found his hand and squeezed it reassuringly. "No, you must stop talking like that—"

"Before I go, I must tell you something that only my wife and I knew. 'Tis knowledge the keepers are allowed to have, and it must never be shared with anyone else."

"Then you must wait to share your secret, for I cannot promise you Espen and I will be the next keepers." In fact, I couldn't even promise him Espen would return. After all, he would soon be putting his life in peril to save the country. Although he was a skilled knight and expert swordsman, it was also true that men were slain when they went to war— sometimes many men.

Orvik paused, as if he was contemplating my

statement. Then he spoke again. "Very well. Even if you and Espen don't take over the light, I must entrust this secret to someone, and I thank the Lord he sent you."

"Whatever it is, I shall pass it along to the new keeper if you are not able to do so yourself."

He shifted his gaze to the window that overlooked the chapel and the light. He likely couldn't see much from his position, but perhaps he could still view the glow, because his countenance took on a faint shine, almost as if he was reflecting the light.

Finally, he turned his attention back to me. "The flames that burn in the chapel are holy flames."

"I have noticed they require no visible fuel. And I wanted to ask you why."

"They are sometimes called the Eternal Flame and represent the presence of Providence. And while he keeps the light burning, he also requires partnership with us."

"Fanning the fire every day?"

"Yes." Orvik's voice grew softer. "If it's not fanned, it will flicker out."

Was that how it was in our lives too? That we needed to do our part to fan the flame of Providence so that then he burned brightly and chased away the darkness? It was an interesting analogy to consider.

"How long does it take to go out?"

"Only one night. By the second, it will surely fade to nothing. And if the flame here in the chapel goes out, the holy lamp will also stop burning as it contains the same light."

I sat forward. This was news Espen would want to know. Although the holy lamp had been stolen from the Chapel Cliff, it was possible Espen might still be able to track it down. Or perhaps Kristoffer would locate it.

But what if they couldn't find it? "We may no longer have the holy lamp in our possession, but can we somehow utilize the chapel flame to fight the Dark Warriors?"

Orvik shook his head. "The holy lamp is the only container that can transport the flame. All others are consumed when the flame touches them."

His eyelids fell, and he expelled a weary breath. I needed to let him slumber again so that he could continue to heal, but I couldn't keep from asking the question that had crossed my mind when I'd considered the mission to find the holy lamp. "How can a single small lamp have the power to defeat the Dark Warriors? I do not understand it."

Orvik nodded but didn't open his eyes. "'Tis a difficult thing to understand. But 'tis always possible for even the smallest light to illuminate darkness and defeat it."

"I hope so."

"Holy Scripture says that the light shines in the darkness and that the darkness cannot comprehend it."

"Comprehend?"

"It cannot extinguish or overcome it."

"Then we must yet find the holy lamp to overcome the Dark Warriors?"

"I don't know enough about the Dark Warriors and their tactics, but yes, if light is important in defeating them, then the holy lamp will help." He expelled another breath, this one shallower and irregular.

I didn't like the sound of it. "I've kept you awake

long enough. Now you must sleep."

He didn't respond, and for a second, I feared he'd stopped breathing altogether, until he expelled a whoosh of air.

I stood and started to move away from the bed when he grasped my hand with more firmness than I expected. I was surprised to see his eyes open and his features earnest.

"Now you understand why you must stay and keep the flame going here in the chapel. Without the source of the light, there is no hope at all."

"Yes, I understand." I pressed a hand against his cheek to reassure him. "I will do everything within my power to keep the flame burning."

He held my gaze for a long moment. Then, apparently seeing what he wanted there, he smiled and closed his eyes.

Once again, his stillness worried me. But at the steady rise and fall of his chest, I assured myself that he was slumbering and would be fine. Besides, he'd told Espen he would stay alive to help me. Surely, he wouldn't break his word.

All the while I washed the dishes and tidied up, my thoughts as usual found their way to Espen. He was my husband. In spite of the unusual circumstances that had brought us together, we were married in the sight of God and man. And I wouldn't let Espen or anyone else convince me to break those vows.

Just as I finished drying the last spoon and placing it back in the cabinet, the clanging bell at the base of the cliff brought my pulse to a halt. Someone had come to Chapel Cliff and was calling to the lightkeeper.

Orvik had indicated that he always heard the bell,

that he'd trained himself to listen for it at all times. But now, he didn't stir, not even slightly.

Should I go to the edge and see who was there?

I folded the damp towel slowly even as my thoughts rushed about hastily.

Answering the summons was the right thing to do. What if Espen was already returning? Or perhaps his squires had come with news. Or maybe his family.

I stepped outside and pulled my cloak on. Though the day was mild, the wind coming from the sea brought a chill. Orvik had said that his wife Anja had never liked the cold wind, that it had been the one thing about dwelling on the cliff that had been hardest for her, even above the isolation.

From what he'd shared, they'd had a difficult life, marked by tragedies in the death of both of their young sons in a boating accident and then losing another baby at birth. The family they'd loved and longed for had been taken from them. Yet through the years, Orvik had done everything he could to counter the harshness, making their lives full and meaningful in other ways.

When I'd previously explored the dwellings, I'd noticed Anja's touch everywhere. Maybe her dreams hadn't materialized the way she'd planned, but she hadn't let that stop her from creating beauty from what she had left.

The bell clanged again, this time longer.

I forced myself to approach the edge where the rope ladder sat in a heap. I was in charge, and no one could ascend unless I permitted it. I didn't have anything to worry about.

But as I knelt in the long grass and dragged my

cloak around me, my heart banged hard anyway. I whispered a prayer, then peeked over the cliff.

At the sight of a familiar flag flying from the bow of the vessel, I jerked back. My father's ship. That meant only one thing. He'd discovered where I was and had come to retrieve me.

I sat back on my heels and pressed my hands to my chest. Maybe if I pretended I wasn't here, he'd sail away and leave me be.

Squaring my shoulders, I rose and began to walk to the house. But at the call of my name in a voice that sounded like Espen's, I halted. As he shouted again, I spun and started back. Something must have happened if he was returning but a day after he'd left. Had my father had a change of heart? Perhaps he'd offered to work with Espen to help him locate the holy lamp. And maybe he'd even accepted that we were married and was inviting me to travel along.

My speculations were too good to be true. But I wanted them to be. I wanted my father to realize he'd been using me. I wanted him to recognize I was more valuable than my beauty. And I wanted him to finally love me for who I was and not for what I could do for the family.

Holding my breath, I lowered myself again and looked over the edge to the ship below.

Espen stood in the center of the main deck and appeared free of harm. My father was also on the main deck and was watching the cliff. At the sight of me, he murmured to Espen.

Espen was peering behind him into the captain's cabin, but his attention jerked up to me. At the desperation on his face, my heart plummeted.

Something was terribly amiss. Though he was too distant for me to distinguish every detail of his countenance, I could tell he was silently pleading with me. But to do what?

My father said something else to Espen, and again, I couldn't hear his words, but I could discern that my father's stiff bearing and curt movements held anger.

The hope that had swelled only seconds ago deflated. I'd been a fool to expect him to show any mercy toward Espen for helping me. And I'd been a fool to believe he'd apologize and tell me he loved me. To him, I remained a bargaining tool that he could exploit and then discard at will.

"Lower the ladder, Sylvi." Espen's command contained a curtness he oft employed with his squires but never with me.

I hesitated.

"Tell her," my father said to him, the sharpness of his tone echoing against the stone.

Espen squared his shoulders as though to brace himself for something he didn't want to do. "I was wrong and selfish to steal you from your father and marry you. I'm giving you an annulment, and now you must wed the man of your father's choosing."

Every word that fell from his mouth was a lie. I knew it. He was too much a man of honor and integrity to declare his love for me so ardently one day and the next, order me to marry Lord Grimsrud. The fact was, Espen hadn't stolen me from my father. I'd run away. And he hadn't been selfish. He'd withheld himself and hadn't wanted to admit his love for fear of exerting undue influence upon me.

Though his voice didn't betray him, his eyes did.

He was only repeating what my father had instructed him to say.

A thousand thoughts rushed through my mind all at once, but one clamored above them all. I had to do whatever I could to protect Espen. He must be in terrible danger if he'd allowed my father and uncle to manipulate him like this. In fact, I suspected he wouldn't have done it, even at the cost of his own life, unless he was protecting someone else. . . .

He cast a glance at the captain's cabin, as though communicating that very message. Someone he loved was in peril, and that was the only reason he was cooperating with my father and uncle. Had my father and uncle perhaps captured his parents? Were they even now torturing them to force Espen to do their bidding?

I shifted my focus to my father. The tall, proud man staring up at me had become a stranger. I'd thought I'd known him, thought I could trust him, thought he loved me. But I had to admit what I'd never wanted to—that I was nothing more than his pawn.

Did he really think he could come to Chapel Cliff and convince me to believe this charade? Surely he didn't view me as so unintelligent that I would fall for Espen's declaration.

I blinked, trying to hold back sudden hot tears. Yes, he truly thought I was naïve and stupid enough to blindly go along with all his plans. The truth was, I'd always been the beautiful but dumb daughter.

For too long, I'd let his view of me shape who I was, and I'd let my fear of being seen as stupid keep me silent. Was it time to prove to myself—and to him— that I wasn't all beauty and no brains?

Narrowing my gaze, I took in the entire scene below me again. If he wanted a dumb but beautiful daughter, then that's the role I'd play. But in doing so, I would find a way to save Espen, his family, and myself. I'd do so or die trying.

Chapter 22

ESPEN

THE SIGHT OF SYLVI AT THE TOP OF THE CLIFF WAS TEARING ME asunder. Yet I was helpless to do anything but what Lord Prestegard and Vilhelm had commanded me.

Even now, Vilhelm had his knife wedged against Terese's finger and had threatened to cut off a finger every time I disobeyed. With the gag tied tightly over her mouth, Terese was struggling to breathe. From the tenseness with which she held herself, I guessed the blade was pressing into her flesh and causing her pain.

I felt every flinch she made and heard every whimper as if it were a whip tearing into me. In fact, I'd offered to let him cut off my hands rather than allow Terese to suffer. But neither Lord Prestegard nor Vilhelm had listened to any of my pleading throughout the night. And now I was left with no choice but to betray Sylvi.

Although I'd spoken the words exactly the way Lord Prestegard had instructed me, I prayed Sylvi understood that I hadn't meant them, that I didn't want her to lower the ladder. If she refused to hand herself over, then Lord

Prestegard couldn't hold me accountable or harm Terese for Sylvi's stubbornness. He'd realize that no matter what I said or did, I wouldn't be able to sway his daughter into cooperating.

Sylvi rose to her feet and held herself regally. "I take full responsibility for this situation, Father. I panicked at the prospect of marrying Lord Grimsrud. I made a rash decision to run away and thrust myself upon Espen."

I shook my head, a sense of dread welling up within me. What was she doing? She surely wasn't contemplating giving in to her father, was she? I wanted to say something to stop her, but I could feel Vilhelm's sharp gaze upon me, watching my every move.

Sylvi lifted her chin. Though she was too far away for me to read her eyes, she held herself in a way that radiated determination. "I pushed him to take me. And I am the one who coerced him into marrying me. He did not want to do it. But he is too kind to resist my ploys."

She was attempting to defer the blame away from me to herself. Did she really think she could make her father believe I held no responsibility for this situation? That I'd allowed her to manipulate me into it without any desire for it on my part?

Lord Prestegard knew me well enough. He'd already guessed how much I cared about Sylvi after the banquet the other night. Even if he understood Sylvi had been the one to run away, he'd realize I wanted to be with Sylvi and hadn't needed any—or at least much—pressing to marry her.

"I overreacted to your decision," Sylvi called. "Leaving was a mistake, and I regret now that I didn't stay and do my duty as a daughter should."

From the sincerity in her tone, I could almost believe

Sylvi was telling the truth, that she believed she'd made a mistake and regretted leaving.

Lord Prestegard studied Sylvi. Did he believe her?

"I shall willingly return with you to Vordinberg and marry the man of your choosing . . ."

Every muscle in my body tensed with the need to shout no, to yell at her to stop, to demand that she stay atop Chapel Cliff and not come down. But as Terese flinched again, I bit back my protest even as it swelled for release.

"But first I want you to allow Espen to climb up here onto Chapel Cliff to take care of the light, since the keeper is injured."

What was she doing? Was she orchestrating a way to be together after all? If I went up, then I could keep Sylvi from descending and handing herself over to her father. Just as quickly as the hope fanned to life, it turned to ashes. I'd never be able to help Sylvi as long as Vilhelm held Terese.

Lord Prestegard glanced from Sylvi to me and then back. "If I allow Espen to go, what will prevent him from coming after you and trying to get you back?"

Aye, he knew me too well. At the moment he set me free, I would indeed do everything I could to extricate her again from his clutches. In fact, I wouldn't rest until I made sure Sylvi was far away from him.

"If you make him ascend, he will have no means of getting away from Chapel Cliff. He will be stranded, at least until I am wed to Lord Grimsrud, and by then it will be too late."

I wouldn't be stranded, and Lord Prestegard would know that too. I was an excellent swimmer. Even without a boat, I'd be able to swim across the channel.

"Will it be too late?" Lord Prestegard studied my expression as though attempting to read the depths of my feelings for Sylvi and discover what lengths I'd go to for her. Then he looked back up at Sylvi. "What will prevent you from abandoning Lord Grimsrud for the man you love?"

"I love Espen as a friend and nothing more."

"The villagers testified to a marriage based on love and affection between you both."

No doubt he and Vilhelm had interviewed many people in my village and gathered as much information as they could about the events that had transpired. Though our wedding had been hasty, my feelings toward Sylvi had been genuine. And when she'd spoken her vows, she'd said them as though she meant every word. Our kiss had certainly been affectionate. We'd given my family and friends no cause to think our marriage was a pretense.

"I was swept up in the emotion of the moment," she responded. "'Twas all too easy to imagine myself with feelings for a good man like Espen. But now that I have been apart from him, I realize I was feebleminded to think I could have a happy future with him. We are simply too different."

My pulse slowed to a crawl. She sounded as though she was speaking the truth. Had she changed her mind about how she felt about me? This was what I'd suspected could happen—that the hasty marriage and spending so much time together would stir her emotions, making her think she cared about me more than she did.

And she wasn't wrong about our differences. She'd given voice to my worry that if we stayed together, eventually she would find herself dissatisfied with the life I could give her.

"Please let him come up to the top," she called. "I vow I shall do everything you require of me. And Espen will too, will you not?"

I hesitated.

"What have you to say for yourself, Espen?" Lord Prestegard's hard gaze bored into me. Did he really care what I had to say, or was he wanting me to confirm Sylvi's declaration?

I had to remember Lord Prestegard could read me well. If I lied to him, he'd likely be able to tell.

"I think you know the truth, my lord." I held his gaze. "And the truth is that Sylvi deserves better than the men you have picked for her." My answer was vague and yet was completely honest.

"So, you believe she should have you instead?"

"She should have someone who loves her."

"And you consider yourself to be that man?"

"I cannot claim to be worthy of her. But I'll not deny that I love her."

Lord Prestegard glanced into the captain's cabin as if needing advice from Vilhelm. A few seconds later, Vilhelm ducked out into the open and stalked over to his brother. The two conversed in whispers for a long moment.

Prickles formed at the back of my neck. I didn't know what they were planning, but I predicted it was something much more sinister than either Sylvi or I could comprehend.

As they broke apart, Lord Prestegard motioned to Sylvi. "If you come down and go through with marrying Lord Grimsrud, then once the deed is accomplished, we vow to send Espen back to Vordinberg."

"You vow to send him away without harm?"

"Yes, but only after your wedding."

They would hold me hostage and use me to manipulate her, the same way they were using Terese to manipulate me. Even if Sylvi didn't love me, she wouldn't want her father or uncle to torture me. If they but laid a knife to one of my fingers the same way they had to Terese's, Sylvi would do anything they asked of her, even something she despised.

"Very well." She spoke pleasantly, as if the matter was settled. "I shall do my duty as a daughter, and you will free Espen and not hold him accountable for my foolishness."

Foolishness. The word slammed against me. Was she merely saying what she thought her father wanted to hear? Or did she believe she'd been foolish to run from her father's match?

I prayed this was just a ploy she was concocting to buy us more time to get away from her father. But a part of me trembled at the prospect that she was truly planning to go through with marrying Lord Grimsrud.

Lord Prestegard gave a curt nod. "I shall uphold my part of the bargain as long as you uphold yours."

While Lord Prestegard had been a man of integrity during my days of training at his household, I didn't know if he was trustworthy anymore, not after coming under the influence of his brother over recent years.

Would he indeed allow me to go free after Sylvi was wed? Somehow, I couldn't quite believe he would. Not if he feared I would chase after Sylvi and attempt to steal her from Lord Grimsrud.

"To ensure that Espen does not conspire further," Lord Prestegard said, "we shall lock him in the hold for the duration of the voyage."

Vilhelm motioned toward the nearest guards. In the next moment, several of them surrounded me, wrenching my arms together and wrapping a rope around them. Once the knot was tightly secured, they shoved me toward the opening in the hull that led to the narrow hold.

As they slid the wood covering away and forced me to climb down inside, I glanced a final time at Sylvi on the edge of Chapel Cliff. I wanted to shout at her not to come down, to stay where she was, but she was already dragging the rope ladder over the side.

As the darkness closed in around me, I expelled a tight breath. Once I no longer had to worry about Terese, I'd get to the bottom of Sylvi's plans and figure out a way to help her. I prayed I could do so before it was too late for either of us.

Chapter
23

Sylvi

I couldn't leave the light or Orvik behind, but I didn't know how else to save Espen. As I dangled from the last rung, two of my father's men assisted me down and steadied my feet upon the deck.

My father waited, and now at this proximity, the skepticism on his face was easy to read. Even though we'd made a bargain, he wasn't convinced I would go through with marrying Lord Grimsrud. Perhaps he thought I'd come down to set Espen free and run away with him.

The truth was, I did intend to liberate Espen and escape with him. But I needed to do better at my pretense of being daft but beautiful if I had any hope of fooling Father into thinking I was going along with him.

"Oh, Father." I pressed a hand against my forehead and feigned weakness. Then I stumbled forward and wrapped my arms around him, clinging to him as if he was my salvation.

He embraced me and gently patted my back.

"I am truly sorry for causing you such distress." I infused relief into my voice. "I did not realize the deprivation that would come as a result of marrying Espen. Now, after meeting his family and seeing the hardships, I cannot imagine that as my future."

None of it was true. The luxuries I'd grown up with had paled in comparison with the joy of being by Espen's side. After meeting his family and experiencing their love and warmth, I was all the more aware of what was lacking in my own family. But I needed to say everything my father would expect of me.

"You are fine now, my dear." My father patted me again.

I pulled back and wiped at my eyes, blinking away the tears I'd forced. I loathed that I must speak so deceptively to my father, but what other choice had he given me?

A movement in the captain's cabin caught my eye. I didn't dare take too much interest. But as I pretended to dab tears from my eyes, I took in now what I'd been unable to see above.

Terese. The young woman was tied to the chair, her mouth gagged. And her eyes filled with both fear and pain.

I sniffled again, tilting my head and pretending to cry silent tears.

My father pressed a linen cloth into my hands.

"Thank you." I made sure my voice wobbled, but all the while I pieced together what had transpired with Espen. He'd clearly made it back to his village yesterday. But at some point, my father and his small army had arrived. Espen had likely been outnumbered and captured. Then in order to gain Espen's cooperation, Father and Uncle had brought Terese along.

The two were despicable.

I couldn't keep a small ache from forming in a corner of my heart. Father hadn't always been this way, had he? Surely he hadn't pretended to care about me and Kristoffer and even Espen while we were children. I hadn't imagined his genuineness, had I?

Whatever the case, now I had two people to set free instead of one. Did I dare ask if we could take Terese and Espen back to their fishing village and leave them there?

My uncle approached, and I launched myself against my father again to hide my face. If either man suspected the depths of my love for Espen, I feared what they might do to him to ensure that we couldn't be together.

Yet, even if I could temporarily keep them from discovering my feelings, it was only a matter of time before the truth came out—the truth that I'd do anything for Espen, including sacrificing my own future to make certain he had his.

Again, my father wrapped me in his arms, this time gathering me closer. I pretended to sob quietly, sniffling and gasping.

"There, there," my father said kindly.

I released a deep shudder. "I think I need to rest now, please." I pulled back and looked at the captain's cabin, attempting to make myself appear weary from my ordeal.

"Take the cabin." Father waved a hand toward it.

Uncle Vilhelm didn't say anything, but from the

tightness of his pursed lips, I suspected he had much to say and would encourage my father to question me in more detail, which meant my rest would need to be lengthy—perhaps the duration of the voyage.

As I took a step in the direction of the cabin, I paused and pretended to notice Terese for the first time. I tilted my head in a way that hopefully made me look confused before turning my wide eyes framed with wet lashes upon them both. "Why have you brought Espen's sister along?"

My father cleared his throat and exchanged an uncomfortable look with Uncle Vilhelm.

"Alas, Espen was giving us a difficult time," Uncle Vilhelm said, "and we knew he would do our bidding better if she accompanied us."

It was as I'd suspected. I could only imagine the terror Espen had felt at knowing my uncle would hurt his sister if he didn't do exactly as they wanted.

"You surely will not object if she serves as my maidservant, will you?" I directed the question to my father, imitating the sweet expression my mother always used to get her way. "I am sorely in need of a maid after these past days without assistance."

My father's expression softened. "Do with her as you please, my dear—"

"No," Uncle Vilhelm spoke at the same time.

Father shot him a narrowed look. "What harm can come of allowing Sylvi to utilize her as a servant?"

The two men gazed at each other severely before Uncle Vilhelm bowed his head in subservience. As the younger brother, my uncle hadn't inherited the land and wealth that had been bestowed upon my father. Though he'd married well and resided in a home that had once belonged to his wife's family, he never would gain the prestige or power of a firstborn son. Instead, he was destined to live in my father's shadow.

"Sylvi may have the girl," my father said again. "But we shall keep her close at hand to continue to control Espen."

I'd already started across the deck toward the captain's cabin and had to force myself not to trip over his words. If Espen attempted an escape or tried to come to my aid, he would not only put himself in danger, but he'd bring harm to Terese.

The merest prospect sent fear charging through every vein. But I forced myself to walk calmly into the cabin. I turned and feigned another weary sigh. "Thank you, Father."

He nodded.

Before he or Uncle Vilhelm could say anything more, I closed the door.

As the darkness of the cabin fell over me, my body trembled so that I sagged and slid down until I sat in a heap upon the floor. I fisted a hand against my mouth to keep myself from crying out with the despair that was rising like the tide, threatening to drown me.

I needed to free Terese from her bindings, but I didn't know if I had the fortitude to push myself up. I feared I'd used every ounce of courage I possessed to playact in front of my father and uncle so that now I had nothing left inside.

As bootsteps approached the cabin, I had no choice but to scramble to my feet. At a firm knock upon the door, I smoothed down my skirt, then opened the door.

Uncle waited without speaking a word, but his dark

look seemed to say he was aware of my duplicity. He brushed past me, his knife in hand. As he crossed to Terese, her eyes rounded.

My heart raced with sudden fear too. What did he intend to do to her? He surely wouldn't defy my father and hurt her, would he?

As he lifted his knife, I couldn't hold back a small cry of alarm. "Do not harm her."

My uncle paused, and his lips curled up into the hint of a smirk. "You may be able to fool your father, but you will never fool me. I see the way you care for this girl, just as I see the way you care for Espen."

"Of course, I care for them both." I needed to walk a fine line between truth and deception, and I was learning it wasn't an easy line to balance. "I am a compassionate person and would not have you needlessly harm anyone."

Without arguing, Uncle Vilhelm slipped the blade into one of the ropes binding Terese's arms to the chair. Only then did I notice the slices in her flesh upon several of her fingers, almost as if Uncle Vilhelm had purposefully positioned his blade there.

Had he threatened to cut off Terese's fingers?

As Uncle Vilhelm finished sawing through the rope on one arm and began the next, I could feel him watching my reactions from the corner of his eyes. Could he see my revulsion?

"There," he said as he finished the second binding. "Now she can do her duties."

"Please release the rag from her mouth."

My uncle sheathed his knife. "Your father has agreed to continue her gag. While this prisoner will need her hands to serve you, she does not need her mouth."

"She needs it removed so that she can breathe better, along with eating and drinking."

"If you remove the binding from her mouth, I shall personally remove her tongue." My uncle leveled a hard, cold stare upon me.

I didn't look away. I wouldn't let him know how frightened I was for Terese and Espen and myself. I had to keep up the pretense for as long as I could. But I couldn't imagine doing anything more difficult.

As he closed the door, I held the handle and listened to his steps retreat. When I was sure he was gone and wouldn't come back, I crossed toward Terese, whose eyes still brimmed with terror.

I fell to my knees before her, gathered her hands in mine, and kissed them, letting my silent tears fall for her, for Espen, and for the love that might never be ours to share.

Chapter 24

Sylvi

I felt no joy upon my first view of Gullkronnen at the end of Frosta Fjord. The elegant turrets rose in varying heights, their steep-sloped roofs glistening in the late-afternoon sunshine. Against the backdrop of the hills and mountain peaks, the castle was picturesque.

It held many happy memories from my childhood—mostly those of Espen and Kristoffer and me playing and exploring together.

But now, as we approached the wharf, I could only think of Espen in the cargo hold. He was there for one reason alone—because he'd tried to help me. He'd sacrificed himself to gain my freedom.

Yes, I'd known I was putting him at risk by stowing away on his boat and especially by suggesting our marriage. But I'd assumed his connection with the king and his position with the Knights of Brethren would protect him. I hadn't expected my father and uncle to so callously disregard him, almost as if they didn't care at all about angering the king.

Clearly I'd been naïve to believe my father would cease his matchmaking once he learned I was married. And I'd misjudged how badly he wanted me as part of the bargain he'd arranged with Lord Grimsrud and how determined he was not to let me get away.

I huddled deeper within the folds of my cloak. Beside me, Terese leaned nearer as though to give me some of her warmth. I'd bandaged her fingers, and I'd loosened her gag as much as I could so that Uncle wouldn't realize I'd done so. All the while, I'd whispered my reassurance that I would do whatever I needed to in order to return her to her family.

If only I'd never involved Espen in the first place. . . .

During the past hours of the voyage, I'd had plenty of time to consider the ramifications of stowing away with Espen. I'd taken advantage of his goodwill, kindness, and willingness to help. The only thing to do now was to pretend to move forward with marrying Lord Grimsrud while plotting an escape—although a part of me feared I wasn't smart enough after all, that I wouldn't conceive a plan that could save us. Because so far, I hadn't been able to think of anything workable.

Apparently, my father had allowed Lord Grimsrud to believe I'd left Vordinberg because I was going ahead to Gullkronnen to prepare for the wedding. Now that I was arriving, Father and Uncle would make sure I was locked away until the beginning of the ceremony. They wouldn't leave anything to chance and give me an opportunity to escape.

"When we dock, I do not know if I shall see you again." I cast a glance behind me to find that Father and Uncle were conversing in the captain's cabin as they'd been doing since I'd emerged a short while ago.

Terese had been attempting to speak with her eyes. They were as wide and expressive as Espen's, and now they seemed to be asking me for instructions on how she could help get us out of our predicament.

"I shall do everything to ensure you and Espen are set free." I tried not to bend too close so that I didn't chance arousing anyone's suspicion that I was conspiring. "Once you are liberated, you need to return to Chapel Cliff with all haste. Orvik is weak, and I fear that he will not have enough strength to fan the flame. Tell Espen to journey there straightaway. That 'tis urgent."

She nodded, a dozen questions swirling in her eyes. Orvik had trusted me with the secrets of the light and holy lamp, and I wanted to tell her the details so that she could relay the information to Espen. He needed to know about the holy lamp being tied to the chapel light. But hopefully, once he returned, Orvik would pass along the secrets to him too.

"We cannot allow the light to go out."

Terese's eyes narrowed, and she tilted her head to one side and seemed to be asking how long it would go without tending.

"Forty-eight hours. You must be there on the morrow at sunset, or we will risk everything." I was likely revealing too much, and I prayed Orvik would forgive me if I was. But for now, with *my* future so uncertain, I could at least make sure *Norvegia's* future wasn't jeopardized.

If only Kristoffer had come along. He'd be able to set everything aright. He was never at a loss for solutions, unlike me. At the very least, he'd be able to find a way to save me from Father's schemes—schemes I desperately wanted to escape so that I could spend my life with Espen.

Maybe I'd initially run away from my father because I wanted to avoid marriage to a man I didn't love, but at some point, I'd realized I was running away to be with a man I loved with all my heart, soul, and strength.

As though recognizing the truth, Terese squeezed my hand. Her eyes held sorrow that brought an ache to my throat.

As the ship docked and I made my way onto the wharf, I tucked my hand into Terese's arm, intending to keep her with me as long as possible. Though I wanted to enjoy the beauty of the rugged land with its steep cliffs, waterfalls, and the thick woodland that covered the hillsides, I couldn't tear my attention away from the slab closing off the cargo hold. I needed to see Espen and beg him to forgive me for bringing him into this situation.

But the cover remained resolutely closed, and none of the sailors or soldiers made a move to open it. I guessed they would transport him directly from the hold to the dungeons. Would they take Terese there as well?

I wouldn't be able to prevent Father and Uncle from locking Espen away in the bowels of Gullkronnen. But I could attempt to keep Terese out of the cold, dank cells.

When Father disembarked moments later, I approached him with what I hoped was a sincere expression. "Since Terese has tended me well, I would like to keep her with me."

He eyed the maiden.

She bowed her head and fixed her gaze on the damp boards of the wharf beneath our feet.

Was Father remembering he'd once shown kindness to Espen by bringing him into the noble house? Or was he thinking only about how much trouble Espen had caused him over recent days by interfering in our family affairs?

"If I am to be beautiful for my wedding, I shall need a woman's touch, and Terese has proven she can work miracles." I twirled enough that Father could see the pretty way Terese had styled my hair.

If compassion for Terese didn't convince Father, then I would dangle my beauty in front of him. After all, he wanted Lord Grimsrud to believe he was getting the most beautiful woman in Norvegia.

"Very well, my dear." He glanced toward Uncle Vilhelm, still on the ship, speaking with the captain. "She may assist you in preparing for your wedding, but then afterward, she will leave with Espen."

I gave him one of my pretty smiles. "Thank you, Father. She will serve me well."

"See that she does." He started away, his boots thumping with authority as he crossed to the end of the wharf.

"She would better assist me if she were able to remove the binding and speak."

Father halted and shook his head. "Vilhelm will already be peeved at me for conceding to you on this. He is afraid the girl will conspire with you and make plans for escaping with Espen. Your uncle believes you love Espen and will run away with him the first chance you get."

My uncle was right. Perhaps he was the only one who believed I had the capability to scheme. If only I weren't proving him wrong. If only I could come up with an elaborate plan to save us. "I don't know how I would accomplish such a feat, even if I wanted it, which I assure you, I do not." I couldn't keep a note of discouragement from lacing my voice.

Father seemed to hear it, for the worry lines at the corners of his eyes disappeared. "I am sorry, Sylvi. I have conceded enough by allowing the maiden to remain as your servant. I cannot allow you to take off her gag."

I would have to accept his offering. 'Twas the best I could do for Terese for the time being.

As Terese and I started up the pathway that led to the gatehouse, I couldn't keep the weight of sadness from slowing my steps. If I failed to scheme, then tonight or on the morrow, I would sign an annulment that would officially end my marriage to Espen. I hadn't been his wife for long, but the prospect of losing him as my husband was suddenly unimaginable and unbearable.

Pain squeezed my chest, and I drew in a breath to ward it off. But I suspected this was the kind of pain that would never go away, no matter how much time passed.

Chapter 25

ESPEN

I PACED THE LENGTH OF THE DUNGEON, NOT ONLY TO KEEP THE cold from seeping into my bones, but also because I was restless. I'd been caged for hours and had no contact with anyone, not even the guards for food.

From what I'd gathered from the conversations I'd overheard while in the cargo hold, Lord Prestegard and Vilhelm had invited Grimsrud to join them at Gullkronnen for his wedding to Sylvi. Grimsrud was to arrive today, and the ceremony would take place with all haste.

I was running out of time. If I had any hope of saving her from the union, I needed to act soon.

The sconce near the stairway was beginning to flicker for want of fuel. Once it burned out, I would be left in the darkness. The windowless underground cavern contained only four dirty cells and was small compared to the dungeons of the royal residence or even the Prestegard castle in Karlstadt.

Though Gullkronnen had seemed massive to me when I'd first come to live here as a boy, I'd since realized it wasn't grandiose, with but a few servants and groundskeepers who stayed year-round. The rest of the staff traveled with the Prestegards when they moved between their several estates, including their hunting lodge at Endressen in the Moors of Many Lakes.

I'd been in Gullkronnen's dungeons as a boy while playing hide-and-seek with Kris and Sylvi. Never had I imagined I'd end up in the cells as a prisoner because I'd attempted to foil Lord Prestegard's matchmaking for Sylvi. And never had I imagined I would become her husband or that she'd declare her love for me.

A time or two, I'd pinched myself to see if I was dreaming, and if so, to awaken. But with each pinch, I realized this was no dream—that I was not only Sylvi's husband, but I was likely to be eliminated because of it.

Sylvi may have believed she'd bargained for my life, but I was under no such illusion. Lord Prestegard and Vilhelm had plans that were more serious and complicated than I'd realized. I still didn't know what they were plotting, but they wouldn't have chased after Sylvi with such resolve for an ordinary match.

As before, I'd attempted to understand why they were collecting signatures and from whom. I'd weighed all the possibilities, including the prospect that they were colluding with King Canute of Swaine. If so, how and why?

Lord Prestegard had always been a staunch nationalist, supporting Norvegia's royal lineages. In fact, last autumn when King Ulrik, the former king, had been dying and the country was without a solid heir, Lord Prestegard had employed a number of wisemen to delve into the royal bloodlines to leave no stone unturned in the effort to find an heir.

Whatever he was conspiring, I wasn't intending to

stand by and let him marry Sylvi off. In spite of her declarations about making a mistake in marrying a man of my status, she still didn't want to wed Grimsrud. And I'd do everything within my power to keep her from having to go forward with the union.

Although the very thought of her being with any other man except for me made me want to punch a stone wall, I didn't want to free her from Grimsrud because of that. If I could never have her, then I wanted to hand her over to someone who would cherish her the way she deserved.

I paced again the length of the cell to the rusty iron door and then back. My speed had picked up, as if that could somehow help me get out of the dungeon faster.

"Fie! Think of something!" My voice echoed in the confines, containing the anguish that had been eating away at my insides since the moment I'd fallen into Lord Prestegard's clutches. How could I have been so foolish that I hadn't paid better attention to signs that something was amiss when I'd returned to Pollock?

I couldn't let my guard down again or allow any detail to pass by me. This time, I had to be more alert, the way I'd been trained.

Alas, I'd tried everything possible to unlock the door since arriving hours ago, but the locks were as foolproof as always. I'd learned that lesson the one time I'd accidentally barred myself inside as a child. I'd had to wait until Kris thought to search for me.

If only a guard would come down to bring me food. I would use one tactic or another to draw him to the door and then find a way to force him to unlock it. Mayhap Lord Prestegard realized I was capable of overcoming his men and had forbidden them from tending to me.

Most likely I would need to rely on Sylvi sending someone to my aid. But if she believed her father would free me after her wedding, then she would wait, counting on her father to follow through with his word. And by then I'd be too late to intervene and to prevent the wedding to Grimsrud.

The annulment paper.

I halted my pacing. That was the solution I needed. The guards would have to come down to the dungeons before the nuptials to gain my signature upon the annulment paper. Once they were within reach, I'd grab them and force them to set me free. I'd destroy the annulment, find Sylvi, and together we'd sneak out of the castle.

I'd already plotted a route, having mentally gone over every inch of the castle. I intended to escape through an underground passageway, the start of which was concealed in a closet behind the dungeon stairway. It had been built to provide a secret way out into the forest should Gullkronnen come under siege. Though I hadn't visited the estate in years, I was counting on the tunnel still being accessible. And I was counting on Sylvi still having a key.

Expelling a deep sigh, I braced myself against the iron bars that formed the door. If Sylvi had given up on us, I could easily forgive her. She'd never been mine to begin with. I'd known that all along and shouldn't have allowed myself to think otherwise.

But I had to admit, the thing that hurt the most was knowing Lord Prestegard had rejected me. I'd spent years seeking his approval, wanting to be taken seriously by him, waiting for him to view me as someone important. But even after becoming one of the Knights of Brethren, his regard for me hadn't changed.

I hadn't expected him to think I was worthy of Sylvi. But I had hoped to see respect in his eyes, one man to another. Mayhap I'd even wanted him to be proud of me for all I'd accomplished, for him to know his efforts and investment in me had been worthwhile.

Yet, after all this time, I'd still failed to gain his acceptance. I'd earned his displeasure instead.

I closed my eyes, weariness overtaking me. I shouldn't care about Lord Prestegard's favor. I had the king's. I had my family's. I had my father's. And I'd even had Sylvi's for a short while. Wasn't that enough? Why did I need one more person to validate me?

I rested another moment, then resumed my pacing. Whether Lord Prestegard approved of me or not, I had to stop him from giving Sylvi to Grimsrud. Her happiness was more important than anything else.

Chapter 26

Sylvi

My elegant gown glittered with seed pearls and my golden hair was piled in curls upon my head. Today for my wedding, I'd most certainly earned the title of Norvegia's most beautiful woman.

But even as I glided down the hallway with the train floating behind me and making me feel like a princess, my insides were churning. I hadn't been smart enough to come up with a viable escape plan. Maybe I was empty-headed and only good for my beauty after all.

I glanced at the guard following behind. I couldn't overcome him now any more than when I'd been locked in my chambers—even if I enlisted Terese's help.

Terese accompanied me toward the small chapel. Though she still wore her gag, I'd removed it as oft as I could over the past twenty-four hours since our arrival. Once we reached the chapel, I would request that Father release Espen and Terese and allow them to be on their way. I'd already secured a rowboat for them so that they wouldn't have to rely upon anyone else and would be able to travel swiftly to Chapel Cliff to make sure Orvik and the light were fine. Terese had agreed to stay with Orvik. No doubt Espen would flag down a ship to take him to Vordinberg.

As I neared the chapel door, I halted and laid a hand over my rapidly thudding heart. Terese stopped several feet behind me, and the guard waited a respectable distance away from her, clearly sensing my need for privacy in this moment before I said my vows.

The walk to my wedding this time was so different than what I'd experienced with Espen. Instead of being escorted by excited and enthusiastic villagers who laughed and smiled and offered encouragement, I felt as though I was on my way to a funeral.

Could I really make myself go through with this?

Lord Grimsrud had arrived but an hour or so ago, and Father had sent a messenger to alert me that the wedding would take place with all haste. Since Terese had already worked all morn and into the afternoon to transform me into a work of art, I hadn't needed much more time to prepare.

Low voices wafted through the half-open doorway.

"Will he give us trouble with the annulment sheet?" My father's whisper was hardly audible but gave me pause.

"I think not." My uncle's whisper was even fainter. "The guards are to tell him that after he signs, they will take him to the waiting ship."

So they intended to carry through with their part of the bargain and were making plans to release him.

I expelled a tight breath. I could admit I'd been worried they wouldn't free Espen. Now, I would have to inform them I'd already secured a boat and that they need not provide Espen transport.

"The captain knows what to do?" My father's voice dropped so low I had to strain to hear.

"I spoke of it yesterday when we docked."

"He knows he must be leagues out to sea before throwing him overboard?"

My heartbeat rolled over itself and crashed to a halt. Had my father just insinuated what I thought he had?

"Yes, I made sure the captain was aware of Espen's skills in the water and that he must be not only away from any place he could swim to, but they must knock him out first, to be certain he doesn't find a way to survive."

My father and uncle were plotting to murder Espen. And they believed I was too dumb to know any better.

I had to go away, had to get back to my chamber, before Father or Uncle realized I'd overheard them.

Terese was studying me, waiting for me to proceed, clearly not having heard what I had.

Without waiting for Terese or giving her any warning, I picked up my skirt and retreated down the hallway past the guard back toward my chamber. My slippered feet hardly made a sound. But I was afraid my father and uncle would hear the distress clanging through my chest and mind.

When I reached my chamber, I paused and addressed the guard. "I have need of the garderobe."

He gave a curt nod before positioning himself by my door.

I walked to the center of the room. Behind me I could hear Terese close the door. Only then did I fall to my knees in the cushion of rushes, letting my gown pool around me.

In the next instant, she was kneeling beside me and clutching my hand.

I cupped my fingers over my mouth, too distressed to do anything else.

Terese squeezed my hand hard to communicate with me.

I tried to gain control of my breathing, but I felt as though I was sinking beneath the waves and drowning. Tears began to slide down my cheeks in earnest. I wasn't surprised my father had lied to me about our bargain. After all, if I'd been able to figure out a way to escape, I wouldn't have kept our bargain either.

Nevertheless, I hadn't expected him to plot murder. Murder.

I had no doubt the captain would perpetuate a story about a storm and Espen being swept overboard. Such a tale would deflect any blame for Espen's untimely death.

How could my father do something so cruel and callous? Was Espen really so expendable?

If my father could so easily dismiss Espen for defying him, then his love didn't run very deep. And maybe his love didn't flow deeply for me either. Was it conditional upon what people accomplished for him?

"Oh, Father." The anguished words slipped from my lips, and the beginning pang of a headache formed in the deep recesses of my mind. "Why?"

"What's happened?" Terese whispered, having pulled down her gag. She eyed the door, likely afraid my uncle would burst in and discover her without her binding in place. The stinging flesh wounds upon her fingers and neck had proven how cruel he was and left no doubt in either of our minds that he would act on his threat to cut out her tongue.

"I just overheard my father and uncle." I swallowed the bitterness that rose swiftly. "They intend to have Espen assassinated as soon as he's out to sea."

Terese's face blanched. "We need to warn him."

I nodded and stood, the room spinning around me.

Terese took hold of my arm and held me steady.

I had to stay strong. Today, in this moment, I needed to finally prove to my father and to myself that my worth wasn't confined to my appearance. I had so much more—I had depth of character, intelligence, and strength.

The first thing I needed to do was make sure neither Espen nor Terese ended up on the ship my father and uncle had arranged to transport them. That meant I had to get Espen out of the dungeons before the guards went to him and escorted him to the awaiting vessel. Once Espen was free and made it to the rowboat I'd left for him, he'd have no trouble escaping. He knew the fjord well and would be able to find places to take shelter.

I wanted to go down to the dungeons myself, free Espen, and stride out of Gullkronnen with him in full view of my father to demonstrate that I would no longer bend to anyone else's will.

But of course, I'd already considered all the options. And Father would never allow me to slip through the gatehouse. His guards would stop me and force me back to the chapel.

Furthermore, if I resisted signing the annulment and refused to say my vows to Lord Grimsrud, I didn't doubt they would torture Terese or another servant until I complied.

The best option was to pretend I was the stupid but beautiful daughter going along with the wedding ceremony. Then at the last moment, I would execute an escape plan, finding a way to elude them.

My gaze landed upon the discarded boy's garments hanging from a peg on the wall, the clothing I'd worn last summer underneath my tunic so that I could get around more freely when I went fishing and hiking and searching for sea glass.

My attention dropped to the old chest underneath the clothing. It still contained the treasures from my childhood, including . . .

My pulse kicked forward with sudden anticipation. I rushed over to the chest, opened the lid, and dug under the collections of rocks and sea glass and shells. As my fingers connected with a familiar iron key, my mind spun with a daring and dangerous idea. Could I truly pull it off? Would I be able to outsmart my father and uncle?

I pushed back the voices of doubt that clamored in my mind, and I met Terese's gaze. "I have a plan. Let us pray it works."

Chapter 27

Espen

THE HEAVY SLAP OF TWO SETS OF BOOTS TOLD ME A PAIR OF guards was coming for me. I threw myself to the cell floor. The thin layer of straw that covered the ground was littered with rat droppings, crusty insects, and tangled cobwebs.

Nevertheless, I closed my eyes and lay absolutely still.

When they reached the bottom of the stairwell, keys clanked against the outer dungeon door. A second later, a key scraped in the lock and the door opened, bringing light into the darkness that had ensconced me hours ago.

The boot steps moved into the passageway that separated the cells, and I could feel the light also fall across my face.

"Time to go," a gravelly voice called to me.

I kept myself from twitching, so that not even my breathing was noticeable.

"The master wants you to sign the annulment. Once you do, then we've got orders to take you to the hold on the ship, and it won't be long before you have your freedom."

At the clink of chains, my resolve hardened. I had to avoid being bound again. That was my main goal. And I knew only one way to do it. I had to draw the guards into my cell and attack them when they least expected it.

The light rose higher outside the bars as the two no doubt took in my body sprawled out in what I hoped was an awkward pose across the floor. I wanted them to think I'd fallen and passed out—or even believe I was dead.

"Come on, get up," the other said in an irritated tone.

I remained where I was, eyes not flickering.

A few moments later, a painful prick through my stockings and into my calf nearly made me flinch. One of the fellows had slipped his sword through the bars and was using the tip of his sword to prod me into action. "Wake up."

Though I could feel the warmth of blood seeping into my leggings, I kept myself from giving any indication I'd felt the prick.

"He's unconscious," came the gravelly voice.

"I told the master he should have a little water," the irritated guard responded.

At the jingle of keys on a ring, I mentally prepared myself for my first few moves. With my weapons having been confiscated, I was unarmed. And though I was proficient at using my fists in a fight, that wouldn't be enough to defeat these two trained guards who wore chainmail and had numerous weapons at their disposal.

The cell door creaked open cautiously.

I hardly dared to breathe.

As the door widened and the light drew nearer, I

cautioned myself to be patient. If I acted first, before both of them were in the cell, I'd lose the element of surprise, my only weapon at the moment.

At another poke of a blade, this one into the back of my upper thigh, I wanted to grit my teeth against the pain. But again, I remained unmoving, giving the guards no cause to think I was conscious.

As boots neared my head and one of the men toed my shoulder, I loosened my muscles so he could prod me easily. When the second footsteps entered the cell and drew closer, my stomach tensed with the need to jump up.

But I held myself back again.

"We can't return to the master without the signed paper," the gravelly voice said above me. "We'll have to carry him up and try to revive him with some water."

"We'll need to chain him first," said the guard who stood furthest away. "The master said he wasn't to go anywhere if he wasn't wearing chains."

"He'll be heavier to carry."

"Don't matter. We can't take any chances."

Chances of what? Disappointing Lord Prestegard? Clearly they hadn't learned what I already had—that pleasing Lord Prestegard was only possible when a person did exactly what the lord commanded and naught less.

I pushed aside the bitterness. Now wasn't the time to think about how I'd fallen short with Lord Prestegard. I had to let my resentment go, otherwise it would weigh me down and cause me to stumble. Wasn't that the way of bitterness and hurt? If we clung to it, it would only make our hearts heavier and hold us back.

As one of the guards bent and grabbed my feet, I kicked up swiftly, placing two well-executed thrusts into his midsection, stunning him, causing him to gasp for breath. In the same instant, I lunged for the knife in the other guard's boot, easily pulling it loose and swiping it across his legs.

He screamed out his pain and toppled backward against the wall behind him. I scrambled up but only in time to parry the irritated guard's sword as it swung toward me, barely missing slicing open my back.

The force of his swing nearly dislodged my knife, but I managed to keep my grasp, maneuvering myself so that I was near the door, the key ring still dangling in the lock. Before he could regain his footing, I aimed the knife for his exposed wrist and sliced him hard so that he, too, stumbled back, momentarily stunned.

I rushed out of the door and slammed it shut. In spite of their injuries, they rushed against the bars, lowering their shoulders together and attempting to push it open.

I threw the full weight of my body into the door and turned the key.

In the next instant, the blade of a sword sliced into my arm. I knew the guard's intent was to weaken me and prevent me from completing my task. But even with the piercing pain, I finished twisting the key and then jerked it free.

As another sword flashed through the bars, this one aimed at my neck, I ducked and dove away, feeling only the slightest graze of the blade. It drew blood but was only a surface wound. Though the injury to my arm was more severe and was now gushing blood, I jogged toward the main door, ignoring their curses and baiting to return.

If they were just now coming to me with the annulment paper, that meant I wasn't too late to stop Sylvi from marrying Lord Grimsrud. They wouldn't be able to legally proceed with the wedding without first bringing our marriage to an end. And I had no intention of signing an annulment. They would have to slay me if they wanted Sylvi to be free to marry Lord Grimsrud.

Without a glance back, I exited the dungeon and closed the outer door. The thick wood muted the guards' calls. Even so, it wouldn't be long ere the noise alerted someone.

At the rapid tap starting down the dungeon stairway, I tensed, then flattened myself against the wall out of sight. I had only a knife and was wounded and losing blood rapidly, which meant that once again I had to use the element of surprise to my advantage.

As the guard finished ascending and hurried past me, I lunged at him from behind, knocking him out in an easy blow to the back of his head.

As a second set of footsteps slowed near the bottom of the stairway, I pressed back against the wall. This time 'twas but a woman or boy coming to check on the ruckus. I would have to lock the two newcomers up with the other men—at least within the dungeon chamber, if not a cell. I couldn't risk any of them notifying Lord Prestegard and Vilhelm of my escape.

Of course, the two would learn soon enough when the guards didn't return with the annulment paper, and they would send more men down to investigate what was taking so long. Then dozens would start searching for me, leaving me little time to locate Terese and Sylvi and guide them out of the castle to the hills beyond.

Though it seemed an impossible task, I was willing to risk everything to see it accomplished and to set Sylvi free.

As the person on the stairs turned the corner, I found

myself face to face with my sister.

I stopped abruptly. "Terese? What are you doing here?" I wasn't sure whether to feel relief or fear, so I used the interlude to slice off a piece of my tunic.

"After returning to the chapel, Sylvi instructed her guard to lock me in the dungeon with you. She was counting on you overcoming him and setting us free. And it looks like you already did so before my asking."

"Aye." I cocked my head to the dungeon door. "Two other guards came to have me sign the annulment. I decided to let them know what I thought about that task."

The sconce on the wall at the base of the steps gave off enough light that I could see her lips curving into a small smile. At my fumbling with the piece of linen I'd sliced, she took it and began to wrap it around my arm, the blood already soaking my sleeve with deep crimson.

"You're cut badly."

"If we can stop the blood flow, I'll be fine."

She worked efficiently, tying it tight and then wrapping the remainder of the linen around my arm. All the while, she relayed Sylvi's escape plans.

I didn't like them, nary one bit. Sylvi was putting herself into too much danger. But from the sound of things, I was too late to stop her. I had no choice but to do as she'd instructed and pray that Providence would come to our aid once again.

Chapter 28

Sylvi

The rush of the waterfall greeted our arrival. I pushed back the last of the branches on the overgrown path and stepped into the clearing on a high rocky cliff to the sight of water cascading from cliffs above down into the tributary below.

Father followed me, and Uncle Vilhelm came after him, swatting the gnats and mosquitoes that swarmed the damp air.

"This is the place." I mustered as much enthusiasm and cheer as I could into my voice. Under normal circumstances, I would have easily found joy at being upon the breathtaking cliff that was but a ten-minute hike from Gullkronnen. 'Twas a place I'd gone oft as I'd tagged along with Kristoffer and Espen, and it held many happy memories.

Several more people, including Lord Grimsrud, a priest, and guards, pushed out of the tangle of shrubs and trees into the waterfall overlook. They, too, slapped at the pesky insects that were out in full force, especially because of the open puddles as well as the spray from the waterfall as it passed nearby.

Although Lord Grimsrud had masked his annoyance at my suggestion to have the wedding outside on the cliff, I could read it in the tenseness of his shoulders and the pinch of his lips. He thought my father a weak man for giving in to my plea. If somehow I ended up wed to him, I sensed he was the type of man who wouldn't be so easily swayed.

"This is preposterous," Uncle Vilhelm muttered under his breath, clearly sharing the same sentiment as Lord Grimsrud.

Thankfully, my father still retained a shred of decency. Or at the very least he was attempting to gain my fullest cooperation in the wedding ceremony. Perhaps he was hoping this excursion would allay any desire to escape. Or perhaps he'd heard of my return to my room and deduced I'd overheard his plans to harm Espen and was appeasing me and assuaging his guilt.

I pretended not to notice any of the disparaging remarks from the others, playing fully the role of the beautiful but brainless bride they expected of me. All the while, my head was aching with a growing ferocity. I couldn't get a headache now, not with so much at stake.

Even if I wasn't able to follow through with making my own escape, I consoled myself with the knowledge that at least Espen and Terese would be free. I was counting on Espen breaking himself and Terese away from the guard and then using my key to slip through the secret tunnel that we'd used as children in our adventures.

I had every faith Espen would know of the one I'd described to Terese. I was also confident he'd find the inlet that was nearby the tunnel's exit. And while I didn't know if the groundskeeper would place the rowboat there as he'd oft done in my childhood, I prayed he would humor me as he always had.

With every passing hour, my muscles were tensing with a growing urgency. Someone needed to get back to Chapel Cliff and check on Orvik and the light by sunset to make sure the flame didn't flicker out. The future of the country could very well depend upon the Eternal Flame.

Of course, I hoped Orvik had regained his strength to tend it for himself. But since leaving him, I couldn't stop worrying that he'd spoken his secrets to me because he'd known he was dying.

"The view is spectacular, is it not?" I waved around, breathing in the fresh air. The cliff towered above a deep channel that emptied into the fjord to the south. From where I stood, I could see the narrow opening. If rowed hard, a boat would reach the fjord in less than five minutes.

The inlet was lined with steep rock walls containing several other waterfalls. Now, with the onset of summer, the vegetation grew out of nearly every crack, spreading and winding over the rock sides with unfettered abandon.

"It is beautiful," Father said absently as he paced back to the path and peered down the way we'd come. He'd wanted to wait for his guards to return with the annulment before leaving for the cliff, but I'd convinced him that they would easily catch up to us, especially since I would need to go slower.

I'd donned a long cloak to cover my attire, and now I fiddled with the tie at the top.

Had I given Terese and Espen enough time to get out of the castle? How long could I stall before everyone began to grow suspicious?

"Thank you for agreeing to have a wedding here, Lord Grimsrud." I wanted my chatter to fill the space so that no one would grow suspicious—at least more so than they already were. "I realize how unconventional this is, but 'tis such a beautiful day, and we should revel in such beauty, should we not?"

Lord Grimsrud came to stand by my side. His dark hair was combed neatly, his beard closely shaven, and his clothing of the finest quality. It was clear he'd wanted to be at his best for this wedding. In spite of the rumors about his involvement in criminal gangs, in this moment he almost seemed like an ordinary man who was simply excited for his wedding day.

He gave the landscape nothing more than a cursory glance before turning his attention upon me. "It truly is beautiful, my lady, but of course, it cannot begin to compare with your beauty."

I smiled at him coyly and fluttered my lashes, pretending his comment was something special. But the truth was, I'd lost count of how oft I'd heard a man say exactly that or something similar.

As with the first time I'd met Lord Grimsrud, I was struck by his relentless stare. He rarely took his eyes from me, as if I were the light for his dark soul. If I went through with marrying him, I guessed he'd take everything he could from me, draining me to make himself feel better, leaving me empty in return.

But with Espen . . . he breathed life into me, making

me a better person. He always had. And I wanted to be with him . . . so that I could pour my life—and beauty—into him, making him happy and satisfied. If I could spend the rest of my life doing that, I could ask for naught else.

Espen was one of the rare people who had taken me seriously and cared about me, not because of something on the outside, but because he'd probed deeply into my innermost self. I hadn't needed to hide who I was, hadn't needed to dress a certain way, hadn't needed to be perfectly put together for him to like who I was. In fact, he'd accepted me when I'd been at my worst, with my boy's clothing, wet hair, and blue lips. I'd been unkempt and uncivilized, but he'd seen me as valuable anyway.

Lord Grimsrud's fingers circled my arm. "Careful now."

His touch had none of the power to affect me the way the merest brush of Espen's fingers did.

"I would not want you to accidentally fall." His fingers slipped lower, gliding over my arm much too intimately.

With what I hoped was a cheerful smile, I tugged out of his hold. "You must not worry over me, my lord. I know these cliffs and inlets better than most. Perhaps you are the one who must take care where you step so that you do not accidentally fall."

Though my words were spoken lightly and with a teasing, flirtatious bent, Lord Grimsrud narrowed his eyes upon me as though I'd just threatened him. Did he think I'd brought him up to the cliff to push him off into the dark depths below?

Instead of letting me get away from his touch, he

wound his arm behind me, almost as though he wanted to prove that he had every right to hold me whenever he wanted. Or maybe he sensed something was amiss and was making sure nothing interrupted our wedding.

Whatever the case, I needed to extract myself from his embrace. Perhaps if I could distract him. Then when the right time came, he'd be too late to stop me. "So, my lord. I should like to hear how you were able to get so many signatures and thus win my hand in marriage."

I spoke quietly but with enough confidence that I hoped he would believe I was knowledgeable of my father's challenge and his scheming. "You must have great sway in the land if you are able to gather the most support."

He slid me a sideways look, his arm still around me. His grasp was neither light nor gentle.

For a moment, panic began to tear at my insides. What if he refused to release me? He was much bigger and stronger than I was, and I wouldn't be able to get away.

The ache in my head pulsed harder.

"I do have great sway," he said after a moment of hesitation, his tone turning hard. "Few can resist my pressure."

I didn't know what he was referring to, but I could playact well. "If men are coerced, will they stay loyal?"

"If they have the assurance Kristoffer will be the type of king who will offer them benefits, then their loyalties will most definitely be assured."

Kristoffer a king? What was Lord Grimsrud talking about?

Sir Ansgar was the new king of Norvegia, chosen by

the sword and Providence as the worthiest to take King Ulrik's place. Surely my father and uncle weren't plotting with Lord Grimsrud against the king. They couldn't be.

My thoughts turned back to the way my father and uncle had searched every script and historical document in Karlstadt during the autumn when the king had been looking for an heir with royal blood. Father and Uncle had discovered that somewhere in our distant past, we had a link to royalty. At the time, I'd supposed the ties were so removed that Kristoffer would be an unlikely candidate.

But what if my father and uncle hadn't considered the connection too slim after all?

While most people in Norvegia loved and supported King Ansgar and Queen Lis, there were those who believed the legend of the sword was nothing more than a fairy tale and that King Ansgar was an imposter. But those people were in the minority . . . weren't they?

I peeked over my shoulder at my father and uncle whispering to one another. What if they'd been conspiring for months? Maybe the signatures they'd gathered were support for their cause, for putting Kristoffer on the throne instead of Ansgar.

Suddenly my blood turned cold as everything became clear. My father and uncle had used me as a reward for the man who could deliver the most signatures of support for making Kristoffer king in place of Ansgar. And Lord Grimsrud had won the challenge.

I blinked hard, trying to stave off the pain that was beginning to radiate through my head. But one thought reverberated through my mind louder than all the others ... I'd unwittingly been a part of a plot of treason against King Ansgar.

Chapter 29

ESPEN

SYLVI WAS MINE.

The thought rammed through me relentlessly as I watched Grimsrud hold her, filling me with a steely rage. The feeling was similar to when I'd watched her with the other men who'd paraded through her life. Only this time it was magnified, so that it threatened to turn me into a raving monster.

Over the past week, all the barriers I'd erected had crumbled. Now I could no longer deny what my heart had known all along . . . Sylvi belonged with me.

I had no right to her. And I'd told her that I wanted her to have the freedom to choose me, not to have our marriage thrust upon her. But now seeing her with Grimsrud, I knew with absolute certainty I didn't want another man to touch her ever again.

Leaning out of the rowboat as far as I could go, I craned my neck past the overgrowth of brush we were hiding behind.

"Stop, Espen," Terese whispered behind me. "You'll tip

over the boat. And then they'll know we're here."

I couldn't force myself to remain secluded in the shelter of the protruding boulder. And I couldn't take my eyes from Sylvi, even if I tried. All the years of secretly loving her and trying to hide my true feelings had been for naught. I'd confessed my love to her, and I couldn't take it back. Didn't want to take it back.

The simple fact was that my life would never be whole or complete without her in it. Even now, as I beheld her standing upon the cliff, my whole body tensed with a deep and powerful longing.

"I need her," I whispered harshly to Terese.

"I know."

The certainty of Terese's statement pulled me back, and I swiveled on my bench. How could Terese accept so readily what I'd denied for years?

As if seeing the question upon my countenance, Terese smiled gently. "I've never seen you more alive than when you are with her."

Terese was right. I *was* alive when I was with Sylvi. Whenever I'd been away from her for long months, I'd tried to forget about her by occupying myself with other women. But I'd always felt as though I was simply getting by.

Every time I saw her again, all it took was one look at her, one word, one smile to revitalize me, as though her blood was flowing through my veins, resurrecting me, and giving me a fresh burst of life.

Maybe that's why I'd loved living with the Prestegards—because Sylvi was my heartbeat. Aye, I'd appreciated my friendship with Kris, but Sylvi was the one who'd made my life bearable, who'd made each difficulty brighter. She brought me a sense of purpose and meaning, and I wanted her not only to be a part of my past but to be in my present and future too.

Terese nodded toward the cliff. "She needs you just as much, Espen."

"I'm not good enough for a woman like her."

"You have to stop letting Lord Prestegard define you. A man's pride can oft cloud his vision so that he can't see others with the value Providence has given them."

The value Providence has given them. I let Terese's words soothe the ache inside—the one I'd nursed for so many years, the one that told me I wasn't good enough, that I didn't quite measure up, that I'd always be inferior.

Mayhap she was right. Mayhap it was time to stop letting Lord Prestegard's opinion of me matter so much. And mayhap it was time to decide the life I wanted to lead and to seek what Providence had in store for me instead of aspiring to be the man Lord Prestegard had chosen for me.

I peeked through the vegetation to find that Grimsrud still had his arm wrapped around Sylvi much too possessively. The beast inside reared its ugly head again, and I wanted nothing more than to climb up, drag her into my arms, then shove him over the cliff.

Even though Terese had relayed Sylvi's instructions to me—that if anything went wrong, I needed to get away— I had no intention of following her directives. If Sylvi wasn't able to free herself, I would do it for her.

I didn't want to get caught again, but this time, Lord Prestegard and Vilhelm wouldn't have Terese to make me comply.

From the stiff way Sylvi held herself, I could sense that she wasn't comfortable with Grimsrud's touch.

I growled out my frustration. I couldn't sit back

another second and do nothing.

"She's a smart woman," Terese said behind me. "Trust her, Espen."

So many people underestimated Sylvi's intelligence. And I didn't want to be one of them. Terese was right. I had to wait and let Sylvi work out her plan in her timing. Even if it tore me up inside to do so.

In the next instant, one of the guards I'd fought in the dungeons broke through the brush and into the clearing. From the blood-soaked bandage tied around his wrist, I guessed the other guard that I'd wounded in the legs was too weak to make the hike to the cliffs.

The newcomer fell to his knees before Lord Prestegard and held out a parchment—the unsigned annulment paper.

My fingers tightened around the oar with the need to go to Sylvi before everyone learned of my escape and rushed back to Gullkronnen to keep her out of my grasp.

Could Sylvi make her next move? Or was it already too late?

Chapter 30

Sylvi

"Sir Espen is gone, my lord." The guard my father had sent to the dungeons spoke in gasps, winded from racing out to the cliff.

My breath snagged. I had to leave. Now.

But how could I free myself from Lord Grimsrud's grasp? And shed my cloak in the same moment?

My thoughts swirled in disarray. Had I overestimated my ability to make an escape? Maybe I wasn't clever enough to plan and execute my scheme after all.

"Did you at least get him to sign the paper?" Lord Grimsrud asked, his grip around me still unyielding.

If I started tugging and trying to break free, Lord Grimsrud would likely guess I wanted to escape from him. Instead, I had to find a way to distract him so that he released me of his own volition.

The guard's wrist was wrapped in a bloody linen, bright crimson still seeping through. "Sir Espen was too quick and managed to injure us and lock us up before we could make him sign the paper."

My father and uncle shared a look that told me they planned to track down Espen, that they'd never let him get away alive. And now I knew why they had no hesitation about killing one of the king's own knights . . . they didn't care what King Ansgar thought of their actions since they intended to oust him and replace him with Kristoffer.

Did Kristoffer know of their aspirations? And would he go along with them? I could only imagine how tempting the prospect of being king would be. Kristoffer was indeed loyal to the family and would have great difficulty in denying Father in this endeavor. Yet Kristoffer was also loyal to the king. How would he be able to turn his back on Ansgar?

The treachery was all the more reason I needed to free myself, so that I could send word to King Ansgar and warn him before it was too late. What if at this very moment, they'd placed a traitor in the royal court, someone willing to help them with assassinating the king?

I wanted to shout at Father to stop this madness. Even if the Prestegards were somehow related to a royal bloodline, this wasn't the time to cause division within Norvegia, not when the country needed to be united in order to fight against King Canute and his invading army. The battle ahead would already be difficult enough. If we were divided, we would surely fall.

Instead of shouting, however, I closed my eyes and inwardly prayed for Providence to bestow upon me an extra measure of wisdom and courage. I would need both if I had any hope of saving my country.

"Tell us what happened," Lord Grimsrud demanded, the frustration evident in each line of his face as he glared at the injured guard.

The guard didn't rise to his feet as he gave the briefest of details about Espen luring them into the cell by feigning unconsciousness before rising and attacking them.

Lord Grimsrud's fingers tightened around the hilt of his sword. And I guessed if the rest of us hadn't been present, he may have taken out his anger upon the guard, punishing him with more injuries, perhaps even death.

As it was, he seemed to rein himself back, albeit stiffly.

"My lord, what shall we do?" I feigned disappointment. "I suppose this means we shall have to postpone the ceremony and return to the castle? You would surely not wish to be out here in the open if Sir Espen chooses to attack."

"Are you insinuating I am no match for Sir Espen?" Lord Grimsrud pulled slightly away but not enough.

Perhaps if I put him on the offensive and made him believe an attack by Espen was imminent, he'd forget to hold me so tightly. "If the rumors about you are true, I am sure you are indeed a fierce fighter." His tactics were less than fair or noble. From what I'd heard, he and his gangs oft attacked unsuspecting travelers. In doing so, he hadn't proven his prowess, only his callousness and cruelty in preying upon those weaker than himself.

"If he attacks, he will be outnumbered." Lord Grimsrud nodded at the half a dozen armed guards who had accompanied us. With Father, Uncle, and

Lord Grimsrud all skilled with the sword, Espen would certainly be in danger, but I couldn't show any weakness with Lord Grimsrud and had to persist in playing upon his pride.

"I have watched Espen with every weapon and know he has indeed earned his spot amongst the king's closest knights. Not only is he skilled, but he is cunning, as you can see from the guard's tale." I nodded toward the injured guard, who'd risen to his feet and was waiting for an order.

"Sir Espen is no match for me." Lord Grimsrud finally released me and unsheathed his sword.

I wasted no time in pretending to lose my balance, stumbling toward the cliff's edge.

His eyes widened, and he lurched after me.

I let myself slide in the gravel, waving my arms as though to stabilize myself but all the while inching to a precarious position.

Seeing my danger, my father started to cross to me, holding out his hand as if to offer me his help—or perhaps he merely wanted to save his prize possession. Whatever the case, I had the briefest urge to tell him I still loved him and that I forgave him for the way he was using me to seek the kingship for Kristoffer. But if I was to succeed in my feat, I needed him to believe I was gone.

I held his gaze, hoping he could see there everything I couldn't say. Then I allowed myself to fall backward off the cliff.

The moment my feet left solid ground, shouts erupted from the men.

In the next instant, I was airborne. I floated, my cloak billowing around me and filling with the wind, slowing my fall only a little.

As the men crowded along the cliff's edge, my father amongst them, their calls of alarm echoed in the ravine. Would any of them jump in and attempt to rescue me? I was counting on the steep drop deterring them from taking heroic measures. But even as my father hung back, not willing to put his life at risk for mine, the hurt inside swelled.

I'd loved him, but he'd never loved me back the way I'd wanted, not even when he believed I was plunging toward my death.

Rather than watch my father or any of the men, I positioned myself for the impact. A second later, my feet slammed into the water. While my cloak cushioned the fall, the impact was still jarring. The stinging surge of the splash encompassed me, and my momentum plunged me deep under the surface.

Water rushed over me, drenching my garments and dragging me down even further. But I immediately set to work freeing myself from my cloak. I'd already loosened the tie, and with a tiny tug it came free the rest of the way. I pushed it downriver, knowing it would make its way out of the ravine and into the main fjord. My hope was that the tide would carry it to the shores of Gullkronnen so that my family would believe I'd drowned.

Staying under water, I propelled myself swiftly toward the opposite cliff, to a spot of vegetation that would hide me as I came up for a breath. While I'd learned to swim in the ravine as a child during the many times I'd jumped from the cliff with Espen and Kristoffer, I'd never had to stay under water for any length.

I didn't know how far I could swim without needing to take a breath, but if I surfaced too soon, everyone would see me. I had to remain submerged until I reached a place where no one would be watching.

As I kicked through the cold, dark water, the pain of my oncoming headache radiated more forcefully. I didn't have long before the throbbing became too consuming to function. I could only pray I'd make it to the hiding place in time.

With swift strokes, I kept going, relying upon the way the water was flowing to guide me in the right direction. My hope was that everyone would have their attention fixed upon the spot where I'd disappeared, waiting for me to surface. When I didn't reappear, they would assume my heavy cloak and gown had dragged me down since I'd done everything I could to hide that I was wearing my lightweight boy's clothing underneath the cloak.

Although my father knew I could swim, I didn't think he was aware I'd accompanied Kristoffer and Espen during their cliff-jumping escapades, especially to this cliff. Even if he'd realized I'd tagged along, he wouldn't know I'd joined in the dangerous and difficult diving feats with them. He most certainly wouldn't know the backward fall off the cliff was one I'd accomplished oft.

My lungs began to burn, but I pushed onward. Never would I have believed that faking my death was the best way to protect myself and those I cared about. But sometimes dying was the only way to gain life.

Chapter 31

ESPEN

"WHERE IS SHE?" I FRANTICALLY SCANNED THE DARK WATERS OF THE inlet.

The place where Sylvi had jumped was completely safe, without any hidden boulders or rocks that she could hit. And she could manage a jump well enough.

But swimming to a secluded area without being detected by onlookers above? That was a new feat, and my muscles tightened with each passing second, especially when I didn't see a sign of her among the rocks where she'd told Terese she would surface.

Above on the cliff, some of the men were still peering down. But from what I could tell, Lord Prestegard, Vilhelm, and Grimsrud had rushed off. I guessed they were hiking back to the wharf and would have someone row them out to the inlet and search for Sylvi by boat.

We had to be well away from the area before then, which didn't leave us much time to make it to the place I planned to stow away—the alcove and the low cleft that was in one of the tributaries branching off from the inlet.

It would keep us hidden until darkness settled.

Sylvi had instructed Terese that we would need to leave right away in order to reach Chapel Cliff by darkness, saying something about Orvik being too weak to keep the flame burning. But if we tried to row out of Frosta Fjord in broad daylight, Lord Prestegard would eventually hear of it and chase after us.

No, if Sylvi truly wanted her father to believe she was dead as Terese had said, then she would have to wait. Even under the cover of night and staying along the edges among the overgrowth, we would still have a difficult time leaving the fjord undetected.

"Come on, Sylvi. Come on." I willed her to break the surface and appear.

Too much time had passed. She couldn't still be underneath. Could she?

Dread began pounding through my veins. Something had happened to her. "We're going out there." I grabbed an oar.

Before I could push away from the rock wall, Terese smacked me in the back with her oar. "No. Now wait, you big oaf."

"I can't." Again, I scoured the sides of the inlet for some sign of her: bubbles in the water, the ripple of movement, her wet head.

Terese was kneeling upon her bench in an effort to see beyond the boulder and growth hemming us in. She locked onto something, and her brows furrowed. "There." She pointed to a rock a hundred feet away.

At first, I didn't see anything. Then I glimpsed slender fingers gripping the rock. They were white and taut, as if the effort to hang on was nearly impossible.

I breathed out my relief and a quick prayer of

gratitude. Then I shoved against the wall with my oar.

Terese whacked my back again, this time harder. "You can't row over to her. They'll see you for sure."

I gauged Sylvi's position to that of the men on the cliff. From their angle and distance, they wouldn't be able to see her. But Terese was right. We couldn't row a boat over to her and risk being seen out in the open. On the other hand, I refused to wait until they left before going after her. She was too weak and wouldn't be able to make it that long.

The only thing left to do was jump in and swim to her.

I unhooked the weapon belt I'd taken from the guard in the dungeon, then began to shed the chain mail hauberk that I'd also pilfered.

"What are you doing?" Terese whispered.

I tugged off one boot then the other. "Something's wrong with Sylvi. And I'm going after her."

This time Terese didn't wallop me, which I took as her approval of my plan. When I slipped over the side of the rowboat a moment later, she braced the vessel to keep it from tipping under my weight.

I sucked in a deep breath, then I wasted no time in submerging and propelling through the water in the direction I'd spotted Sylvi. I was a fast swimmer, better than Kris. And within seconds, I made it to the rock where I'd seen her hand. Since I usually swam with my eyes open, I spotted her before I surfaced.

As I reached her, I cautiously poked my head out of the water. At the same time, I grabbed hold of her. The moment I did, her head lolled, and she groaned. "Espen?"

I didn't realize my pulse was thudding in a deafening rhythm until I pulled her safely against my body and ensconced her in my embrace. I pressed a hard kiss against her temple, one containing the angst of the past few days.

"I have one of my headaches," she mumbled.

For as long as I'd known her, she'd suffered from debilitating headaches. Thankfully, they didn't occur oft, but when they did, they rendered her useless. "How bad is it?"

"I cannot move any farther."

"'Twill not be long ere the men return to this area via boat to search the inlet for you. We must be away by then."

She groaned again and rested her head against my chest.

"We will need to swim underwater to reach the boat."

"Leave me and save yourself."

My arms tightened, having a will of their own as always. "I'll never leave you."

"You must. I cannot swim to the boat."

"We'll go together."

"No—"

"You are my life. Without you I have nothing."

My words silenced her.

I kissed her head once more. "On the count of three, we're going under, and we won't come up until we reach the boat."

Either she didn't have the energy left to protest, or my words had rendered her speechless. Whatever the case, I counted softly. Then I ducked under the water, guiding her down with me.

I sensed her weakness the moment we started the swim. She was in pain and could hardly move. But I wrapped my arm around her and tugged her along at my side. I couldn't go as deep as I had on the swim over to her, and I prayed none of the observers from above would spot us.

The swim back to the boat took more time, and I wasn't sure how much longer I could hold my breath when, thankfully, I bumped into the boat. As I pushed Sylvi up and out of the water, her body sagged, unconscious.

Terese was at the side pulling Sylvi over the edge. By the time I hauled myself out of the water, Terese had already started pumping Sylvi's chest in an attempt to empty it. Having grown up on the sea, Terese knew all the tips as well as I did on how to clear water out of someone's lungs.

I joined in the effort, and within a few seconds, Sylvi sputtered, and water gushed out of her mouth. She didn't awaken, but I could feel the rush of her breath, and I knew she'd be fine. Even so, I grabbed her into a hug, holding her to my chest, unable to contain the fierceness of my love.

I had to stop worrying whether others knew I loved Sylvi. In fact, I had to stop letting the opinions and regard of men be of any importance to me. And I'd start by casting aside my feelings of unworthiness and embracing the value that came from Providence.

After a moment more, I released Sylvi, and with Terese's help, I situated her in the bottom of the boat. Then we rowed swiftly up the tributary until we reached the crevice. We had to crouch low to fit the boat underneath. But once we were tucked away, I hoped none of the search parties would see us even if they came up this particular tributary among the dozens that branched off from the inlet. I didn't think they would make their way this far and would instead focus their search efforts closer to the cliff where she'd fallen.

Terese lay down on the floor and promptly fell asleep. I wouldn't allow myself to slumber, knowing I needed to remain alert to any soldiers who might come our way. We wouldn't be able to outrun them, but I'd fight until the death to protect Sylvi.

As I situated myself and stretched out my legs, I reached for Sylvi's hand and threaded my fingers through hers. I didn't know how we'd ever be able to live public lives, not without her family discovering she was still alive and attempting to manipulate us again. Maybe I needed to consider Orvik's offer to take the lightkeeper position. But would even that be safe enough? Regardless of what the future would bring, I was determined to find a way to keep Sylvi by my side.

Chapter
32

Sylvi

I awoke to the gentle rocking of a boat and the sight of a black sky overhead giving almost no light past a layer of clouds. The rhythmic slapping of oars and the lapping of waves told me I was at sea, as did the heavy scent of fish and brine.

At the low pounding in my head, I rubbed my temple. My headache was almost gone, but I was weak. As I pushed myself up to my elbow, I was distinctly aware of my wet garments. Cold, wet garments. I shuddered and sat up further.

"How are you feeling?" Espen's whisper came from behind me.

I shifted to find him at the oars. I couldn't see him clearly, but from his ragged breathing, I could tell he was rowing hard and had likely been doing so for quite a while.

A second pair of oars dipped in and out of the water at the stern. Though the darkness prevented me from seeing clearly, I knew Terese was rowing with just as much effort as Espen.

Where were we? Had we evaded my father's men? Or were they even now pursuing us?

"I should take a turn rowing," I whispered, crawling up to my knees. But as soon as I did, I swayed, overcome with dizziness and nausea. I sat back on my heels and pressed both hands to my head.

"Is the headache still bothering you?" Espen's voice was laced with concern.

"Just a little." I breathed in a lungful of air, trying to quell my nausea. The chilly air seemed to clear my mind, and as I took in the darkness of night, panic began to set in. "The Chapel Cliff Light. We have to make haste to it."

"I believe we're almost there," Terese said over her shoulder.

I stared all around, seeing nothing. If we were indeed close and couldn't view the beam coming from the lighthouse that meant only one thing—the flame was out.

Tears sprang to my eyes. "You should have left Gullkronnen right away as I instructed." But even as I spoke my rebuke, I knew it wasn't fair. With my father's treasonous plans, he would have sent out guards to seek not only me but also Espen. In fact, I was surprised we'd escaped, even under the cover of darkness.

Regardless, the tears began to slide down my cheeks. "'Tis my fault the light has gone out. And 'twill be my fault that Norvegia will not be able to defeat the enemy as they invade."

"No, Sylvi," Espen started.

"Orvik revealed to me that the flame is the source

of light for the holy lamp, that once it is extinguished then the holy lamp cannot burn." The pain in my chest welled into an unbearable tension. "If only I had been smarter, I would have understood my father's scheming all along and would have done something much sooner—"

"You orchestrated this brilliant escape."

"But I should have discovered a way to save the light too."

He was silent a moment, as though taking his time formulating his answer. "You and I are alike, Sylvi. For too many years we've let the opinions of others dictate how we see ourselves."

He was right. And though I was trying not to yield to my old insecurities, it was too easy to let them taunt me.

"'Tis time for both of us to see ourselves in a new light."

A new light? And what might that be?

Before I could say anything more, Terese stopped rowing. "We're here."

Through the dark, the outline of the cliff wall rose from the water in front of us.

"How will we get up?" I asked.

In the bow, Espen was maneuvering the boat around. "I see something. Mayhap the rope ladder is still hanging down."

If so, that meant Orvik hadn't been able to get to the cliff's edge to retrieve it. My heart gave a painful squeeze. "I should not have left him alone."

"I could say likewise." Espen stood on the bench and grabbed the bottom rung. "Perhaps I should have stayed and sent a message with my squires to the king instead."

"You did what you thought was honorable."

"And so did you."

I let his words settle inside, sifting them and finding a small measure of encouragement. We'd both acted as honorably as we could. Our motives had been pure. We'd wanted the best. And perhaps that was all we could ask from ourselves.

"Are you strong enough to make the climb?" Espen's hand brushed my shoulder.

"Yes." I clasped it and let him help me to my feet. As he guided my hands to the bottom rung of the ladder, I paused and clutched him instead. "We need to inform the king with all haste that my father is plotting treason against him."

"How?" Espen's question held no doubt, only a demand.

"The signatures he is collecting? He was using me as a reward for the suitor who could bring him the most signatures from men throughout Norvegia, calling them to support a new king."

"Himself?" Espen's voice was low. "Or Kris?"

"Kristoffer. But how did you guess?"

"He told Kris last autumn that he'd discovered the Prestegard lineage hails from the Fairhair dynasty, an old royal bloodline that was in place long before the House of Oldenberg came into power."

"So Father started conspiring then?"

"He made the discovery after Queen Lis came forward as the rightful heir and was wedded to King Ansgar. But he made no mention of challenging their claim to the throne."

"He has changed his mind."

"Or mayhap he intended to bring this about all

along but was waiting until everyone was distracted by the imminence of war to set his plans into motion."

I nodded. With Father, I'd learned anything was possible. "And what of Kristoffer? What does he think of Father's plan?"

"We've been so busy, I don't think he's aware of your father's ambitions."

"Once he learns of the plans, do you think he will join Father?"

Espen hesitated. "I wish I could say no. But your father has great sway over Kris."

I grasped Espen's hands more urgently. "Then all the more reason we must alert the king of the treachery."

"I'll leave at once for Vordinberg." Of course, Espen would say so. I'd known he would need to go.

"But my father will be searching for you now more than ever. 'Tis possible he fears you have learned of his treachery—or at least suspects it. Can you not send someone else with a message?"

"I cannot entrust anyone else with the warning. I must deliver the news myself."

I understood. But my pulse thudded in protest anyway.

"Terese can stay with you here at Chapel Cliff. 'Twill be safer for her to remain hidden from your father for the present."

A new urgency radiated from Espen, and I sensed he wanted to be on his way as soon as possible to take advantage of the blackness of the night for his escape.

Espen gave Terese a hug, then turned to me. As his arms surrounded me, I clung to him, relishing the solid length of his body and the strength emanating from him. We'd only just been reunited, and there was so much I longed to tell him, especially that I wanted him to come back, that I'd wait for him.

But I'd thrust myself upon him already and brought him undue trouble. This time, I had to let him go. I wouldn't entangle him in the problems and dangers of my life any longer.

"Farewell, Sylvi," he said against my ear.

Somehow his whisper felt final. I wanted to ask him if he would return after the war, but I bit back my question. He'd helped free me from my father's grasp—hopefully for good this time. And now his job was done. He no longer needed to remain married to me.

Moreover, I couldn't ask him to forfeit his work for the king and live at Chapel Cliff with me. Because that's where I would have to stay, pretending I was dead, perhaps indefinitely—at least until my father no longer had need of me.

A courageous knight like him was made for more than hiding away at a remote lighthouse. He was needed for bigger and more important duties to the country.

"Farewell, Espen." I pressed closer to him, needing this last contact to sustain me. I was tempted to wrap my arms around his neck and pull him down into a kiss. But I didn't want to encourage him any more than I already had.

His fingers fisted at my back, and his breathing in my ear turned ragged.

Oh my. I loved this man. But because I loved him, I wanted him to be free in a way I couldn't be.

I took a deep breath to fortify myself to do what

was necessary. I pried myself loose.

A cold breeze sent chills over me. I had the urge to bend over and be sick. Instead, I fumbled for the rope ladder. As I grabbed on and began to climb, I didn't dare let myself look back.

Chapter 33

Sylvi

Tears slid down my cheeks, and I didn't bother to brush them away.

As Terese climbed the final distance of the ladder and scrambled onto the cliff beside me, I couldn't make myself move from the heap where I'd landed once I'd reached the top.

Thankfully, she didn't try to console me, and instead followed the instructions Espen had called to us as we'd ascended. He'd told us to pull up the ladder right away. And he'd said that if anyone came to the cliff, I should stay hidden, and Terese should be the one to interact with the outside world. We didn't know whom we could trust, and so it was best if everyone assumed I'd died.

When Terese finished, she knelt beside me and waited quietly.

I wiped my cheeks. Now wasn't the time to grieve over my parting with Espen. I needed to check on Orvik. There was a small chance he might still be alive and that he'd simply been too weak to get out of his bed. In that case, time was of the essence, and I would do all I could to help him recover. Maybe there was even a slight chance we could yet fan the flame and bring it back to life. I had to at least try, in spite of Orvik's dire prediction that it would fade to nothing.

I led Terese to the low stone house to find that the door was ajar. All was dark and silent except for the clink of seashells hanging in an open window.

Stepping inside, I held back a shudder at the prospect of seeing him dead upon his bed, lying just where I'd left him.

"Orvik?" I called softly.

I waited, hoping for his response, but I wasn't surprised when one wasn't forthcoming.

Terese went to the hearth and stirred the ashes, likely trying to find an ember so that we could have light.

I didn't wait, guessing the last sparks of any heat inside the house had gone out too. Instead, I crossed toward the bed. As I bumped into it, I reached down carefully, searching for Orvik's mouth to see if the breath of life remained in even the slightest.

But my fingers made contact with bare sheets. I skimmed my hand over the rest of the bed, finding only emptiness.

"He's not here."

Terese stood. "If not here, where could he be?"

He wouldn't have been able to climb down the ladder, not in his weakened condition. If he'd had the fortitude, there was only one place he would have gone.

I jogged across the room, not caring that I was

bumping into furniture and baskets and overturning them. Once outside, I darted across the span of long grass to the chapel.

I knew what had happened. When I hadn't returned, Orvik had crawled out of bed and across the yard to the lantern. He'd probably used every last ounce of his strength to reach the chapel. When he'd arrived, he'd had none left to fan the flames.

Sure enough, the door was open. And as I stepped inside, I stumbled over Orvik stretched out on the floor.

I fell to my knees beside him. Once again, tears pricked my eyes, and I gently caressed his cheek. "I'm sorry."

He twitched.

"Orvik?" Was he alive?

I started to shift him, but he kept his face pressed against the stone, resisting my effort with surprising strength. His chest rose and then fell as he expelled a deep breath . . . into a small opening at the base of the lantern.

A second later, a faint glow of blue came from inside the stone pit.

I gasped.

"What?" Terese stood in the doorway.

"Make haste. Hand me the bellows."

Terese grabbed the hand-held pump from the floor near the door and tossed it to me. I caught and opened it in one motion, then sent a puff of air into the stone pit.

This time the blue within fanned brighter.

"The flame isn't dead." Excitement began to course through me. I pumped the bellows again. A spark spluttered to life.

I worked the bellows over and over for several minutes, until at last, bright tongues of fire burned within.

Terese was kneeling now beside the old lightkeeper. "It looks like Orvik kept a flicker of the light alive by fanning it with his own breathing."

With the flames bursting higher with every passing moment, I released a final pump to the fire, then lowered myself beside Orvik. This time as I gently shifted him away from the base of the pit, his head rolled to one side, his chest motionless. I held my hand against his mouth and felt nothing.

With a sob, I bent and buried my face into his chest. He'd spent his last and dying breaths to keep the flame alive. He hadn't had much left to give, but he'd given it all anyway.

He hadn't known if or when I'd return, but he'd lived and died fulfilling his purpose, doing so with great honor and sacrifice.

"You did it, Orvik," I whispered through another sob. "You did it."

Now it was my turn to keep the flame burning at all costs, even if I had to sacrifice the man I loved in order to do so.

Chapter 34

ESPEN

NIGH TO A WEEK AWAY FROM SYLVI WAS TOO LONG. HOW HAD I ever gone for weeks at a time?

In the darkness, the boat swayed as I assisted Terese down the last of the rope ladder.

"How is she?" I asked.

"She's faring well. And I'm doing well too. Thanks for asking." Terese's voice held a teasing note.

I released a tense breath.

Behind me, my father's hand clamped upon my shoulder. "Told you they were well."

I could only nod, my relief clogging my throat. After the past days of traveling and hiding, with scant sleep, I was exhausted, but I knew I wouldn't rest until I saw for myself that Sylvi was safe.

During my mission, I'd only been able to travel part of the way by ship to Vordinberg before running into Swaine's vessels trolling the sea. At the sight of them, I'd realized what had happened. While Ansgar and Norvegia's army had been distracted by the belief that the war would occur in the Valley of Red Dragons, King Canute and his fleet had managed to sneak into Ostby Sound and lay siege to the city.

I'd known then that any effort to reach the king and the Knights of Brethren would be futile. I'd decided the only thing I could do was pray that Kris would get my missive about Swaine having captured the holy lamp. And I prayed he would persist in searching for the sacred relic, even traversing into Swaine to retrieve it.

The more I'd thought about Lord Prestegard's plans to take the throne, the more convinced I'd become that Kris was innocent of any involvement. We were too close for him to hide such plans from me without giving something away. Nevertheless, I needed to proceed with caution. Even if he wasn't colluding with his father, he wouldn't be happy when he learned of my marriage to Sylvi.

Although I'd been hindered from taking my warning to the royal city, I'd decided to make it my goal to thwart Lord Prestegard's efforts to wrest the kingship from Ansgar. I didn't know how I'd do that, but I had to try, especially since I was the only one who knew of the danger to the king.

Before I embarked on my new mission, I'd needed to see Sylvi one last time. Now, as I glanced up again at the bright light beaming from the top of the cliff, I hesitated.

My father had already assured me that the chapel light was still burning, but he didn't know anything about Orvik's fate. "Does the burning light mean Orvik is also alive?"

Terese shook her head. "He lasted only until we arrived."

Orvik had been ready to go be with his wife. I didn't blame him. The question plaguing me over the past league of rowing was whether Sylvi would rejoice in my coming or find frustration in the uncertainty of my livelihood. "Will Sylvi receive me gladly?"

Terese didn't immediately answer.

My pulse skittered. "No?"

"She is determined to stay and keep the light." The resignation in Terese's tone didn't bode well for me.

From what my father had said, the word circulating throughout The Hundreds was that Lady Sylvi Prestegard had drowned in the dark depths of Frosta Fjord, and only her cloak had been recovered. So far, no one knew she'd survived and lived on Chapel Cliff.

But how long before someone guessed the truth? If anyone learned I'd visited Chapel Cliff, word would eventually reach Lord Prestegard, and he would send men to try to capture me. In the process, I didn't want them to chance discovering her. 'Twas why I'd had my father row me out in the dark of night. I couldn't risk leaving even a boat at the base of the cliff—not when there hadn't been one over recent weeks.

I glanced up the ladder gleaming in the moonlight. "Mayhap seeing her is a mistake. Mayhap I should be on my way to locate Kris."

"Stop cowering like a scared pup." My father socked me in the arm. "Get on up there and win her over."

I situated the pack of supplies on my back.

"Then once you win her over, you keep on doing it every day that you have breath."

"Aye, I will."

"Good then."

I swallowed past the uncertainties that came out to whisper I wasn't enough for Sylvi and I shouldn't even try. I'd been getting better at ignoring those voices, but they still clamored for my attention once in a while.

"You've got two days," my father said. "Then I'll bring Terese back."

I hesitated once more. Lord Prestegard's men had already been to Pollock to search for me and Terese. They wouldn't go back, not any time soon. Terese would be safe, and the villagers would remain silent about her presence to protect her. Even so, I didn't want to put her in jeopardy. Her cuts and my father's bandaged neck were a glaring reminder of the danger that I could so easily bring them.

"I'll be fine, Espen," my sister said. "You need to be with Sylvi."

I've never seen you more alive than when you are with her. Terese's words from when we'd waited in the rowboat during our escape came back to me.

Aye, I needed Sylvi. But now that she was free, did she still need me? Or would she relish her freedom?

The questions had plagued me more with each passing day so that I knew I couldn't function until I discovered the answers. Even with the fate of the country hanging in the balance, I had to do this.

I gave my father and Terese each a final embrace before latching onto the rungs and climbing. I was glad Terese had been the one awake and tending the light tonight. She'd heard us ring the bell and had lowered the ladder, explaining that Sylvi was asleep.

When I reached the top, I sucked in the first full breath I'd taken since I'd left her behind last week. I stood and stared at the stone house, the door closed against the breeze blowing off the sea. I'd vowed I wouldn't go in and wake her tonight, that I'd wait until morn.

But my feet carried me to the house, and my hands

found the door handle. Before I could force myself to go somewhere else, I was inside.

My heart pounded hard, as though wanting to break free from my chest. The fact was, I needed to see her more than anything else, needed to assure myself she was here and doing well. That was all. Then I'd leave her be until morn.

Light from the chapel poured in through the thick glass in the windowpanes and illuminated my path to the bed.

As I stopped at the edge and took in her beauty, every coherent thought fled from my mind. Her hair was unbound and spread out around her, her long lashes rested against her high cheeks, and her lips were slightly parted with even breathing.

I could only behold her, reveling in this unguarded moment. She seemed at peace, content with her new place in life.

The truth smacked me hard, sending me back a step. She didn't need me. Not only that, but my work for the king was too dangerous and would disrupt this peace she'd finally gained. I'd been foolish to come and needed to go now, before Terese and my father rowed too far away. It was for the best.

Sylvi's lashes fluttered open.

I retreated another step.

But as her gaze landed upon me, I halted.

She blinked as though trying to decide if I was real or merely a dream.

I held myself motionless, but my insides parried in a brutal swordfight, telling me to go and stay all at once.

She took me in with a hungry eagerness that only added to the battle within.

I waited for her to smile and welcome me. But she didn't say anything and instead let the silence stretch between us.

"I brought supplies." I let the pack slide from my back to the floor.

"How long?"

I wanted to pretend I didn't know what she was asking, but I was done with my days of trying to hide my feelings. "Only two days until my father returns for me."

She nodded.

What was she thinking? Had she realized she didn't love me after all? It was as I'd feared.

"You're safe now. You don't need me anymore."

"Oh, Espen . . ." Her voice contained an agony I'd never heard there before.

"'Tis alright. I understand—"

"No." Her whisper was sharp. "I shall never stop needing and loving you."

At her confession, my chest seized. Would she still have me after all?

She shook her head. "Even so, we cannot be together. I will only endanger you. . . ."

Her statement mirrored my sentiments from moments ago. But now, hearing her echo the same fear, I knew that I wouldn't run away from her in fear any more than I would ask her to do likewise. If she meant what she said about loving me, then didn't we deserve to fight for our love and the chance to be together?

"I will endanger you too," I said softly. "But we've already faced adversity and come through it stronger. We'll continue to do that." Aye, I knew in my heart that I'd rather be with her to face whatever might come than to miss out on the love we could share.

Her eyes were wide and still filled with agony . . . and hope.

Did I dare believe she might yet be willing to have me?

As though hearing my unasked question, she shook her head. "I have been the cause of all your trouble, and I cannot bear the thought of heaping more upon you."

She was rejecting me to keep me safe. And I couldn't let her do it.

"I would rather have you for one day than not all." The words came out harshly. I should have been embarrassed by my passionate plea, but the feelings I'd stuffed away for so long came tumbling out. "I cannot bear the thought of living my life without you in it."

Her pretty lips stalled around her retort.

"Please, Sylvi. Let me love you as long as I am able."

Again, she studied my face.

"The past week away from you was unbearable, and I cannot leave you without the assurance that you will be waiting here for me when the war is over."

She released a soft breath, and I felt as though it had the power to snap me in half. "What if my father one day learns I am alive? If we are together, he will endeavor to kill you again."

I'd let Lord Prestegard stand in my way of having and loving Sylvi for too long. I couldn't let him have that control any longer. "We don't know whether your father will succeed in his plans. And we don't know what the future will bring. But we do have this moment."

This time she didn't respond.

I took hope from her silence and pressed on, needing to say everything and hold nothing back. "I pray we will have many more days in the future, that perhaps I will even be able to come live with you here at Chapel Cliff." I could think of naught I would like better than returning to the sea and spending my days with her in this windswept oasis.

"Nevertheless," I continued, "if tonight and the next two days are all we'll ever get, I will take them rather than nothing at all."

"Espen . . ." My name on her lips was breathless and filled with longing.

I fisted my hands to keep from reaching for her. "I would rather love you than be safe. Will you give me the chance to do so?"

She tilted her head in that pretty way that made her irresistible. For a long moment, she studied me. Then she held out her hand. I could see in her eyes that it was her invitation to a life together.

I folded my hand around hers. "You're certain?"

"I shall never be satisfied with only two days. But I shall never be satisfied with less either. I want the chance to love you too, Espen. As long as I'm able."

"Good then." I dragged in my first full breath since the start of our conversation.

Finally, she smiled that beautiful smile of hers, the one that never failed to melt my insides and turn me into an incoherent dolt.

I started to pull my hand loose, knowing I needed to put some space between us and allow her to go back to sleep.

She didn't release me. Instead, her lashes fluttered halfway down, making my stomach flutter right along with them. Then she tugged me toward her.

I didn't budge. But my mouth went completely dry. What was she doing?

"I thought you wanted a chance to love me," she

whispered in a husky voice.

"Aye."

"Then come here and kiss me."

I needed no further invitation. I dropped to the edge of the bed, dragged her into my arms, and crushed my lips to hers.

This woman I'd always loved . . . she was finally and completely mine.

As she slipped her arms around me and wound her fingers into my hair, her mouth moved against mine with crackles of heat and sparks of fire that set me ablaze. She was the fire that enflamed me—a fire I would cherish and keep burning brightly. Until eternity.

JODY HEDLUND

ENTRUSTED

KNIGHTS OF **6** BRETHREN

**Take a peek as the real story
of the Holy Lamp continues . . .**

Chapter
1

KRISTOFFER

A HAZE OF destruction hung in the air, sending prickles up my spine.

I toed a blackened cauldron left amongst the rubble of the lofthouse. Bright embers glowed in the fading light of the June day, and smoke swirled up, stinging my eyes and nostrils.

Though the dwelling was charred along with every possession within, I saw no human remains.

"Looks the same as the last place." Next to me, Stefan, one of my squires, shifted a scorched board with his boot.

"I concur." Since crossing the Blood River and heading east toward the Valley of Red Dragons, we'd come across several such burned homes.

My other two squires, Finnseth and Jansen, waited on their mounts, their keen gazes roving over the hills that were covered by thick woodland. Like me, my men were attired in chain mail with a number of weapons at hand, ready for any situation.

"More Dark Warriors?" Stefan rubbed a hand over his

weary eyes. The long hard hours of riding without much sleep were taking their toll on us. But as the youngest of my squires at seventeen years old, Stefan was faring the worst.

'Twas easy to see the place had been set ablaze hours ago, before dawn. All the evidence did indeed point to another attack by Dark Warriors, who fought in the darkness. Not only did they have night vision, but they could extinguish all lights so that victims were left to fight blindly in the dark. Once finished with their onslaught, the Dark Warriors set everything aflame in a twisted effort to illuminate their destruction and possibly prove they were in control of the light.

However, the absence of any victims was unusual, since the Dark Warriors were known for ruthlessly slaying everyone they caught. In fact, the recent slew of victimless burned homes and villages was puzzling. From what we could tell, no one had died in any of the skirmishes, and the Dark Warriors hadn't taken prisoners. If so, we surely would have come across evidence of the captivity.

"My guess is Dark Warriors." I used the tip of my sword to prod asunder the darkened fireplace stones that had collapsed into a heap. "Yet I still cannot grasp the change in their methodology in allowing their victims to live."

"Maybe the Ice Men?"

I stepped back from the shell of the lofthouse. The surrounding buildings—a small stable, smokehouse, chicken coop, and the privy—were burned to the ground too. "If Ice Men, we would surely have seen them and their draco by now." Though King Canute of neighboring Swaine had used fierce Ice Men and their red draco during the war last autumn, we'd seen no evidence of the Ice Men joining with Canute over recent weeks in his effort to invade Norvegia again.

Instead, this time, Canute had enlisted the aid of the Dark Warriors from the far northern reaches of Swaine. Of course, we'd believed the Dark Warriors had long since become extinct and so we had been heartily surprised when we'd learned they'd joined forces with Canute.

At another strange prickling on the back of my neck, I scanned the base of the foothills, the bright lush green of summer always a welcome sight after the long months of winter. The majestic peaks of the Snowden Mountain Range rose above the hills, their pinnacles still a brilliant white with thick snow, the reminder that Norvegia's northern climate was harsh and even deadly.

I shifted my scrutiny to the woodland that covered the higher elevations of the foothills. Someone was out there, watching us. I had no proof of it. Only my intuition.

With our coat of arms, a dragon head on a background of royal red, we were easily identified as King Ansgar's men. If the Dark Warriors were hiding in the woods nearby and recognized the emblem, then they would confront us once darkness gave them their advantage.

I spun from the smoldering rubble and stalked toward my steed. "Tonight, we shall take shelter and rest."

At my proclamation, Stefan turned his startled gaze upon me, as did Finnseth and Jansen.

At eighteen, my other two squires also seemed young compared to my twenty-three years. They had to undergo several more years of training before they would be eligible for knighthood. They were loyal and helpful companions, and I'd been grateful they'd taken our quest to find the holy lamp as seriously as I had.

When we'd left Vordinberg nigh to a fortnight ago, none of the men had uttered one complaint when I'd indicated we wouldn't have a respite until we arrived at our final destination, a remote abbey along the Atlas River in the mountains.

It was our last hope for finding the holy lamp. If we didn't locate the ancient relic there, then I could only pray my fellow Knight of Brethren and best friend Espen had found it during his searching of the western locations.

Whatever the case, my squires and I would fare better during the coming night if we hid ourselves away at a tavern rather than staying out in the open. Perhaps doing so would help us dodge the interest of whoever was watching us.

"'Twould do us all good to rest," I offered, although I suspected my squires already knew that I was merely making an excuse. As we'd ridden farther and farther south, they'd seen the danger we were heading into every bit as much as I had.

"There's a tavern at the crossroads less than a league from here." Finnseth's youthful face was etched with determination to please me. As the broadest and burliest of my squires, he resembled Espen the most in his physical appearance. And I prayed again, as I had been doing every day, that Espen had experienced better fortune than I had in locating the holy lamp that could help save Norvegia from the Dark Warriors.

I hoisted myself into my saddle, alert to the distant eyes that were calculating my every move. As I gathered my reins, I dared another look, hoping to catch someone in the act of staring.

But again, as with before, no one was visible. 'Twas possibly in my exhaustion that my imagination was overwrought.

"Let us be off." I nudged my horse onward. "We shall do our best to cover our trail so that we keep anyone from following us to the tavern."

Less than an hour later, as the shadows of eve began to lengthen, we arrived at the lodging, a tall three-story structure painted a bright blue. If anyone had attempted to follow us, we'd given them a difficult task.

Once inside, I took the first guard shift, letting my squires get a few hours of slumber in the quarters above. I situated myself at a corner table so that I could keep an eye on both the front and back doors.

Though I'd hoped for solitude while eating a warm meal and sipping ale, 'twas not meant to be. Within minutes of my taking a seat, the few old farmers who were already gathered at the other tables turned on their benches, taking me in with part admiration and part suspicion.

I wasn't surprised they'd identified me as Kristoffer Prestegard. After being one of the twelve noblemen chosen to participate in Princess Elinor's courtship week last autumn, I'd gained a measure of popularity. Coupled with my status as an elite knight, I was unable to travel anywhere in Norvegia without someone recognizing me.

Hungry for news, the farmers peppered me with questions about the war with Swaine and what was happening in Vordinberg. Of course, I could only give them the news from the king and capital from two weeks ago when I'd left on my quest. At that point, King Ansgar had been rallying knights and chieftains from all over Norvegia. The men had been arriving in the capital and preparing to leave for the Valley of Red Dragons. But since the bulk of Canute's army hadn't yet crossed over the border into Norvegia, Ansgar was holding off from advancing, giving Espen and me time to find the holy lamp to aid us in the fight against Swaine and the Dark Warriors.

Without the specially blessed relic, we all feared a battle would go poorly, and we'd risk losing too many lives. But we couldn't prevent war with Swaine for much longer. I expected that any day we'd get word Canute's army had finally reached the border and was beginning to cross over.

As I spoke with the farmers, I asked them questions in return about the attacks in the area, gleaning as much information as I could. They confirmed what I'd already surmised—the Dark Warriors were behind the devastation but hadn't resorted to any killing, at least not yet.

The fire on the hearth crackled in lively flames, lighting the room along with candles glowing upon the tables which were still laden with the remains of supper— a simple fare of brown goat cheese, crusty bread, and roasted hen. The scent of the meat lingered in the air, along with the spiciness of pipe smoke.

With my appetite sated and my thirst quenched, my eyelids began growing heavy. The warmth of the room surrounded me, and I suddenly wanted nothing more than to rest my head and gain a few hours of sleep.

Not yet. I would let my squires slumber another hour or so and then take my turn.

"Suppose now that Swaine has the holy lamp, you'll be going over the border to get it," a stoop-shouldered farmer said before puffing perfect rings of smoke from his long-handled pipe.

Everywhere I'd gone, I'd offered a reward to anyone who could give me information about the ancient relic. Clearly the word of my mission had spread. I'd heard plenty of hearsay over the past days, and none had been true. I had no reason to believe this man now either, but I had to investigate. "And what leads you to believe Swaine has it?"

"The letter."

"What letter?"

"Courier came riding through the area this morn carrying news to you from Sir Espen."

I sat up straight. News from Espen? "Do you have the missive?"

"We told him we hadn't seen you, and he continued on his way. You being this close, figured he'd found you after leaving here."

"Did he read you the letter?"

The stoop-shouldered farmer paused, his pipe halfway to his mouth. My tone was terse and aggressive. Such an attitude would get me nowhere. 'Twas not this farmer's, the proprietor's, nor anyone else's fault that I'd missed being here when the letter arrived. The courier wouldn't know our exact location, especially since we'd been moving so quickly. He'd likely been relying on other travelers and their descriptions of our whereabouts.

I swallowed my growing frustration and forced a calmness to my tone. "I would be obliged if you can give me any further information the letter contained."

The farmer finished a draw on his pipe, then shrugged. "Only news we learned is that Swaine has the holy lamp."

If that was true, then Norvegia was in dire peril.

I pushed back and stood, arching and stretching my arms, but even then, anxiousness pumped my blood into a frenzy.

What should I do? If Espen knew with certainty that Swaine had the lamp, then my pursuit of it in Norvegia was over. There was no need to go to the last abbey.

But that didn't mean the quest for the holy lamp had ended. We still had need of it, and the farmer's suggestion to cross the border and continue the search in Swaine held great merit. The trouble was that I wouldn't know where in Swaine to begin looking. And of course, even if I disguised myself, I would draw suspicion anywhere I went.

I needed to think of a viable plan. And quickly. Time was already running short, and having to ride into Swaine and hunt for the relic there would only put Norvegia at a further disadvantage.

"The water barrel?" I asked the proprietor, who was sitting at the table with the farmers.

"You be needing to wash up, my lord?" He pushed up from his bench. "I can heat water and fill the tub."

As much as I longed for a bath to scrub away the grime of travel, right now I simply needed to wake myself up. "Cold water will be sufficient this time."

The proprietor plopped down and cocked his head at the back door. "Just outside."

With a nod of thanks, I let myself out into the cool night, the heat of the summer day long gone with the onset of darkness. The black sky overhead was clear and dotted with a million stars. A lone sliver of moon gave off enough light that I could see the wooden barrel next to the door. Grooved slats from the roof slanted down to the open container—a way to catch rainwater and have a steady supply of fresh water always at hand rather than having to transport from a nearby stream or well.

I bent over the water. The clear surface mirrored the endless array of stars. I longed to identify the various constellations in the reflection, with the extra test of finding them even though they were backward. But now was neither the time nor place for such a challenge.

I loosened the golden pin upon my cloak—the pin Ansgar had given to each of the ten elite Knights of Brethren. In the shape of the Sword of the Magi, it signified our brotherhood and our willingness to serve one another unto death.

A soft bird call rose into the night air from the woodland not far from the tavern, and my weariness evaporated. The sound, though meant to imitate a willow warbler, didn't contain enough of a descent in the slightly diminishing trill.

My mind sped with the implications. Most likely a group of Dark Warriors was in the forest and planning to attack. If I acted like I knew they were there, they'd stop me from going back in. But if I pretended to be unaware of their presence and made my way casually inside, I could warn everyone and awaken my squires. If the Dark Warriors entered the tavern, they'd snuff out all the flames, and we would be hard pressed to see anything in the blackness. But if we could force the warriors to remain outside, at least we'd have the starlight to aid us.

I splashed water on my face—twice for good measure. Then with a dripping face, I returned to the door, shaking away the droplets. With as much nonchalance as I could muster, I entered the tavern and closed the door with a measure of composure that belied the storm now raging in my chest.

As soon as I was no longer visible to the enemy, I bolted across the room. "Arm yourselves." I tossed the warning to the men still lounging on their benches. "We are about to face an attack."

I prayed I hadn't been the one to bring our foes to the business. Even if I had, 'twas also likely the Dark Warriors would have found the place and descended upon it anyway. Regardless, I would do what I could to protect the inhabitants. If the earlier strikes were the precedent of what was to come, then we need not fear for our lives, although in this case, since I was one of the king's knights, I couldn't count on them sparing me.

I took the simple ladder-like stairs two at a time, and as I reached the top, I found my three squires already pushing up from their pallets and donning their chain mail and weapon belts. They'd obviously heard my warning, which meant they were sleeping the way they needed to—lightly while staying alert to their surroundings.

"We need to do our best to keep the combat outside." I tugged up the mail hood of my hauberk. "If we face Dark Warriors in the open, at least we'll have some natural light to guide us."

At the rattle of the back door, I hopped down the stairs and retraced my steps. The scuffle of bootsteps on the stairs told me my squires were on my trail.

Before I could open the door, it burst loose from its latch and banged against the wall. A gust of wind blew inside with a shrill whistling. It swirled around us, and then in the next instant the flames on the hearth disappeared and the candles on the table flickered out.

"Outside. Now." I wasted no time in barging into the black night, my weapons at the ready, a sword in one hand and a knife in the other.

The moment my feet hit the ground, a long blade sliced the air toward my throat, aimed as though to sever my head from my neck.

Author's Note

Hi friends!

I know you're probably thinking that the old medieval tales don't reference a quest for a holy lamp the same way that they do Excalibur and the Holy Grail. And you would be right!

However, in keeping with the pattern of the first four books, I wanted to have our handsome and daring final two knights have the opportunity for their quests . . . and of course, to find true love along the way! So I invented the holy lamp and sent them on a mission to locate it. That's the beauty of writing fiction . . . you can make up whatever strikes your fancy!

Even though this story isn't inspired quite as directly by Arthurian legends as the previous books in the series, I hope you still enjoyed getting to know another Knight of Brethren. Espen's longtime unrequited love of Sylvi was very fun to write since he was so determined to be noble. I hope you ended up having as big of a crush on him as Sylvi did!

Stay tuned for the final book in the story involving the regal and intelligent Kristoffer. Will he be able to resist his father's offer to take the kingship? Will he resist the love that is casting a spell over him? And how will the confrontation with King Canute and the Dark Warriors end? Keep reading to discover the answers in the riveting series conclusion, *Entrusted*!

If you want to find out more about the other books in this series, please visit my website at jodyhedlund.com or check out my Facebook Reader Room where I chat with readers and post news about my books.

Until next time . . .

Jody Hedlund is the best-selling author of over thirty historicals for both adults and teens and is the winner of numerous awards including the Christy, Carol, and Christian Book Award. She lives in central Michigan with her husband, busy family, and five spoiled cats. Learn more at jodyhedlund.com.

More Young Adult Fiction from Jody Hedlund
Knights of Brethren

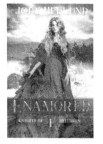

Enamored

Having been raised by her childless aunt and uncle, the king and queen, Princess Elinor finds herself the only heir to the throne of Norvegia. As she comes of age, she must choose a husband to rule beside her, but she struggles to make her selection from among a dozen noblemen during a weeklong courtship.

Entwined

After growing up on a remote farm, Lis learns she is the rightful heir to the throne of Norvegia. Even as she does her part to thwart a dangerous plot against the king, she resists pursuing her new identity and resigns herself to a simple life helping her elderly father with their farm.

Ensnared

Nursemaid to the Earl of Likness's two young daughters, Mikaela despises the earl for his cruelty to his subjects, and she longs for the day when she can make a difference in the lives of her suffering friends and family.

Enriched

Lady Karina lives in a convent and expects to become a nun someday. When her wealthy father asks her to help his textile business become more successful by marrying one of the popular Knights of Brethren, Karina complies, ever the dutiful daughter.

Enflamed

When Sylvi Prestegard discovers that her father has arranged for her to marry a wealthy nobleman known for his thieving ways, she's desperate to avoid the union. She turns to her childhood friend Espen, a Knight of Brethren, counting on his loyalty and kindness to help her escape.

Entrusted

Hoping to minimize the death and destruction of the coming war, Princess Birgitta of Swaine leads the Dark Warriors as part of her brother King Canute's efforts to take the throne of Norvegia. As she engages in a skirmish with a band of elite Knights of Brethren, she's kidnapped by Kristoffer Prestegard, a cunning warrior.

The Fairest Maidens

Beholden

Upon the death of her wealthy father, Lady Gabriella is condemned to work in Warwick's gem mine. As she struggles to survive the dangerous conditions, her kindness and beauty shine as brightly as the jewels the slaves excavate. While laboring, Gabriella plots how to avenge her father's death and stop Queen Margery's cruelty.

Beguiled

Princess Pearl flees for her life after her mother, Queen Margery, tries to have her killed during a hunting expedition. Pearl finds refuge on the Isle of Outcasts among criminals and misfits, disguising her face with a veil so no one recognizes her. She lives for the day when she can return to Warwick and rescue her sister, Ruby, from the queen's clutches.

Besotted

Queen Aurora of Mercia has spent her entire life deep in Inglewood Forest, hiding from Warwick's Queen Margery, who seeks her demise. As the time draws near for Aurora to take the throne, she happens upon a handsome woodcutter. Although friendship with outsiders is forbidden and dangerous, she cannot stay away from the charming stranger.

The Lost Princesses

Always: Prequel Novella

On the verge of dying after giving birth to twins, the queen of Mercia pleads with Lady Felicia to save her infant daughters. With the castle overrun by King Ethelwulf's invading army, Lady Felicia vows to do whatever she can to take the newborn princesses and their three-year-old sister to safety, even though it means sacrificing everything she holds dear, possibly her own life.

Evermore

Raised by a noble family, Lady Adelaide has always known she's an orphan. Little does she realize she's one of the lost princesses and the true heir to Mercia's throne . . . until a visitor arrives at her family estate, reveals her birthright as queen, and thrusts her into a quest for the throne whether she's ready or not.

Foremost

Raised in an isolated abbey, Lady Maribel desires nothing more than to become a nun and continue practicing her healing arts. She's carefree and happy with her life . . . until a visitor comes to the abbey and reveals her true identity as one of the lost princesses.

Hereafter

Forced into marriage, Emmeline has one goal—to escape. But Ethelrex takes his marriage vows seriously, including his promise to love and cherish his wife, and he has no intention of letting Emmeline get away. As the battle for the throne rages, will the prince be able to win the battle for Emmeline's heart?

The Noble Knights

The Vow

Young Rosemarie finds herself drawn to Thomas, the son of the nearby baron. But just as her feelings begin to grow, a man carrying the Plague interrupts their hunting party. While in forced isolation, Rosemarie begins to contemplate her future—could it include Thomas? Could he be the perfect man to one day rule beside her and oversee her parents' lands?

An Uncertain Choice

Due to her parents' promise at her birth, Lady Rosemarie has been prepared to become a nun on the day she turns eighteen. Then, shortly before her birthday, a friend of her father's enters the kingdom and proclaims her parents' will left a second choice—if Rosemarie can marry before the eve of her eighteenth year, she will be exempt from the ancient vow.

A Daring Sacrifice

In a reverse twist on the Robin Hood story, a young medieval maiden stands up for the rights of the mistreated, stealing from the rich to give to the poor. All the while, she fights against her cruel uncle who has taken over the land that is rightfully hers.

For Love & Honor

Lady Sabine is harboring a skin blemish, one that if revealed could cause her to be branded as a witch, put her life in danger, and damage her chances of making a good marriage. After all, what nobleman would want to marry a woman so flawed?

A Loyal Heart

When Lady Olivia's castle is besieged, she and her sister are taken captive and held for ransom by her father's enemy, Lord Pitt. Loyalty to family means everything to Olivia. She'll save her sister at any cost and do whatever her father asks—even if that means obeying his order to steal a sacred relic from her captor.

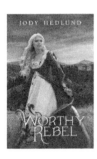

A Worthy Rebel

While fleeing an arranged betrothal to a heartless lord, Lady Isabelle becomes injured and lost. Rescued by a young peasant man, she hides her identity as a noblewoman for fear of reprisal from the peasants who are bitter and angry toward the nobility.

A complete list of my novels can be found at jodyhedlund.com.

Would you like to know when my next book is available? You can sign up for my newsletter, become my friend on Goodreads, like me on Facebook, or follow me on Twitter.

Newsletter: jodyhedlund.com
Goodreads:
goodreads.com/author/show/3358829.Jody_Hedlund
Facebook: facebook.com/AuthorJodyHedlund
Twitter: @JodyHedlund

The more reviews a book has, the more likely other readers are to find it. If you have a minute, please leave a rating or review. I appreciate all reviews, whether positive or negative.

Made in the USA
Las Vegas, NV
19 November 2022

59806526R00173